THE DUKE'S MAN-AT-ARMS

The Duke's Guard Series
Book Eleven

C.H. Admirand

ARE YOU SIGNED UP FOR DRAGONBLADE'S BLOG?

You'll get the latest news and information on exclusive giveaways, exclusive excerpts, coming releases, sales, free books, cover reveals and more.

Check out our complete list of authors, too!

No spam, no junk. That's a promise!

Sign Up Here

www.dragonbladepublishing.com

Dearest Reader;

Thank you for your support of a small press. At Dragonblade Publishing, we strive to bring you the highest quality Historical Romance from some of the best authors in the business. Without your support, there is no 'us', so we sincerely hope you adore these stories and find some new favorite authors along the way.

Happy Reading!

CEO, Dragonblade Publishing

Additional Dragonblade books by Author C.H. Admirand

The Ladies of the Keep Series
Liberating the Lady of Loughmoe (Book 1)
Bargaining with the Lady of Merewood (Book 2)
Rescuing the Lady of Sedgeworth (Book 3)

The Duke's Guard Series
The Duke's Sword (Book 1)
The Duke's Protector (Book 2)
The Duke's Shield (Book 3)
The Duke's Dragoon (Book 4)
The Duke's Hammer (Book 5)
The Duke's Defender (Book 6)
The Duke's Saber (Book 7)
The Duke's Enforcer (Book 8)
The Duke's Mercenary (Book 9)
The Duke's Rapier (Book 10)
The Duke's Man-at-Arms (Book 11)

The Lords of Vice Series
Mending the Duke's Pride (Book 1)
Avoiding the Earl's Lust (Book 2)
Tempering the Viscount's Envy (Book 3)
Redirecting the Baron's Greed (Book 4)
His Vow to Keep (Novella)
The Merry Wife of Wyndmere (Novella)

The Lyon's Den Series
Rescued by the Lyon
Captivated by the Lyon
The Lyon's Saving Grace

Historical Cookbook
Dragonblade's Historical Recipe Cookbook:
Recipes from some of your favorite Historical Romance Authors

Dedication

There are precious moments in life that live in your heart forever…

That night you walked me to my parents' back door and said goodnight. I turned around to go inside, and you called my name and said, "I've got a great idea!" You pulled me into your arms and kissed me…for the very first time.

Acknowledgments

A special thank you to my wonderful editor Arran McNicol. I truly appreciate your "nitpickery and such." My books are stronger because of you, Arran. Thank you. You are the best!

Author's Note

I have suspended time by forty years in order to use the early method of chest compressions to restart a heart. While it was mentioned that artificial respiration was first used in 1732 in Scotland to resuscitate a suffocated coal miner, it wasn't until 1856 that London physician Marshall Hall introduced his technique. It involved moving the patient and later adding pressure on the thorax.

My information from the American Heart Association regarding CPR was fascinating. cpr.heart.org/en/resources/history-of-cpr#1800s Here is more information from The American Heart Association's footnotes in this article: 6 Baskett TF. Silvester's technique of artificial respiration. Resuscitation.2007;74:8-10. www.resuscitationjournal.com/article/S0300-9572(07)00019-6/abstract

Book eleven is finished! Only one more of the O'Malleys to write about before the last four books: the Flaherty brothers. What seemed unreal when I began this series is close to becoming a reality. Although *The Duke's Guard series* will end after I have written the last of the Flahertys' stories, before then, I'll be writing a novella for an upcoming Dragonblade anthology. The novella features Lady Farnsworth, Persephone, Duchess of Wyndmere's mother. After that, I have another Lyon's Den book: *A Lyon's Promise*. Then I'll begin a new four-book series: ***Wyndmere's Warriors***, featuring wounded military men whom you have already met reading The Duke's Guard series.

Thank you for joining me on this wild ride, and the biggest series I have ever written. Your encouragement and support mean the world to me. That you love my hardheaded, stubborn Irishmen is a bonus.

C.H.

PROLOGUE

THE ANGEL OF the streets slowly opened her eyes and blinked. Her vision did not clear, and for a moment, she feared she was still inside that musty-smelling rug. The insistent, painful throb at the back of her head made itself known now that she regained consciousness. She tried to raise her hand to touch the back of her head, to see if it was bleeding, but couldn't. She could not move. The instinctive urge to cry for help was stifled by the foul-tasting gag covering her mouth.

Digging deep for strength, she tried to recall what happened, but for the life of her she could not. Where was she? Who had hit her? Her belly roiled and sweat broke out on the back of her neck and behind her knees. The telltale signs, and her body's warning, that she was about to vomit! Desperate to take back control from whomever had wrested it from her, she knew she had to hang on. She could not cast up her accounts now... Not when she was bound and gagged! She'd choke to death!

Tears welled up as she felt her will slipping. *Concentrate!* her mind screamed. She needed to think of something... Anything! She had to calm down. Closing her eyes, she breathed in and out through her nose three times. Reaching for calm, her mind called up the image of a giant of a man with broad shoulders—his physique, heavily muscled. His eyes, an intense emerald green. The memory of his carrying two little girls who clung to him as if he were their savior filled her mind's eye. The sudden thought that he could be hers too, if only she would let him, calmed her. Her stomach finally settled and the nausea disappeared.

How could she have been so careless after nearly a decade spent living a double life? She'd skirted discovery many times, but had never been injured or abducted. It was as if a private guard followed in her wake. But she only had one guard, not five, nor ten. By day, she was the quiet daughter of one of the *ton*'s favorite widowed physicians. Oh, she would attend the odd musicale or visit to a museum now and again, but when dusk fell, she moved in and around the edges of the stews of London, helping those who thought they were beyond it. Giving aid to women whose families had tossed them out. It had been her mission in life since that night...

She blocked off the memory, shoving it back to the back of her mind with the rest of that nightmare. She had been cautious when necessary, enlisting the aid of one or two men she trusted with her secret—and her life—when she could see no other way to protect the young women she had rescued.

To her shame, she realized that she had not only been self-righteous, but arrogant. Being so sure of her cause, positive no one but her could do what she did, had led her to believe herself invincible. Determined not to let the men who violated women, tossed them aside, and ruined their lives further by maligning them to all who would listen get away, she gave herself fully to her cause. These women still had value. They mattered... *She* mattered. What had been stolen from them could never be replaced, but she had helped heal the scars on their bodies until they were strong enough to begin healing the scars on their hearts. She helped them find employment and a chance to regain their self-respect. If only she could finally find a way to heal her own heart.

The pain in her head increased with each beat of her heart, as the reality of her situation hit home. No one would be coming for her. It had always been essential that no one know who she was, or her location. Whenever she felt the prickle of awareness and fear on the back of her neck, it was time to move. Time to find new rooms in a different building. No one knew of her location except her current guard, Greenwood. Had he been gravely injured? Dear Lord, had he survived the attack?

Trussed up and lying on the cold floor, she had naught to do but try to reason out what had happened. She quickly came to the conclusion that it had to have been intentional. Surely no footpad would be plying his trade at that hour of the day! She had heard a scuffle and knew Greenwood was trying to protect her. Then pain exploded in the back of her head. The rest of the fog in her brain lifted as her circumstances became perfectly clear. She had never been attacked before, but now that she had, the first prickles of awareness tinged with fear filled her. Though she could not see it or touch it, it felt as if her abductor's net slowly closed around her.

Her secret had been uncovered. Someone without a conscience, a heart, or a soul knew of her crusade and wanted to bring it to an end. The only reason that made sense to her was that whoever it had been was either trying to hide or cover their tracks by eliminating her.

Michaela was strong, and she would survive whatever her captor had planned for her. She had survived that long-ago night in the garden, determined that it would not define her future. She had kept her secret for years, until recently, when a wounded kindred soul needed to hear that she was not the only one who had been taken against her will. Aimee had been so brave insisting that Garahan and O'Malley go back and rescue the others, with little thought to her own safety. Those two little mites came to mind again, clinging to the handsome Irishman who had sparked what she thought had died inside of her. *Hope.* Hope that she, too, deserved a chance at a life where she would eventually be able to forgive herself for being too weak to fight off the despicable man who had stolen not only her virtue, but her dignity and her dreams. Those women did not deserve what happened to them, and neither did she.

She shoved that memory aside and whispered O'Malley's name in her head. He was a healer like herself, but also a warrior, the duke's man-at-arms, protector of innocents…as well as those who'd had their innocence stripped from them. Her heartbeat returned to normal, and her tears dried. She opened her eyes with renewed purpose—she had to escape! Wriggling her jaw from side to side was painful at first, but she kept at it. Opening and closing her mouth, she finally loosened the gag.

The pain in her head increased, but she ignored it by bringing up the memory of the helpless look in O'Malley's eyes when he tried to extract himself from the two little girls he and his cousin had rescued along with the others. At last she worked the gag off her mouth and took in great gulps of air. It wasn't fresh, and smelled oddly of the Thames, but at least the disgusting taste of the gag was gone.

She shifted one shoulder forward and then the other, pulling against the ropes binding her wrists together, fighting to loosen them. It took all of her willpower to keep working at the ropes. When she felt the trickle of warmth on her hands, she realized her attempts were all in vain. The ropes had not budged, and she'd rubbed her wrists raw. Whoever had tied the rope did not intend for her to escape. But the need to free herself overrode the pain in her bleeding wrists. She refused to give up and give in! Michaela twisted, tugged, wriggled, and pulled, but to no avail. She may have managed to remove her gag, and calm her roiling belly, but she hadn't been able to loosen her bonds.

Exhaustion crept up from the soles of her feet, threatening to claim her. She fought against it, knowing she needed to stay awake. The throb in her head, blurred vision, and nausea had returned, and the possibility that she was concussed was not to be ignored. Studying at her father's side, assisting him with his patients, had taught her that and more, and it enabled her to save those whom Society deemed unfit. Had anyone discovered what had happened to her that night, not only would her reputation have been in shreds, but her father's as well.

The *ton* would have refused to allow a physician with a pariah for a daughter to tend to them. What if her father had demanded satisfaction and called Lord Haversham out, demanding that they meet on the field of honor? She could never have let that happen. So she'd kept silent and lived with the shame that threatened to eat her alive until she paid attention to what was happening around her. She was not the only young woman to suffer such a fate. From that moment on, her life had had a new mission. She no longer hoped to study to become a physician and work alongside her father—a dream unheard of at the time. She would be the hand that lifted others who suffered such treatment out of their guilt and misery. Heal them, clothe them, find employment for them as they learned what she had had to do—forge a new path for her life.

Michaela bit the inside of her cheek when she felt her eyes closing again. She had to stay awake. *Botheration!* She could not do this alone. She rarely asked for help because it could be dangerous to those she gave aid to. But lying on the floor in the dark, unable to free herself, she knew of only one man who could rescue her and tend to her head injury. Michaela needed Emmett O'Malley!

Though the memory wasn't clear, she vaguely recalled Greenwood fighting to protect her. She had been grabbed not two steps from the door to her new building, where she'd recently procured rooms to continue her work, and had been struck on the back of her head.

Unless something horrible had happened to her guard, she was confident he would send word to Garahan and O'Malley, mayhap even Gavin King of Bow Street. She bit her lip, trying to decide who would be able to reach her first. Garahan was recovering, adjusting to the injury he'd received after rescuing Aimee, his new wife. Though she would never discount Garahan's strength and ability to regain the balance and acute sense of awareness necessary to perform his duties with the partial loss of eyesight in one eye, she wondered if O'Malley would be the one to find her.

Lost between the pain in her head and her thoughts, she heard the echo of footsteps coming toward her. Would she meet the person responsible for this travesty, or would it be one of his henchmen? Trepidation filled her as the footsteps drew near and stopped. A key scraped in the lock, and the hinges squeaked as the door opened. A tall man holding a lantern at his side stood there, but it was too dark to see his face. The shadowed hallway hid it from her. She felt his gaze on her, and the wild hope that mayhap this was all a mistake filled her. Had they grabbed the wrong woman? Was he here to set her free?

"So the rumors in the stews of this city are true. There is an angel who sweeps in to rescue fallen women… A fallen woman herself."

Her heart began to pound. It was the voice from her nightmare! How in God's name had he found her?

"I wondered where you disappeared to after that night in the garden. I confess I was surprised *not* to hear that your body had been found floating in the Thames. Isn't that what most women unable to bear the loss of their only valuable asset resort to?"

His questions battered her as he intended them to, but she refused to answer. The sudden silence after the rasp of his voice slashed through her hard-won confidence, chilling her to the bone.

"Do you remember what happened that night, Miss Colborne?"

The acid in her empty belly roiled and his voice had her skin crawling. She remembered his anger and harsh words, the violence that followed, as if it had happened hours ago instead of years.

"When I heard that a certain boarding house had been closed down and young women had been rescued, I wondered if the rumored angel of the streets could possibly be you." He stepped over the threshold and lifted the lantern in his hand so the light shone on him. "I dismissed it because I knew you to believe yourself above others…above men such as myself. You would never stoop so low as to help damaged goods."

Lord Haversham looked just as she remembered him, impeccably dressed in a dark blue frockcoat of the finest wool, and a pale blue jacquard waistcoat shot with threads of gold that glistened in the soft light. The stark white of his cravat was crisply folded to achieve the waterfall effect, giving the appearance of a gentleman, but she knew it was just the outside shell. A shell that hid the demon within. Everything about him was unchanged, even what she had not noticed until it was too late…his hollow black eyes.

Had she made the wrong decision all those years ago by not telling her father what Lord Haversham had done? Her lack of action at the time had left her guilt ridden. Had he gone on to ruin more than one young woman, or had his anger been focused solely on her because of her dream to become a doctor? Rage began to build inside of her as she recalled all he had stolen from her. She curled her hands into tight fists and clenched her teeth. He was in for a surprise if he thought he would touch her again! Her legs were unbound, so she was not totally defenseless.

He continued to stare at her without speaking until, finally, he said, "I cannot allow you to continue to interfere in my most profitable business, Miss Colborne. What a pity your looks seem to have deserted you along with your innocence." He sniffed and lifted his chin as if disgusted by her very appearance. *Thank God!* Fear that he would touch her dissipated. "I had thought to see if you had learned how to pleasure a man since our diverting time in the garden." His lip curled in disdain. "You'll need a bath and fresh clothes first."

"You are despicable."

"I see that your temperament has not improved. Let us see if it improves after another day spent locked in with the rats."

"Rats?"

His laugh had ice sprinting up her spine. "Surely you recognized the scratching and scurrying in the corners of the room, the hole in the wall near the floor."

When she did not answer, he smiled. "They hunt here at night, sometimes in the middle of the day. Whenever hunger strikes." His eyes bored into her. "Are *you* hungry, Miss Colborne? Thirsty?"

She refused to give him the satisfaction of answering. It had taken her years to recover from his attack. Though she had been raised to believe in forgiveness and knew it would lift part of the heavy burden she carried, she had not been able to do so.

With her anger bolstering her, her pride back in place, she spat at his highly polished Hessians. His shocked expression and quick step back was a small strike at him for what he was trying to do to her again. He had not changed—he was still a handsome man, rotten to the core. In her heart she knew that he would continue to take, and by taking destroy another gentle heart, another fragile soul.

"There is a place in Hell for the likes of you, Haversham."

His posture changed in a heartbeat—he squared his shoulders and vibrated with anger as he took a step closer. Raising the lantern above his head, he snarled, "It is *Lord* Haversham! I demand that you respect me and my title!"

"Only a weak man demands respect. Strong men earn it by their actions and good deeds."

As soon as the words left her lips, she realized too late that she had pushed him too far. She guessed his intention a heartbeat before his foot connected with her ribs. The pain registered as he kicked her again, harder this time. "Bloody. Filthy. Trollop!"

The third kick to her ribs stole her breath. She felt two of them give way, and heard the deep echoing crack of their breaking in her pounding head.

The light blinded her as Haversham leaned down and growled, "Another day in here, and you'll be willing to do anything for your freedom."

The pain in her ribs rolled over her in waves, increasing in intensity. Each breath she struggled to take was torture. The door slammed, and the key turning in the lock echoed around her. Alone she prayed for a miracle…

She prayed for Emmett O'Malley.

CHAPTER ONE

G AVIN KING LOOKED up as Emmett O'Malley walked into his office. "Thank you for coming so quickly."

"I'd never ignore a summons from Bow Street. Does it involve His Grace or Earl Lippincott?"

"Neither," the Bow Street Runner replied. "And before you ask, it doesn't involve Viscount Chattsworth or Baron Summerfield."

O'Malley knew of another connection he and the famed runner had, a woman whose good works kept her in constant danger in her quest to save as many young women off the streets of London as possible. The darkest sections of the city, where there used to be despair, now held hope with the merest whisper of the name she had been given by those she had saved—*angel of the streets*. The angel had been instrumental in saving the lives of three of his Garahan cousins' wives. But O'Malley knew better than to jump to conclusions. He waited for King to continue.

King rose from the seat behind his desk, walked to the door, and closed it. "What I have to say must never leave this room."

"Ye have me word," O'Malley promised.

"Dr. Robert Colborne's daughter did not return home last night."

"The name sounds familiar. Is he a colleague of Dr. McIntyre or Lieutenant Sampson?"

"Aye, they are known to one another."

O'Malley digested the information, then asked, "Is she somehow connected to Miss Michaela?"

King's eyes flashed with temper, and O'Malley sensed there was a strong connection between the missing physician's daughter and Michaela. At King's continued silence, O'Malley had to stifle a groan of pain. "Miss Michaela *is* the physician's daughter?"

"Aye, and Colborne is more aware of her good works than she realizes. He prefers to keep it that way. He has had two men keeping watch over her since she began her crusade to rescue and heal those who cannot help themselves."

"Does he have any idea how much danger his daughter is in?" O'Malley asked.

"He is well aware, which is why he has contacted me more than once over the last few years when he feels she is in over her head."

"Why doesn't he demand the lass stop?"

King's gaze met O'Malley's. "Have you been present whenever His Grace has tried to tell Her Grace what to do?"

O'Malley stifled a snort of laughter. "Aye."

"Well then, you understand what would happen should the good doctor try to tell Miss Michaela what to do. She is just as stubborn as the duchess, if not more." Clasping his hands behind his back, King paced.

"I've heard tales from the Garahans and have met Miss Michaela more than once," O'Malley said. "Her size has ye thinking she's weak. But she's strong and has a heart of gold, even if she seems to be a bit on the stubborn side. What else have ye heard?"

"Nothing. Which is why I brought you in. Your contacts and Garahan's have deeper connections in the stews and on the docks." King hesitated before adding, "I need you to press them for information. I cannot shake the feeling that we do not have long to find her."

Emmett's eyes locked on King's. "I won't rest until I find her."

King's expression changed to one of relief. "I have a handful of men on the case. To put more runners out there asking questions may do more harm than good."

"'Twould bring attention to who ye're looking for. No matter if ye use her nickname or real name, the lass would be in even more danger."

"Exactly. I'm thinking of bringing Cameron in on this."

O'Malley shook his head. "Miss Michaela wouldn't want Cameron, or his new wife and her family, exposed to rumor and innuendo if word gets out he's helped her in the past. Not all those of the *ton* believe her mission is warranted or in their best interests. They protect their own, even if they're twisted and bent on destroying others." His mind was screaming to leave now, not his normal reaction when called to help. He waited a beat before adding, "I'll speak to Cameron and Greenwood, her newest guard. See if I can unravel any threads that will lead back to who has kidnapped her and where she's being held."

King stopped pacing and said, "Colborne did not send word immediately, as she often works long hours, arriving home near dawn."

"Bloody hell! 'Tis now nigh on eight o'clock in the morning. She could have gone missing anytime yesterday!" O'Malley stalked to the door, yanked it open, and glanced over his shoulder. "Have ye spoken to Garahan?"

"Given his condition—"

O'Malley spun around and glowered at King. "Are ye saying Darby isn't fit to do his job?"

The runner shook his head. "I am sure that he is still capable—"

O'Malley interrupted him, "Garahan's been training with Coventry and is just as lethal wearing an eyepatch as when he had perfect vision!"

King remained silent.

"Ye'll see how wrong ye are to think to exclude him. I will find Miss Michaela with Garahan's help. When I do, ye'll owe me cousin an apology."

The two men glared at one another, neither capitulating. Finally King barked, "Keep me posted."

O'Malley grunted, turned around, and stalked out of the door. He strode along the hallway with the single-minded thought: rescue the lass…no matter the cost! The bloody bugger who dared to lay hands on Michaela would live to regret it.

He nodded to the runner stationed outside the front of the building. Stalking over to where he tied his horse, he scratched behind the animal's ear. "We've a mission, laddie." He untied the reins and mounted his horse. O'Malley's thoughts settled into place as he rode toward the duke's town house. He'd speak to Findley and Garahan. Findley would have no problem being left in charge. Though one of the newer men hired, he was more than capable. He'd be sure to add two footmen who would man Garahan and O'Malley's positions guarding the town house until further notice. They had done it before and would no doubt do it again when circumstances warranted it.

O'Malley and Darby would split up and gather information from their contacts. Someone would know *something*, anything, that would lead him to Michaela. The overwhelming need to find and save the lass was his mission. A calm filled him at having a workable rescue plan that included Garahan. As he neared Grosvenor Square, he murmured, "Hang on, lass, we'll find ye!"

O'Malley whistled as he dismounted on the fly, handing the reins of his horse to one of the stable lads. Garahan rounded the corner of the house from the servants' entrance as Findley strode toward them from the front. Even when one of them gave the urgent signal—the three-note whistle—it was agreed no one would run out of the front of the town house. It could cause alarm should anyone observe one of the duke's guard running.

"What's the emergency?" Findley asked.

Garahan asked, "Have you heard?"

"Michela's missing!" O'Malley said.

Findley frowned. "*The* Miss Michaela?"

"Aye," Garahan bit out. "Burke sent a message."

"She moved to the new location a week or so ago," O'Malley said. "She should have been safe."

"Who told you?" Garahan demanded.

"King sent for me." O'Malley held up a hand when Garahan's face flamed with anger. "I let him know that he'd made a mistake trying to exclude ye. Ye're as fit as ever, and have the balance of a cat."

Garahan raked a hand through his dark hair. "Bugger it!"

O'Malley shoved his cousin with his shoulder. "I told him that Coventry taught ye well."

Garahan's stance relaxed. "Thank ye."

"I'll have two of the footmen take your positions while you are away," Findley said. "Do you expect trouble to find its way here?"

O'Malley met the other man's direct look. "Nay, but be on guard for it. Darby and I are going hunting. We'll find the lass and bring her back here."

Garahan shook his head. "Not here."

"And why not?" It felt right to O'Malley, but he valued his cousin's point of view.

"Too many people living on this bloody square cannot keep their noses out of the duke's affairs."

O'Malley sighed. Mayhap Garahan was right. Time would tell. "Where, then?"

"Bring her to Aimee. We're well protected living in Captain Coventry's building." When O'Malley did not answer right away, Garahan pressed him, "Ye know me wife would do anything for Michaela. She saved her life and gave her back her self-respect."

"I'm thinking marriage to ye did that, boy-o," O'Malley replied.

"I don't—"

"Want to waste anymore time," he finished for Garahan.

"We'll be in touch, Findley. Send word through Coventry or King if ye need us."

"Aye. I'll tell the footmen we may need to have a rotating shift until you return." Findley took off at a lope around the back of the building to the servants' entrance.

The stable lad had two geldings saddled and ready to go when Garahan and O'Malley approached the stables. "I was going to saddle another horse for you," the young man told O'Malley, "but this one here wasn't ready to go back in his stall."

O'Malley accepted the reins from the younger man and scratched behind his horse's ear. "He knows we've a lass to rescue." He mounted his horse and turned to Garahan, who was speaking to his horse in low tones. "Are ye asking him what scuttlebutt he's heard?"

"Aye," Garahan replied. "Ye'd be surprised how efficient the rumor mill is straight from the horse's mouth, stable to stable, throughout the city."

O'Malley shook his head. "Now that ye mention it, this lad wasn't surprised to hear about Michaela." Vibrating with anger, worried that too much time had passed, increasing the possibility that the lass had been injured, he took the lead.

Garahan pulled alongside of him and said, "I'm going to speak with Burke. See if he's learned anything more since he sent his message."

O'Malley nodded. "I'll head over to the docks and see if I can find Leach or yer man O'Shaughnessy."

"We'll report back here in three hours at the latest," Garahan said. "Agreed?"

"Aye."

"And whoever finds the lass first will bring her to Coventry's building," Garahan reminded his cousin.

"Ye have me word," O'Malley rasped.

The hand on his shoulder surprised him, though Garahan's words of encouragement did not. "We'll find Michaela before the night is over."

Worry for the angel of the streets nearly distracted O'Malley. With each beat of his heart it increased until he accepted the fact that she was more than just a worry. She mattered to him. The few times he'd witnessed her care for those they'd rescued, most recently Darby's wife and the little lasses, the connection between them had grown stronger. She was not just the angel of the streets... She was *his* angel. "At what cost to the lass?"

Garahan squeezed O'Malley's shoulder, then gave him a shove. "Less than could happen if ye keep shooting off yer gob, delaying us further."

For a moment, O'Malley was so wrapped up in thoughts of Michaela and what could be happening to her that he hadn't realized he'd frozen in place. His mind reeled just thinking of all that could happen to the petite but strong beauty with the soft brown hair and moss-green eyes. "Three hours," he ground out as they parted ways and headed off in opposite directions.

"Three hours," Garahan echoed.

CHAPTER TWO

O'MALLEY FOUND LEACH loitering in Covent Garden. The dark walk wasn't a worry this time of day, though after dusk, it would be. He rode toward the big man, noting the purple bruise along his jaw. Leach's size alone would be an open invitation to all comers that he was ready to brawl. It appeared as if someone recently accepted that invitation.

Leach nodded as O'Malley approached. "I was about to come looking for you."

O'Malley dismounted. "What have ye heard?"

Leach motioned for O'Malley to follow him. They walked a distance away from those strolling along the paths. "The angel's guard was fighting off three men, just two steps away from her, when she was struck from behind."

O'Malley's gut iced over. He curled his hands into tight fists, as the need to physically release the anger and frustration inside of him was a living, breathing thing. "Is that all ye heard?"

"Aye."

Urgency had him by the bollocks. "Someone must have seen something. Was she hoisted over a man's shoulder? Across a horse? Tossed into a carriage?"

"A lead pipe to her guard's temple dazed him. He didn't know she'd been struck, too, until he regained his senses and found her gone."

O'Malley nodded. "Did anyone summon the Watch?"

"Nay."

"Bloody hell! I need more than that to go on."

"I have put the word out. Should hear something in a few hours."

O'Malley wondered what else had happened to her. A head injury could be lethal, if it went unchecked. Was she concussed? Was her head split open and bleeding? Did she need threads to close the wound? Impatience surged through him. Where in the bloody hell *was* she?

"It'll take longer to find out more information because of who she is."

"Aye, though I hate to agree with ye, and bloody hell don't like it." O'Malley met Leach's steady gaze. "Ye know how to get word to me."

"Are you headed to the docks next?"

"Aye. Garahan's in the stews."

The large hand on O'Malley's shoulder snapped him back to the present. "I've already alerted eyes and ears near the Saracen's Head."

The inn was near Newgate. O'Malley's dark thoughts cleared at the news. He hadn't even considered that whoever had taken the angel would whisk her out of London. "Ye're one step ahead of me. Faith, I'm grateful for it. Thank ye."

"I'll never be able to repay yerself, nor Garahan, for putting in a good word for me with your man with the runners."

"Ye won't be falsely accused again, Leach. Ye have me word."

"I'll let you know what I hear from the coaching inn."

They parted, and O'Malley mounted his horse, heading in the direction of the docks. He knew his way in and around the newer warehouses that had been built, as well as the older buildings—a few of which were derelict, left standing. He hoped to run into O'Shaughnessy, one of Garahan's contacts there. If he did not find the man, he would make his way over to the Prospect of Whitby pub. O'Shaughnessy enjoyed bare-knuckle fighting, and preferred to engage in it when there was coin to be earned. He could find both there.

"Ye're either lost, or have *shite* for brains!" a deep voice challenged from behind as he arrived at the docks.

Relief filled O'Malley as he turned around. "I'm glad I found ye, O'Shaughnessy."

The man motioned for O'Malley to dismount and walk beside him. "Bad business, someone snatching the angel right off the street."

O'Malley knew the Irishman tended to be long-winded. He ignored the need clawing at his insides and asked, "What can ye tell me?"

"Nothing concrete, just whispers that I heard early this morning."

O'Malley was tempted to reach out, grab the man by the throat, and demand he spit out what he knew, but held on to his control. "Whatever it is could lead us to the angel."

"'Twas a fair lass who confirmed the whisper as we were…" O'Shaughnessy paused and smiled. "Well now, I won't be telling tales. The lass favors me among her regulars, as I treat her like a lady."

O'Malley knew a few of the bits o' muslin who plied their trade near the docks. Some had hearts of gold… The others, he couldn't trust. "What did the lass have to say?"

"She was afraid."

"Has someone injured her? Get the description," O'Malley told him. "I'll take care of the bloody bugger!"

O'Shaughnessy's eyes lit from within as he slowly smiled. "It does me heart good to know that you'd offer to defend her honor. She was not injured, but I told her she needed to go into hiding until this blows over. I fear for her safety when words gets out that there is a witness, as ye know it will."

O'Malley sensed that whatever O'Shaughnessy's friend heard could be tied to Michaela's disappearance. "Tell me."

"'Twas an hour or so before I arrived to see her that she witnessed a toff's carriage pulled by a beautiful pair of grays—her words—slowing down by the alleyway. A tall man dressed like he had no business being on the docks stepped out of the carriage with a rolled-up rug on his shoulder."

O'Malley controlled the need to pound something—nay, some*one*. "Rug?"

"Aye. The lass said she's seen the like a time or two before. And same as before, she heard a muffled cry for help when the man headed down a nearby alley."

O'Malley's reaction was volatile, but he controlled it. He would not break his vow to the duke. He would injure—but not kill—whomever they fought against. "What else did yer lass say?"

"The toff had only been gone for about a quarter of an hour when he returned to his carriage—without the rug—and rode off."

"Can ye take me to the alleyway?"

O'Shaughnessy nodded. "There's a gang that has been known to frequent the area around that alley. Ye may want Garahan with ye."

He had to find Michaela…now! "If there's a chance the angel is being held in one of the buildings in that alley, I'm not waiting for Garahan!"

"I'll get word to Garahan for ye, then," O'Shaughnessy promised. "Follow me."

The two men made their way past the newer section of the docks to the older, where O'Shaughnessy had been hours earlier. "This was where she saw the coach."

"Did it have any distinct markings? A crest?"

"Nay. 'Twas black, well sprung. The coachman's livery was dark blue…no fancy trim."

"Indistinguishable," O'Malley muttered, wishing there had at least been markings on the carriage—it would be easier to trace.

O'Shaughnessy nodded. "Ye'll want to leave yer horse out here."

"Me gelding comes with me. I may need to leave quickly."

"This way." O'Shaughnessy passed the first alley and stopped at the entrance to the next. After scanning the length and breadth of it, he entered. "I searched earlier, but did not notice a sign that any of the buildings were occupied."

"They would be smart enough to cover their tracks and not leave any outward sign that he'd dropped off his...*rug*."

"I'll leave ye to explore while I send one of me friends in search of Garahan." O'Shaughnessy looked over his shoulder and warned, "Watch yer back."

O'Malley nodded and began a systematic search of the buildings. Most of them appeared vacant. He tried windows and doors, entering one building at a time. The ones with upper levels, but missing stairs, were the quickest to rule out. Finally he stood in front of the last building. There was something different about it. He couldn't put his finger on it, but the sense that it was not empty filled him.

Not wasting any time, he slipped in through a broken window and felt a sharp jab where a shard of glass cut through his coat into his side. Ignoring it, he dropped to the floor in a crouch, slowly straightened, and cautiously crossed the threshold into the hallway. An odd sound had him freezing. Cocking his head to one side, he cupped a hand to his ear and listened. It sounded like someone was tapping...rapidly. He walked past a series of open doors toward the back of the building, where the sound grew louder. Less like tapping now, but he couldn't quite place it.

The last door on the right was closed. He touched the doorknob, and the sound stopped abruptly, quickly followed by a barely audible gasp. He turned the knob, but it was locked. Before he could ask whoever was inside to step away from the door, a shaky voice rasped, "I will never change my mind!"

He knew that husky voice! "Michaela, are ye hurt?"

"O'Malley, is it really you?" The shaky reply was music to his ears.

"Aye! Step away from the door, lass. I need to break it down."

"I... I'm not near the door."

He grunted in reply. "Now's not the time to get yer gumption up and argue. Step back—"

"I can't move. I'm sorry, Emmett." Her voice broke. "I would if I could."

"How close are ye to the door?"

"A few feet away."

"Are ye in the middle of the room?"

"Nay, to the left of the door… Your right."

"Cover yer head, lass!"

"I can't."

His blood ran cold. Someone had tied her up. "I'll kill the bloody bugger! Close yer eyes, in case the door splinters."

"They're closed."

"Don't open them until I tell ye, Michaela." O'Malley took two steps back and rammed the door with his shoulder. The lock held, but the middle of the door broke apart. His heart stuttered in his chest as he took in the sight of the woman he loved—aye, *loved*! Rushing to Michaela, he knelt by her side and realized the odd sound he'd heard was her teeth chattering. "Open yer eyes, darling lass. Tell me where ye're hurt."

Thick, dark lashes fluttered open, revealing her pain-filled, pale green eyes. "The back of my head aches. I don't remember, but I think someone must have struck me from behind. How did you find me? Where is Greenwood?"

"One thing at a time. I'm going to untie ye and wrap ye in me coat—ye're chilled to the bone. 'Twas yer chattering teeth that led me to ye."

He watched her gather her composure around her like a cloak. *Brave lass.* "I wouldn't have clenched my jaw for so long, trying to be quiet, if I knew you were coming."

"Ye know I will always come if ye need me."

Her eyes held the soul-deep conviction he'd hoped to see. "Yes. It gave me strength."

"How long have ye been here?"

She bit her bottom lip, hesitating, before answering, "Sometime yesterday. I watched the room grow light a few hours ago."

"We'll have to hurry. I'm not sure how much time we have before someone finds us." He felt his gut clench at what he had to do. "I'll apologize to ye now, lass. Yer shoulders and arms may feel sharp pain when I release yer bonds until yer muscles and tendons loosen, but 'twill be easier if ye can wrap yer arms around me neck when I carry ye out of here."

Her hesitation was replaced by her determination. "Don't worry about me, Emmett. I'm fine."

She was in pain and trying to hide it. By God, she was an angel and a warrior! "The hell ye are…but ye will be."

Tears welled up at the tone of his voice, but she blinked them back. "Do not yell at me."

"God help me, lass, I didn't mean to. Hold on now while I cut ye free." He slipped the knife out of his boot and easily sliced through the ropes, carefully avoiding the bloody, torn skin. "Ah, lass, yer poor wrists."

Arms freed, she clenched her jaw. He expected her to complain about the pain he knew she had to be experiencing. She surprised him yet again. "I did that to myself, trying to work the knot free."

He slipped out of his frockcoat and gently massaged her shoulders before lifting her to a sitting position. "I'll help ye with the sleeves." As soon as he moved her arm, her sharp gasp of pain seared through him. "I'm sorry, lass. I hate hurting ye, but 'tis necessary. Ye feel cold as sleet, and we need to get ye warm." He managed to get her arms in the sleeves. "Just another moment." He wrapped his coat around her and brushed against her side. She gasped, and he cursed. "Ye didn't tell me ye'd hurt yer ribs."

"Didn't hurt them," she panted, trying to catch her breath. "Was kicked."

"Someone kicked ye in the ribs? I'll skin him alive!" O'Malley promised.

"Later. I'll be fine. Please take me away from here before he comes back."

Emmett noticed the tone of her voice changed, and suspicion took hold of him. "Ye know who did this to ye."

She did not answer.

Anger such as he'd ever known shot from his gut to his head. "Ye'll tell me his name—"

"Later," she promised. "I don't want to be here when he returns."

"How do yer arms feel? Can ye move them?"

She closed her eyes, tried to do as he asked, and moaned.

"It'll feel like ye've a fire in yer shoulders, but it will go away." He moved closer and slipped an arm around her back, the other beneath her knees. "Wrap yer arms around me neck, Michaela. There's a lass. That's the way. I'll take a closer look at yer head when we're outside. The light is too dim in here."

He lifted her and held her against his pounding heart. Feelings he must have been carrying, but ignoring, added to the overwhelming need to protect the woman in his arms. Bloodlust raged through him as he planned where he would start skinning whoever did this to his angel. They were going to die, slowly, painfully, for what they'd done to her.

Though she made no sound, he felt her trembling a heartbeat before she stiffened, fighting to conquer what he sensed she would consider a weakness. He promised, "I've got ye, lass. I won't be letting ye go."

"Thank you for coming for me, Emmett. I prayed you would."

His heart filled and his head spun at her words. "I'm sorry that I didn't know what happened until a little while ago." He tried the back door. It wasn't locked, so he opened it and glanced to the left and then the right before moving. "I would have been here sooner."

"You're here now." She shifted and sucked in a breath, trying to cover her moan of pain. "That's all that matters."

He stepped outside with his precious burden. O'Shaughnessy had yet to return, so he started walking toward where he'd left his horse. "Try not to move or speak again until we tend to yer ribs. I don't want them to poke—"

"Through a lung," she interrupted. "I have tended to enough cracked and broken ribs to know the risks. I promise to be as still as I can."

He gently brushed the tips of his fingers to the back of her head and found a huge lump, but it wasn't bleeding. "We'll need a poultice for that. 'Tis a good thing ye have a hard head, Michaela. Are ye seeing double?"

"It was blurry at first, but then it cleared."

"Nausea?"

"I was nauseated last night, but it subsided."

His horse watched him approach and whickered as if to ask what had kept him. O'Malley was relieved his gelding was in the same spot halfway down the alley. "I found her, laddie. Now then, I'll need ye to carry us to the corner of Hart and Lumley." Glancing at Michaela, he said, "I'm going to put ye in the saddle— can ye hold yerself up?"

She didn't hesitate to answer, "Yes."

O'Malley was gentle settling her on the back of his horse. He knew she suffered from sitting without his support, so he quickly leapt into the saddle. Pulling her onto his lap, he tucked his coat more firmly around her trembling body. "Try to hang on for a bit longer."

O'Shaughnessy appeared a few minutes later and looked at the woman in O'Malley's arms. "I'm sorry for the circumstances, but 'tis an honor to meet the angel of the streets." He nodded to O'Malley. "I should hear from Garahan soon. Where should I tell him ye'll be?"

"Tell him to meet me as planned."

"Best go quickly now," O'Shaughnessy said.

"Aye. Thank ye for yer help, O'Shaughnessy, and please thank yer friend. Let her know I wouldn't have found the angel without her. If she decides she's ready to make a change, ye let us know. We'll help her."

"Thank ye, O'Malley."

"Is there a young woman who needs my help?" Michaela asked.

O'Malley was even more impressed by how quickly the lass ignored her injuries, as if she had a mere bump on the head instead of a possible concussion. Scraped wrists instead of bleeding. Ribs bruised instead of broken. His admiration grew, tangling with the depth of his feelings for her.

"We'll speak of it later. 'Tis time to let someone take care of ye, lass." He stared into her moss-green eyes and rasped, "Let it be me."

O'Shaughnessy motioned for them to wait a moment while he checked to see that it was safe to leave the alley. "Rest now, miss. Ye're in good hands."

"Thank you, O'Shaughnessy," Michaela replied. "Please tell your friend I have many connections and am certain I can be of help finding her a new—and safe—situation with honest people that I would trust with my life."

The big man promised to pass on her message, thanked her, and said to O'Malley, "Best leave now, before things get busy around here."

O'Malley nodded. "I'll be in touch."

Garahan's contact waved and slipped into one of the buildings as they rode past. O'Malley pressed his lips to the top of Michaela's head and urged, "Close yer eyes, darling lass. We'll be there soon."

"Emmett?"

"Aye?"

"Will there be a woman at the captain's?"

"Aye, why?"

"I think he broke three of my ribs," she whispered.

He clenched his jaw, then relaxed it to ask, "Is that what ye're worrying over?" O'Malley could not believe it wasn't the worry of a concussion or a rib piercing her lung. "Ye're worried about yer modesty when I take care of yer ribs?"

"Yes," she whispered.

"Ye must know I'd never willingly hurt ye, lass, and I'd never do anything to compromise yer reputation." She relaxed against him, and he added, "Darby and Aimee live in Coventry's building. Coventry's wife Miranda will be there with their little daughter, Emma. One of the women will be there with ye to preserve yer modesty while I wrap yer ribs."

When Michaela fell silent, he thought she'd fallen asleep, until he heard her rasp, "I no longer have a reputation to worry about."

The impression that someone in the past had hurt Michaela resurfaced. The thought of a man violating the beautiful lass in his arms gutted him. She had the gift of healing, made it her mission to save others, was precious, stubborn, and brave. If it took the rest of his life, he planned to show the lass how much he valued her. How much he cared… More than cared.

Ye broke down the door to get to her! his heart reminded him. *Bloody hell, don't sugarcoat it. Admit it, ye eedjit! Ye've been intrigued with the lass since ye helped rescue James's wife, Melinda. Yer interest stirred to the surface once more when ye heard the lass had been a witness to the murder of Aiden's father-in-law. Ye were already half in love the her when ye went with Darby to rescue those five lasses, two of them no more than eight or ten summers, from the boarding house where Aimee had been held captive.*

All right, I admit it…but I'm not halfway *in love with the lass,* his head told his heart.

Aye, his heart agreed, *ye're arse over head in love with her!*

CHAPTER THREE

Masterson was lounging outside Coventry's building on the corner of Hart and Lumley when they approached. The gaunt former soldier straightened to attention when he saw O'Malley riding toward him. "Is that who I think it is?"

O'Malley gave a slight nod and pitched his voice low. "We need to get her inside quickly."

The former colonel in Wellington's Fighting Fifth held out his arms. "Hand her to me."

O'Malley hesitated. As one of the wounded warriors Captain Coventry had hired, Masterson was eminently trustworthy. But O'Malley's heart refused to let go of the lass, while his head urged him to hurry. "I've got her, if ye'll grab hold of me horse's bridle to hold him steady." He dismounted and stood next to Masterson. "She has more than one rib broken, and been clubbed on the back of the head. We need to get her warm, before a fever sets in."

"I'll take care of your horse and will alert you if necessary."

"Thank ye, Masterson." O'Malley entered the building and strode down the hallway past Darby's rooms to Coventry's. He adjusted the lass in his arms and knocked on the door. When it only opened a crack, he rasped, "'Tis Emmett. I need yer help."

The door swung open and the captain's wife ushered him inside. "The poor woman. Aimee, would you please put Emma down for her"—she paused—"N-A-P?"

Aimee didn't move at first, staring at the woman in Emmett's arms. "Michaela? What happened?"

Michaela opened her eyes, and O'Malley noted they were red-rimmed and glassy. He didn't think it was from crying. Before he could lift his hand to feel her forehead, the lass locked gazes with Aimee and whispered, "It was him," before going limp in his arms.

"Aimee!" Miranda's tone got her attention. "Please see to Emma—she's too little to see this."

O'Malley sensed what Miranda did not say, that her little one should not be exposed to the bruised and battered woman in his arms. He nodded, silently agreeing with the captain's wife.

Aimee scooped up the toddler. "Let's go find your blocks, Emma."

"Play with me?"

"Of course," Aimee assured her. "Until your mum needs me, then I may have to help while you play quietly. Can you do that?"

Emma laid her head on Aimee's shoulder. "Uh huh."

As soon as they were out of the room, Miranda cleared off the kitchen table. "Lay her here."

"She has a big lump on the back of her head," O'Malley said. "I knew she wasn't bleeding, and thought I would have had time to examine it more closely once outside the building, but I only had enough time to search for a lump with me fingertips. Do ye have something to cushion her head?"

Miranda grabbed a pillow off the chair by the settee and placed it on the table. "Is that the worst of her injuries?"

"Nay—two, mayhap three of her ribs are broken." He ignored the pull toward the lovely woman as he laid her down. "The lass was worried about me seeing her while tending to her ribs. Can ye help me preserve her modesty by draping a cloth over her chest? I'll be able to cut the sides of her chemise away and check for bruising. That'll indicate which spots to press lightly on checking for breaks before I bind them."

Miranda's worry was evident. "Emmett, let me get Aimee to help. The two of us can bathe Michaela quickly, wrap her ribs, and put her chemise back on. That way we can check for injuries"—she glanced down at Michaela—"elsewhere."

O'Malley couldn't contain the tortured groan that escaped. Why hadn't he thought of that possibility? "I didn't ask… She didn't say…"

The captain's wife laid a hand to his forearm. "She may not have wanted to tell you. Let me get Aimee. Stay with Michaela. I'll return in a moment."

O'Malley's heart absorbed the hit it took from the image Miranda had unknowingly planted in his brain. "God in Heaven, lass," he whispered, bending over Michaela. "Did he violate ye, too?"

She didn't bat an eyelash, nor did she open her eyes to answer him.

Miranda and Aimee joined him in the kitchen a few minutes later. He nodded to the women. "I'd feel better if I can see her ribs for meself," he admitted. "The way her fever came on, 'tis a worry. We'll need to ensure that her ribs are immobilized, but not so tightly that she cannot draw in a proper breath. A lung ailment would be a worry then."

"Give us a few moments of privacy to bathe her," Miranda said.

"From the looks of things," Aimee said, "Michaela was not being held prisoner in a town house on Mayfair."

"'Twas near the docks. Dank and dark," O'Malley said. "I found her in an abandoned warehouse."

When he could not bear to tear himself from her side, Aimee urged, "I know what you must be feeling, but please let us take care of her. I owe her my life and promise to treat her with the utmost care and respect."

"I give my word to do the same," Miranda said. "Please, Emmett. I promise we will not be long."

O'Malley wondered why Aimee was staring so intently at

Michaela's face, but pushed the thought aside. The lass needed her injuries tended to immediately. "And you'll call me once you bathe her torso, so I can inspect the bruising?"

"After we bathe the rest of her," Miranda reminded him.

"I can be present when ye bathe her arms and legs," O'Malley insisted. "When I broke down the door, her gown was twisted above her knees from her attempts to free herself from her bonds. Don't be telling the lass that, though—I wouldn't want to shock her tender sensibilities." He brushed the tips of his fingers along the curve of Michaela's cheek, wishing she would rouse and open her eyes. "Best hurry—she's even warmer to the touch now." With that, he turned and walked to the door, opened it, and closed it firmly behind him.

"You can open your eyes now, Michaela," Aimee said. "O'Malley's gone.

Michaela's eyelashes fluttered. "He never touched me other than to kick me…three times."

"Please do not be embarrassed," Miranda said, brushing a lock of hair off Michaela's forehead. "I had to mention that we needed to check for *all* injuries, and wanted privacy in order to question you."

"Thank you."

Miranda hesitated, then said, "O'Malley's very protective of you."

Michaela had no idea what to say to that. His reaction to her being injured was not unexpected. He was a member of the duke's guard, and protecting others was second nature to them. Though she had to admit the intensity in his eyes and depth of emotion had had her wondering if he could possibly care for her.

When she didn't respond, Aimee asked, "Did you see who struck you on the head?"

"I never saw who hit me. I remember stepping out of the door, then vicious pain in my head. I did not realize how dark one's thoughts could be, trussed up lying on the floor in a dark room, scurrying noises in the corners. The longer I lay there, different injuries made themselves known until I found myself taking stock of them. Aside from my ribs and my head, my wrists are a mess from my trying to loosen the ropes."

Miranda sighed. "What you tell us will never be repeated. Won't you please trust me not to repeat what happened to you while you were held captive?"

Michaela understood her insistence and appreciated her promise to be discreet. She had done the same not more than a fortnight ago when the tables were turned, and Aimee was the one injured. "Nothing other than what I already told you," Michaela said calmly. "I confided what happened to me years ago to Aimee. It was just the one time."

The captain's wife used a fresh cloth to bathe Michaela's face. "Thank you for trusting me. I am in awe of what you have accomplished, and how many women you have saved. If you ever need my help, you have but to ask, and you shall have it."

"Close your eyes," Aimee said. "Let us bathe you while we see if you have any other injuries. You may have bruising on your back that you are not aware of. The pain in your ribs could eclipse minor bruises."

When Michaela complied, Miranda shared a determined look with Aimee. "Help me get this chemise off her."

Their soft voices and ministrations had Michaela dozing.

MINDFUL OF THE deep purple bruises mottling Michaela's pale flesh, they surveyed the bruises and scrapes on her body as they bathed her. The scent of lavender wafted off the soapy cloth as Miranda and Aimee cataloged her injuries to relay to O'Malley.

Miranda had to rouse Michaela again to lift her and wash her back. "We're almost finished. Why don't you close your eyes again?"

When Michaela's eyes were closed, Miranda motioned for Aimee to follow her. When they were on the other side of the room, she fought to hold on to her composure. "I have seen what the ravages of war can do to a man. But abducting her, holding her tied up for hours…and her ribs… That was done out of anger, mayhap pride."

"Retaliation for the loss of coin," Aimee added. "While I was being held, before Darby rescued me, I saw bruises like that and received more than my share."

Miranda slid her arm around Aimee's waist and urged her back over to where Michaela was quietly resting. "O'Malley will be champing at the bit. Let me see if I can rouse her again and let her know I have a nightrail for her to put on, but that O'Malley will need to see her ribs first."

Aimee's eyes welled with tears as she stared at the area where the deep bruising was the worst. "How do you think he will react to seeing this? Emmett seems overly worried."

"I don't think he realizes how much he cares for her yet." Miranda leaned down and called Michaela's name. She slowly opened her eyes. "We will make absolutely certain that you will only have your ribcage exposed. I trust Emmett. He is a healer and will never treat you with anything but respect and care."

Michaela sighed and moaned softly. "I know it. I think it's a reaction left over from…"

Her voice trailed off, and Aimee grabbed hold of her hand. "I understand. If it wasn't for the worry that one of your ribs could shift and cause more damage, Miranda and I would wrap them for you."

Miranda nodded. "I'm going to get one of my nightrails, a shawl, and two bed linens to cover you. I shall be right back."

When she returned, Aimee draped the bed linen from Michaela's waist down, while Miranda draped another linen over the top half of Michaela, covering her breasts completely.

"I couldn't help but notice that the size and shape of the bruises on your ribs look like the imprint of a large foot," Aimee noted.

Miranda asked, "Do you have any idea who could have done this?"

When Michaela did not answer, Aimee reminded her, "We both heard you whisper that it was *him* before you fainted."

"With what you have been doing these last few years," Miranda said, "I am certain there could be any number of unscrupulous people who could be angry with you. Which *him* was it?"

Aimee's eyes welled with tears, though she held them back. "I would never break your confidence, and you must believe me that I would not press you for a name if it wasn't necessary. You could have succumbed to a fever and died, and the person or persons responsible would have gotten away with your murder!"

"Do you want him to kidnap another young woman, repeat this crime?" When Michaela remained silent, Miranda's eyes filled with tears. "I cannot even begin to imagine the reason you would protect this blackguard, but I do know that a person's actions are often motivated by an event, something from their past that compels them to act. Is that why you have made it your mission to save other young women?"

Aimee told Miranda, "I was on my way to Gretna Green to marry the man who swept me off my feet."

Miranda didn't reply. She had a feeling what she was about to hear would break her heart, so she waited for Aimee to continue.

"I did not encourage him," the younger woman said, "but he…he anticipated our vows. When I did not agree to become his mistress, instead of marrying me as he promised, he dumped me in an innyard."

Miranda reached for her hand. "Oh, Aimee. I cannot imagine what you went through. You are so brave to have turned your life around."

Aimee locked gazes with Michaela and waited for a sign from her to continue. Michaela nodded. "I would not have been brave enough to do so, or felt that I was worthy of another chance, had Michaela not confided what happened to her."

"Then Garahan found you and set you free," Miranda reminded her.

"When I asked him to go back and rescue the three other young women at the boarding house, he gave his word that he would. It was a good thing he went back with Emmett to help him, because I did not know about the two little girls."

The captain's wife shook her head. "Three young women *and* two little girls. Garahan and O'Malley would give their lives to protect the duke and his family…and anyone else they discover that needs rescuing." Miranda hugged Aimee. "You are so brave, and so lucky to have been rescued by Garahan. He is honest, brave, and would never judge another for something that was out of their control." She turned to Michaela and asked, "Are you certain you do not know the man's name?"

"I know him. I'm not certain that I'm ready to confide in Emmett, but I know that I will have to. Lives and reputations are at stake."

"I'll go let him in."

When Miranda rushed over to the door, Aimee straightened the linens covering Michaela and reached for her hand. "Trust O'Malley with what happened. He will not judge you—he may want to go after the man and exact revenge on your behalf, but he will not judge you."

"That is what I am worried about," Michaela whispered.

"WHAT KEPT YE?" O'Malley demanded, entering the room. The withering look directed at him had O'Malley immediately apologizing to the captain's wife. "Begging yer pardon, but I'm anxious to see to Michaela's ribs."

"I understand, but you have to realize taking care of a woman who has been brutally injured requires a bit more consideration than if it were a man."

The firm tone of Miranda's voice did not keep him from replying, "Not if the man has a lead ball in his *arse*."

Aimee gasped in shock, but Miranda smiled. "You are so like Gordon that it warms my heart."

"Well then, let me see to Michaela."

"It took a bit more time, and gentle encouragement, to ascertain if there were hidden injuries."

O'Malley's face lost every ounce of color. "Is the lass awake?"

"Yes. She told us that she had not been harmed other than her head, ribs, and wrists, which she said she said she managed to do on her own."

O'Malley blew out the breath he hadn't realized he'd held. "Michaela's a strong woman, and a gifted healer—she would know the importance of telling ye about all of her injuries."

He walked over to the kitchen table and had to fight his reaction at seeing Michaela draped in bed linen with her torso exposed. Her skin was pale and smooth. Tamping down his body's reaction, he focused on her side and the deep bruising. His heart began to pound as worry took hold of him. "God in Heaven, lass! I am so sorry I did not know ye were missing. I could have saved ye from suffering."

Michaela licked her parched lips and rasped, "I know Greenwood got word to Mr. King as soon as he was able to." Her eyes opened and locked on his. "Let Miranda and Aimee wrap my ribs."

"That I will, but after ye let me examine them more closely." When she looked away from him, he added, "I'll be fetching Lieutenant Sampson otherwise. 'Tis me or him."

Michaela frowned. "I do not need a physician—even one who served in the King's Dragoons."

O'Malley was nearly out of patience. "Well then, let us all sit down and wait for ye to find the strength to sit up and wrap yer own ribs!"

"Turn your back," Michaela ordered him, "and I will."

"Ye'll roll off the table and crack yer hard head if ye try." He grumbled, "Lie still," then looked deep into eyes the color of moss in the spring. "What I need to do will pain ye, but know that it pains me as well." He hated like bloody hell to cause the lass more pain, but it had to be done. He had to exert a bit of pressure to see if her ribs shifted, indicating they were cracked or broken.

"I'm not used to receiving care," she whispered. "Giving it is another story. Forgive me, Emmett. I will try not to vex you while you press on my ribs."

He felt sweat bead on his brow and was about to press down on the bottom of her ribcage when she said, "It's the two ribs in the middle that are broken." He nodded and pressed on the ribs she indicated. When she sucked in a breath and held it, he said, "Forgive me, lass. I felt movement that would indicate there are breaks. The good news is that the bones are intact, not shattered."

Her eyes met his. "Thank you, Emmett. I'm sorry to be a difficult patient."

The need for vengeance swamped him. "All I need is the man's name, and I'll ensure he never uses that foot again." The blood of ancient warriors surged through his veins as he planned which blade he'd use.

"O'Malley. *O'Malley*," Miranda called before he noticed she was standing beside him. "Let me raise Michaela into an upright position and support her, while Aimee holds the cloth covering the upper half of her torso in place."

O'Malley frowned. It would take twice as long to do as she suggested, but he didn't see any other way to preserve the lass's modesty. And he sure as hell didn't trust anyone else to wrap her ribs properly. The danger of one of her ribs poking through a lung scared the life out of him. He'd had broken ribs himself and never had a problem, but this was the angel of the streets, the woman who'd unknowingly caught his interest from the moment they'd met, and now it seemed had grabbed hold of his heart.

He could not let go of the idea that he could have spared her from this beating. To begin to make it up to her, he knew he needed to acquiesce to the captain's wife. He inclined his head. "Aye, lift her carefully now."

The trio worked together, and surprisingly, it did not take as long as he'd envisioned.

"If you would turn your back, Emmett," Miranda said, "we'll slip this nightrail over her head and wrap a shawl around her to keep her warm."

He rolled his eyes heavenward, but did as she asked.

"Would you mind supporting Michaela for a few minutes? I'll fetch her a cup of water."

He slipped an arm around Michaela's back and tried to ignore the whisper-soft cotton nightrail and brush of the woolen shawl she wore. "Are ye thirsty, lass?"

"Mayhap just a sip or two. My stomach is unsettled."

"With all the worry over yer ribs, I neglected to check yer eyes to see if one pupil's dilated more than the other." He placed a knuckle beneath her chin, and she raised her gaze to his. Her soft eyes were riddled with pain, but the pupils were the same size. She was able to follow his instructions when he tested her ability to focus on his finger as he moved it side to side and up and down. "When was the last time ye ate?"

"I had breakfast."

"Yesterday," he ground out.

Her eyes flashed with temper, and his heart soared with relief. If the lass was vexed with him, she wasn't as badly injured as he feared! His admiration for her grew.

"Astute observation, O'Malley. As I was otherwise occupied most of yesterday, and then today, until you discovered where I had been taken."

He snorted to cover his laughter, then asked Miranda, "Do ye have a bit of bread that we can soak in some broth, milk, or tea?

I'm thinking her stomach may be unsettled from lack of food."

"I need to send my son to fetch milk for us, but I do have tea. Let me get that for you," Miranda said, then turned to Aimee. "Would you please check on Emma?"

The young woman smiled. "I checked on her twice, and she was quietly playing. But I'd be happy to check again."

While the two women were busy with their tasks, Emmett lifted Michaela into his arms and carried her over to the settee. His body reacted instantly as her rounded hip brushed against him. He gritted his teeth and drew in a breath, digging deep for control. Finding it, he said, "Ye may be more comfortable sitting here while ye have a bite to eat. Something that won't upset yer belly." He settled her on the settee and, though there was plenty of room, sat in the chair next to her. It wouldn't do her any good if he jolted her by sitting beside her.

"I'm sorry I snapped at you, Emmett."

He traced the tips of his fingers along the curve of her cheek, tucking a silky brown strand behind her ear. "I've been known to growl meself when I've cracked a rib or two." The earnest expression on her face nearly brought him to his knees. "Whatever is on yer mind, let it go for a bit longer. I promise, I won't go hunting for whoever did this to ye until ye're ready to confide why ye'd withhold the bloody bugger's name."

She sighed and closed her eyes. "I'm not trying to protect him."

In that moment, he thought he understood. "Whatever happened in the past has no bearing on the present."

Tears welled in her eyes, and she blinked them away. "The past has the ability to destroy my father's reputation. And that I cannot allow."

He fought to control his anger at what had likely been done to the lass. "What of yer reputation?"

Her eyes met his. "I no longer have one."

"Ye'd be wrong about that. I'm not the only one who's seen ye put yer life on the line daily to help those no one else would think to. Ye're strong, capable, determined, and have a code of honor I have only seen in me brothers and cousins."

She looked away from him and gathered her composure.

"Ah, lass, I did not mean to make ye sad." He gently nudged her chin until she was looking at him once more. A tear slid past her guard, and he brushed it away and pressed a kiss to her forehead.

"See if you can get this down, Michaela." Miranda handed her a bowl with a spoon. "Something in your stomach will go a long way to helping you feel better."

"Thank you, Miranda. I'm in your debt."

The captain's wife shook her head. "You have it all turned around. I'm in yours. If you finish that, I have a scone and weak tea that you can eat."

"Scones?" O'Malley asked.

Miranda's soft laughter was soothing as she told him, "I'll bring a plate over."

"Thank ye, Miranda."

The door opened and Coventry entered, followed by Garahan. "Miss Michaela, a word."

CHAPTER FOUR

MICHAELA PAUSED WITH a spoonful of tea-soaked bread halfway to her lips and stared at Garahan and the captain. She nodded, pleased that Garahan seemed to have mastered his balance while wearing an eyepatch since the last time she saw him. When her eyes met the captain's she could not explain her reaction to a man she had never met before. She sensed his steely determination, but it was the innate sense of power radiating off him that had her worrying somehow he knew who had held her against her will and was here to confirm his suspicions. Fear—fear that if the lord's name were revealed, her father would fall out of favor with the capricious *ton* and lose his livelihood—washed over her. He would know of her activities through the men of his guard and Gavin King of Bow Street. What else could the Duke of Wyndmere's London man-of-affairs need to speak with her about?

Lost in the vortex of fear twined with worry, she did not realize her hands were trembling until the warm, callused hand cupped hers, steadying the bowl before it could shake out of her grasp. When she was steady, Emmett O'Malley released her hand and turned to face the captain. "Not now, Coventry. The lass has been badly injured—two broken ribs and a hard blow to the head."

She felt the intensity of the captain's gaze, but could not seem to pry her eyes from the unspoken promise in Emmett's angry green eyes. Was O'Malley offering more than trust? She wished she had the courage to ask him. O'Malley was a man she had come to admire for his ability to heal, his compassion for those in need. She remembered the helpless look in his eyes when the two little poppets he'd carried to safety refused to let go of him when he tried to put them down. If those two little girls could trust him after being locked away in that vile boarding house for a purpose no little one should ever have to face, then she could too. For the first time in far too long to recall, Michaela was willing to share her heavy burden…and mayhap her dark secret.

The captain's frown was fierce. "Are you challenging me, O'Malley?"

"Ye always were quick to catch on, Coventry."

Garahan snorted with laughter. "Well now, it seems that me cousin has complimented ye, captain. What do ye say to that?"

"Bloody hell!"

"Gordon! Emma can hear you!"

Michaela watched, fascinated by the scolding tone Miranda used speaking to her husband, and the byplay between the duke's men and the captain. Unsure if she should speak now or wait for the men to stop challenging one another, she decided to wait. It was difficult to tell whether they did so in jest. The last thing she wanted to do was get in the middle of an argument between these three formidable men.

Captain Coventry ignored everyone and turned to stare at her. Distinctly uncomfortable under his scrutiny, she stared at her lap. She didn't see O'Malley move, but felt the heat pouring off his back when he became her shield, stepping between her and the captain. "Ye can address yer concerns to Miss Michaela through me."

"May I?" Coventry drawled.

"Aye. I am her sworn protector. I will track down the man who kidnapped her, bound her hands behind her back, gagged her, broke her ribs, and left her locked in a room in a derelict warehouse with rats scurrying in and out of a hole in the wall."

"Do you plan to be more than her protector, O'Malley?" Coventry asked.

O'Malley ignored the question and turned to Garahan. "Do ye have room for the lass while she recovers?"

Garahan nodded. "Of course. Aimee and I would do anything for ye, Miss Michaela."

"You do not need to leave," Miranda protested. "Emma can stay in our room, or if my husband continues to be rude, he can spend the night upstairs in his office and you will have Emma and me for company."

Michaela dared a glance at the captain, whose mouth hung open, and then at Miranda, who was smiling.

"Despite my husband's rude behavior just now, know that he only has your best interests in mind, Michaela."

"Ye know he wants to batter the lass with one question after another," O'Malley muttered. "Until he extracts every last bit he thinks she knows, but doesn't realize she remembers."

"If I do not ask questions, how do you expect me to uncover the answers?" Coventry demanded.

O'Malley crossed his arms over his broad chest and glared at the captain. "If it were Miranda in this situation, what would ye do? Allow her to rest and recover for a few hours, or drag her through her ordeal all over again by asking pointed questions?"

Coventry took a menacing step closer to O'Malley, and Michaela's heart began to pound. From what she'd heard about the captain, he was not a man to underestimate. He had been instrumental in uncovering vital information concerning some of the women Michaela had helped to rescue, ensuring they would not fall to another predator. London had far too many of those.

The captain locked gazes with his wife as he replied, "I would protect Miranda at all costs. She is my life."

"I intend to convince Michaela that I feel the same for her."

The breath whooshed out of Michaela's lungs at O'Malley's statement. Her hope rekindled. Did he mean that? Could he care for her in that way? They'd only met a few times, and each time they were tending to others and barely conversed.

Black dots swam before her eyes... She needed air! On the brink of losing consciousness, she found herself plucked off the settee and held firmly against a rock-hard chest. His scent was familiar, though his whispered words were not.

"Close yer mouth and inhale through yer nose, lass. That's the way. Nay," he warned when she found herself struggling, unable to do as he suggested. "Ye can breathe. Look into me eyes, now. Aye, see me. Hear me words. Trust me, Michaela. Ye're safe now. Trust me, lass."

A feeling of wonderment washed over her, knowing that she was truly safe in Emmett O'Malley's arms. She'd had the protection of Cameron first, then Greenwood. Both men had been recommended by Gavin King, and both she'd trusted to guard the women who found their way to her door, and those *she* had found in their time of need. But she had never *fully* put herself under anyone's protection.

O'Malley was different. The way she felt in his presence was different. It was the soul-deep knowledge that he would guard her with his life. Cut off his hand before he would raise it to her. What worried her was the possibility he would not want her once he found out what had happened to her before she became known as the angel of the streets. A warrior and protector as noble as the duke's man-at-arms would never choose a woman with such a dark past—a secret she would take to the grave, because if she did not, her father's life would be ruined. She could not do that to Papa.

"Much better, lass." O'Malley tilted her chin up so she could once more stare into the brilliant green of his expressive eyes. Anger was replaced by concern and a hint of something she had never seen before. She blinked, but the emotion in the depths of his eyes remained. He cared deeply for her and meant every word he said to the captain. Emmett the healer planned to convince her that she would be his wife.

Could she let him into her heart? Had the tenuous bond between them solidified to the point where she could willingly open her heart to the possibility that a man truly cared for her? Could she take the chance that he would not spurn her?

God, she was so tired of walking that fine line between the quiet daughter of one of the *ton*'s favored physicians, and the stews of London where she spent her nights, helping young women regain that fragile emotion that had deserted her ten years ago... Hope. If she put her heart on the line, and took a chance that Emmet would not scorn her, nor trample her pride and her heart, would she regain a tiny part of herself that she kept under lock and key?

Tears welled up and spilled over.

"*Mo chroí,*" he murmured, pressing his lips to her brow. "'Tis all right to cry."

She bit her lip to stem the tears too close to the surface to hold back for long. Desperately afraid to give in to them, she had held them back for so long...ever since that night in the garden. She feared once she started that she may not be able to stop.

"Ah, lass. If ye've been storing up yer tears, then have a good cry. Ma always says two things are cleansing: fire and tears. Trust that I won't let go until ye've run dry, *mo ghrá.*"

When he tucked her head beneath his chin, hiding her face from the others, she wished she had the courage to do as O'Malley's mum said, but she just couldn't. Though she sensed that she was secure in his arms, and she believed he would keep his word, she could not bring herself to give in to the weakness of tears.

O'MALLEY CRADLED HER head in his hand, mindful of her injury, and felt three sets of eyes on him. He sensed the lass would not unburden her soul with an audience. Not wanting her to hear him ask for privacy, he gave a nod toward Michaela's head, which he hoped his cousin would understand. Garahan's frown wasn't what he'd hoped to see.

Aimee walked toward the sitting area from Emma's bedroom and moved to stand beside her husband. Her questioning gaze quickly changed to one of understanding. "Darby, don't you and the captain have plans to go over with Masterson?"

Miranda urged her husband, "Aimee and I will be here to chaperone Miss Michaela until you return. O'Malley can guard us."

"He can't take his eyes off Michaela for one moment—how in the bloody hell can he protect you?" the captain thundered. Emma's wail echoed from her bedchamber, earning Coventry a fierce frown from his wife before she rushed to comfort their daughter. He left the room with Garahan in his wake a moment later.

Aimee stared at O'Malley until he felt the need to ask, "What?"

"I'm going to brew more tea and see about reheating the stew Miranda made earlier. While I'm doing that, why don't you let Michaela rest on the settee? See if you can convince her to let go of her ferocious need to hold back her tears."

He appreciated the interference. "Thank ye, Aimee."

She smiled and hurried over to the other side of the large apartment. When he heard her bustling about the kitchen, O'Malley asked Michaela, "Would you like to lie down?" When she didn't answer, he added, "I could sit and hold ye."

Her gaze met his. "Please."

Warmth spread through him, squeezing his heart. Didn't the lass realize that she needed him for more than protection? Careful not to jostle her, he sat with her cradled against him. "Shall I tell ye about me parents' farm back home?"

He felt her head move up and down and took it to mean she did. Pitching his voice low, he began to tell her about the house his great-great-grandparents built, their milk cow—they only ever had one—sheep, and chickens. Gradually she relaxed in his arms, and he heard a soft hiccup. Her hot tears soaked through three layers of fabric, dampening his chest. The overwhelming need to carry her away from Coventry's building on his gelding, not stopping until they reached his quarters at the duke's town house on Grosvenor Square, was foreign to him. He had bedded his share of willing women, but never in his quarters, and not one of them had ever tempted him to wrap his arms around her to shelter her, protect her, give his life for her, until this moment. *This* woman.

Had his three brothers felt the same about the women they rescued and fell in love with?

She burrowed closer, and he dropped his chin to the top of her head. "That's it, lass. Let it all go. I've got ye."

※

CHAPTER FIVE

HER STORM OF tears ended as abruptly as it had begun. Michaela sighed, comforted by the weight and strength of O'Malley's arms wrapped around her, the rhythmic thud of his heart beneath her cheek.

"Better?" His voice resonated inside of his broad chest, the soothing vibration adding to the mix of emotions swirling inside of her. What she felt for O'Malley stirred in her breast. If she let go of the hold she had on her feelings, she was afraid that she would lose her heart to him.

Was he feeling even the tiniest bit of the attraction that threatened to swallow her whole? She braced her hand to his waist, leaned back, and gasped. "You're bleeding!"

He frowned at her. "I'd know if I were bleeding, lass."

"Take off your coat!"

His laugh was low and sensual. "We aren't alone, *mo ghrá*."

Worry snaked through her irritation at the teasing tone of his voice. "Bloody hell, O'Malley! Take. Off. Your. Coat!"

Aimee rushed over to the settee. "Let me help, O'Malley. I am so sorry we did not realize you were injured. What happened?"

"I'm not hurt, and I'm not…"

Michaela held up her blood-smeared hand. "Something cut you near your waist. How can you not feel it?"

"Me strapping physique, for one. Haven't ye noticed I've more than a bit of muscle on me frame than most? Me tolerance for pain is another. 'Tis probably just a scratch."

Michaela scooted off his lap and grabbed hold of his sleeve. "Aimee, we'll need more hot water and bandages."

"What's wrong?" Miranda asked, rushing toward them.

"Emmett's bleeding and refuses to cooperate," Michaela said, struggling to catch her breath.

"For heaven's sake, Michaela, sit down!" Miranda ordered her.

"Only if O'Malley takes off his coat."

He growled at her and stripped it off. "Happy now?"

"No," Michaela answered. "Black hides most stains, especially blood." She put her hand gently to his side, and he winced. She showed him her bloody hand a second time. "Proof that you're still bleeding, Emmett. Please cooperate, and let us see how badly you're cut."

The blond giant rolled his eyes, endearing him to her. "Fine." Before she could ask, he stripped off his waistcoat. His cravat followed, but he paused before taking off his shirt. "Being as how I'm not unconscious, I don't think yer husbands would like ye seeing me without me shirt on. I know I wouldn't want Michaela to be seeing Darby or the captain without theirs."

"I'm a healer, for heaven's sake," Michaela muttered, then what he'd said about husbands hit her. "You cannot tell me what to do. We aren't married."

"Ah, but we could be, lass. Even if we aren't…yet. Ye're not supposed to lift yer arms, twist, bend at the waist—"

"Or anything," Michaela interrupted as his words elicited twin emotions inside of her—irritation and wonder. "I'll sit, but you cannot bend to inspect or tend your wound. You will either let me, an unmarried healer, or someone else cleanse and wrap your wound." She bit her lip. "Masterson is standing guard outside. Aimee, would you poke your head out the door and see if he will come inside for a moment?"

Aimee left to do her bidding, and O'Malley turned to the captain's wife. "It would be best if you went into Emma's room, Miranda. Don't be thinking it is like the time we carried the captain home after we found him beaten, lying in that alley. 'Tisn't a prodigious amount of blood—I'd have passed out by now from the loss otherwise."

She sighed. "Since you put it that way, I'll go. Call me if you need me."

The sound of heavy footsteps ascending on the stairs was followed by two sets of heavy footsteps descending, and a knock on the door. "It's Masterson—I'm coming in." He walked into the room and stared at O'Malley. "What happened?"

"Damned if I know, but apparently I'm bleeding."

Aimee scooted around Masterson, who stood just inside the door, to the cook stove. She filled two bowls from the hot kettle and carried them over, setting them on the table next to the settee. "I'll just fetch the bandages and soap."

When she returned with the items, Masterson thanked her. "On his way outside to man my post, Garahan asked me to see that you join Miranda in Emma's bedchamber."

Aimee hesitated. "Are you sure you don't need my help?"

Masterson smiled. "Between Miss Michaela telling me what to do, and the number of times I have given aid to the men in my regiment, I doubt it."

Aimee nodded. "If you need me, just give a shout."

"I will," Masterson promised.

When the room had cleared, the colonel turned to Michaela and surprised her by frowning. "We're going to do this my way, Miss Michaela. You will sit in the chair next to the settee or be relegated to the back room with the others. Between O'Malley and myself, there is no room for anyone else. Especially a headstrong healer poking her nose under my arm and getting elbowed in the head, or risking being bumped in her broken ribs."

She reacted to the command in his tone. It was the only reason she did not question Masterson. Well, other than the fact that she was not physically able to push her weight around at the moment, nor did she want to be sent from the room. Michaela glanced at the supplies Aimee had set out on the table and noticed there was no needle. No threads. She started to rise from her seat but was immediately blocked by a broad chest garbed in dark blue.

"When I give an order, Miss Michaela, I expect it to be obeyed."

O'Malley cleared his throat. "Ye'll stay seated, lass, or else Colonel Masterson will carry ye into Emma's bedroom to wait with the others."

"I can sit after I fetch the boiled threads and needle," she insisted.

"As you seem to have assumed responsibility for Miss Michaela, O'Malley," Masterson grumbled, "and I would not want to have to go a few rounds with you for raising my voice to her, I suggest you tell her to obey, or I will *lock* her in Emma's bedchamber!"

O'Malley snorted with laughter. "I'm thinking it must be killing ye to be so gracious, colonel." He turned to Michaela. "'Tis yer choice, lass. Sit, or be locked in Emma's room."

"That is not a choice," she huffed. She had never been told to sit or leave before, and did not like it one bit. Both men outweighed her and were twice as tall—and wide—as she was. She knew that she had to listen, though it irked her. "Fine!" She tried to cross her arms beneath her bosom and ended up gasping as pain radiated from her broken ribs up her side.

Strong hands settled on her shoulders. "Just breathe, lass. In through yer nose and exhale through yer sweet lips."

She must be suffering from lack of air. O'Malley could not have just said her lips were sweet in front of Masterson, could he? When she had her breathing, and the sharp pain, under control, O'Malley lifted his hands from her shoulders and trailed the tip of one finger along the curve of her cheek before returning to the settee.

With his gaze riveted on hers, he stripped off his shirt, and every blessed thought in her brain simply evaporated. The glorious display of musculature had her breath catching in her lungs again. His well-defined pectoral muscles were sprinkled with dark blond hair that narrowed beneath his breastbone, forming a V that accentuated the muscles of his abdomen before disappearing beneath the waistband of his trousers.

"You'd think she never saw a man's chest before," Masterson mumbled.

Michaela blinked, but the sheer masculine beauty of O'Malley's body had cast a spell around her that she did not want to break. Hand to her breast, she lifted her gaze to his and got lost in the swirling emotions in the depths of his brilliant green eyes. The unspoken promise twined with desire was clear, but she wasn't sure how she felt about it. After what had happened to her, she accepted that she would never marry. She had vowed to never suffer the pain that she knew would await her in the marriage bed. Closing her eyes, she was finally able to turn away.

By the time she opened her eyes, Masterson had cleaned out the jagged wound in O'Malley's side. O'Malley was right—it wasn't as deep as she had feared. The amount of time that had passed, between when he had been injured and when they had returned, was a worry. It should have been cleansed and taken care of long before now.

"When did this happen?" the colonel asked.

"I remember feeling a bit of jab when I climbed through a broken window but didn't think anything of it."

Guilt swept up from her toes. The wound in his side was her fault. "I am so sorry you were injured rescuing me," Michaela rasped.

"'Tis but a scratch, and nothing to worry about."

Masterson shook his head and stared at O'Malley's side long enough for Michaela to scoot to the edge of her seat. He lifted his head and locked gazes with her.

"I promise not to get up," she said, "if you tell me what has you worried."

"Have I mentioned that stubborn women irritate me?"

She fought the urge to smile. "Have I told you that military men are like a rash that won't go away?"

Masterson snorted with laughter. "Good God, I do not envy your being leg-shackled to the angel of the streets, O'Malley."

"I never said I was going to *marry* Emmett," Michaela protested.

"But ye will, lass," O'Malley said with an easy confidence that had her bristling. Before she could contradict him, he added, "When I get around to asking ye."

Incensed that the two men believed she would simply capitulate, she drew in her breath to lambast them, and ended up placing a hand to her side, bracing it against the pain. At O'Malley's direct stare, she silently reminded herself to breathe in and out through her nose until she had her breath back.

"She's stubborn to the bone, O'Malley." The irritating colonel sounded as if being stubborn was a count against her.

But O'Malley's reply warmed her heart. "Some of the finest women I know are stubborn."

Masterson stared at her. "I prefer a quiet woman. One who will spend all of her time catering to my every need."

O'Malley sat up straight and squared his shoulders. "Ye'll apologize for poking fun at the lass when she isn't up to fighting form and able to continue the battle of words with ye."

"Forgive me, Miss Michaela," Masterson rumbled. "I could not seem to help myself."

He sounded sincere, but Michaela had learned long ago not to trust men. There were a few exceptions: Cameron, Greenwood, O'Malley, and three of the Garahan brothers. She never intended to trust another man, but when Cameron first came to her aid, when she was rescuing a young woman, she'd lowered her guard and trusted the Scotsman. When Cameron married, he had suggested Greenwood as a man he trusted as his replacement, and she accepted his word. James and his brother Darby were instrumental in rescuing two women whom they later married, and their brother Aiden had kept Michaela's identity secret when she contacted Gavin King with the damning information of who had murdered Emily Montrose's father.

Her most recent rescues were tied to shutting down a notorious boarding house that lured young women to London with the promise of employment, but was in fact a cover for a brothel. After the attempted kidnapping that occurred as a result of her involvement, she could not in good conscience keep lending aid, unless she had protection to ensure those she helped were not recaptured by those who saw them simply as a way to put coin in their pockets.

"Lass? Are ye all right?"

O'Malley's voice snapped her back to the present. "Pardon me. I was woolgathering." She turned to meet Masterson's questioning gaze and remembered his comment…and apology. "Apology accepted, but I should warn you that once my ribs are healed, I will be merciless if you taunt me again."

His smile transformed the man from austere to approachable. "I have no doubt that you will. May I say that I can see how you have snagged the attention of the one O'Malley I never thought would take the fall."

She had no idea what the colonel was referring to. "The fall?"

"Aye. I believe it best to let O'Malley explain after I add a few stitches to his hide. That is what I was contemplating before you interrupted my train of thought."

"Forgive me." Concerned that she would not be able to inspect Emmett's wound to see for herself how many stitches *she* would recommend, she could not help asking, "What can I do to help?"

Masterson lifted his eyes to the ceiling. When he finally looked at her, he was frowning again. "Stay put in that chair."

She was about to respond when O'Malley distracted her. He reached for her hand and said, "Ye need to try to remain calm. When ye get riled, ye draw in deep gulps of air. Ye really should avoid doing so with yer ribs wrapped. Please try, lass. If not fer yer own sake, will ye do it for mine?"

Humbled by his concern and quiet request, how could she refuse? She could not help how she reacted whenever a man tried to tell her what to do. Masterson was no different than her father and the way he spoke to her—

Good Lord, *her father*!

"Emmett, I need to send word immediately to my father. He must be beyond worried by now. I haven't been home in almost forty-eight hours."

"Let me finish patching up O'Malley," Masterson said. "Then the two of you can discuss matters. Garahan needs me to relieve him. One of his contacts sent word that he has information."

O'Malley nodded. "I hope he has a name for me."

Michaela put a hand to her throat. "God help me if he has." O'Malley stared at her. She shook her head and tugged her hand free. "Let Masterson sew your wound closed. The last thing you need is an infection."

He brushed the tips of his fingers along the line of her jaw, turning her to fully face him. "The last thing I need is ye worrying about something that has always been out of yer control. Let me handle the matter. Ye know what I need ye to do. Ye know what I need ye to confide in me."

"Don't move," Masterson warned, "while I bandage your side."

Michaela's mind raced as she stared at O'Malley. Did he know? Had he guessed? She shook her head, not ready to have that particular conversation with him—nor would she tell him the name of the man who took her virtue all those years ago.

She suddenly felt every one of those years weighing her down. She had lived her life on a knife's edge for a decade, worrying that someone would find out and spread the ugly truth. It would not matter that she had done nothing wrong, that she was the victim. The *ton* would never see it that way.

Lord, she was tired. Just once, she wondered if mayhap she

should unburden herself to someone who would protect her from the wrath of the man responsible. Though she was proud of the fact that she had helped so many young women since, it had cost her the close relationship she'd had with her father. Since then, Papa rarely had the time for conversations over afternoon tea…and neither did she.

Haversham had not only taken something she had been saving for the man she one day hoped to wed, but he had robbed her of a decade of conversations, and a warm relationship, with her father. Knowing Haversham had the power and connections to tear away her father's hard-won reputation as an excellent surgeon, most of whose patients were members of elite Society, to shreds, she had never uttered his name to her father. To anyone.

With a determined look, she met O'Malley's gaze with defiance.

While he clearly tried to think of a way to extract the name, Masterson handed O'Malley his shirt. "Do you need help putting it on?"

Michaela blew out a frustrated breath. "Do you have attics to let? You just cleaned his wound. Even though you covered the wound, you cannot seriously expect him to don the same shirt. I am quite certain the captain or Garahan will have a clean shirt O'Malley could borrow."

"Forget the blasted shirt, lass. I'm needing the name of the bastard that did this to ye."

She ignored the hard edge in O'Malley's voice. "There is no need to use that language with me."

"Tell me his name, lass,"

She glared at O'Malley. She would not tell him. Not now. Not ever.

CHAPTER SIX

O'MALLEY RECOGNIZED THE expression on Michaela's face. He'd seen it often on his ma's. The lass had no intention of telling him. The need to have the name, to track the man down and exact revenge, had him by the bollocks. If she were a man, he'd use force to extract the information—a quick jab with his left or a right cross usually did the trick. But she wasn't a man—she was a strong, vibrant woman dedicated to helping those Society shunned. At the moment she was weak from her injuries, but he would not use her current weakness as a way to get her to confide in him. He needed her to tell him of her own accord.

He wanted her to trust him with the truth of what happened—and the name of the bloody blackguard who compromised her. She hadn't said as much, but the hints dropped into conversations he'd heard snatches of were all there. As was the way she'd retreated from Society. The very women she chose to help. He'd suspected Garahan's wife had suffered from such an attack, though he would never speak of something that would only bring heartache to Aimee and his cousin. Marriage to Garahan had helped her to blossom into a stronger version of the woman rescued from that boarding house a few weeks ago.

O'Malley didn't try to hide his frustration as he locked gazes with Michaela and put the damned bloodstained shirt on. It was not only dirty, but cold where the blood had yet to dry.

Masterson shook his head and said, "There are times when I forget I am no longer on the battlefield, where we did not have a ready change of clothes for those we patched back together." He inclined his head to Michaela and told O'Malley, "I need to resume my post."

The door opened and closed quietly behind the colonel. O'Malley rose from where he was seated and walked to the back of the apartment. He knocked on the doorframe to Emma's bedchamber. "Masterson patched me up, and I'm decent, wearing me shirt."

Miranda walked toward him with her little girl on her hip. "Thank you for letting us know." She stepped around him and proceeded to the kitchen.

Aimee followed him to the sitting area, and was near the door when someone knocked. "'Twill be Garahan," O'Malley said.

Aimee opened the door and smiled at her husband, though he stood in the doorway frowning. "I've news."

"I am certain we'd all love to hear it," Michaela replied.

Garahan's one-eyed gaze met hers. "'Tis an official missive, Miss Michaela, or I'd share it with ye."

O'Malley was standing near her chair as he echoed Garahan's statement. "Once we've been given leave to share information, and not before, we will." The two men shared a telling look before O'Malley followed Garahan out into the hallway.

Closing the door behind him, he asked, "What did O'Shaughnessy find out?"

"'Tis as we suspected, and it's either a connection to her good works as the angel of the streets, or a connection to her past."

Frustration surged through O'Malley along with the need to pummel something. Garahan's expression mirrored his own when Darby added, "There's more. Word is, he's a member of the bloody *fecking ton*, and has his fingers in the same pies as Farrell, Robertson, and Ashbrook."

O'Malley's gut clenched at hearing the names of the men directly connected to Garahan's wife being lured to London with the promise of employment on Bond Street. It had only been a few weeks since the men instrumental in luring Aimee from the country had been apprehended. She'd answered that advert and traveled to London, only to be duped, and held against her will at Underwood's boarding house. "Are ye certain there's a connection to the boarding house and the brothels?"

"Aye," Garahan answered. "Heard it from three sources. I'm biding me time, but I mean to see that all three pay for what me wife endured."

"I need his fecking name!" O'Malley growled. He needed to find the bastard—not stand in the hallway talking about it!

"If I had it, ye know I'd give it to ye, and I'd hold yer coat while ye beat the *shite* out the *fecking bugger* for every tear Aimee cried, and what Miss Michaela suffered."

O'Malley drew in a breath to stifle his anger. He couldn't go off half-cocked in his bid to extract the name of the man responsible for kidnapping and then imprisoning Michaela. Then he remembered the rug. "You don't know the whole of it, and I haven't had the time to tell ye. After Michaela was hit on the back of the head, they rolled her up in a rug and transported her to the docks before dumping her in that abandoned warehouse, bound and gagged! I mean to make every man who had a part in it pay dearly for that. But I know from what the lass *hasn't* said…she knows the man who tied that filthy gag around her mouth, bound her hands behind her back, and kicked her in the ribs."

Garahan placed his hand on O'Malley's shoulder and squeezed. "I've a new whetstone. Put a fine, sharp edge on both me blades." He reached into his waistcoat pocket and pulled it out. "Here. Use it before ye leave."

O'Malley spat on the stone and rubbed until it was ready to use. Withdrawing the blade from his boot, he placed the edge of the knife against the stone and added a little pressure before swiping the blade across the stone. He pictured using both of his knives on the nameless, faceless lord who'd injured the lass as he pressed both sides of the blade against the whetstone. He lifted his gaze to Garahan's before testing the blade against the pad of his thumb. It drew blood. "Didn't feel a thing," O'Malley said with a grin.

He pulled the knife from his belt and repeated the steps. A few swipes of the blade against the stone, and he tested it against his other thumb, with the same results. This time he felt his temper calm. He would be using his knife on the nameless man…and soon. "When I find the bastard responsible for kidnapping and harming the lass, I'll need someone to hold him down while I take me payment from him." He held the whetstone out to his cousin, who returned it to his waistcoat pocket.

Garahan's eyes narrowed. "Done! We'll find him. But when we do, ye can't kill the man. Ye know how His Grace feels about that."

"I only plan to extract me payment with a pound or two of his flesh."

Garahan shook his head. "I wish we could, but ye know 'twould be a bloody mess. 'Tis best if we stick to our normal punishment. I'll hold him down while ye kick him in the ribs three times. Ye'll be breaking more than a few."

O'Malley shook his head. "An eye for an eye won't be enough. Not this time, Darby."

His cousin stared at him. "Do ye realize how deep ye are?"

"Deep?"

Garahan nodded. "Aye, ye're so deep in love with the lass, it would take ye a week to claw yer way back to the surface. Admit ye love Michaela aloud; it'll ease some of the tension inside of ye. Don't fight it. Life's too short."

O'Malley drew in a breath and blew it out before meeting Garahan's fierce one-eyed stare. "Faith, I wish life hadn't been so short for me da."

Garahan threw his arm around O'Malley's shoulders. "I miss him too." He waited a beat, then said, "O'Shaughnessy has another lead that he's following. We should have a name in the next few hours."

O'Malley's calm snapped. They'd been discussing it in the hallway long enough. "I'm not waiting!" He turned around and yanked open the door to the captain's apartments. Anger such as he'd never known slid like a noxious oil through his veins. He grabbed his waistcoat and put it on, but didn't bother buttoning it, then snatched his cravat and frockcoat.

"Where are you going?"

O'Malley met Michaela's worried look with a fierce frown. "Out."

Surely the lass remembered asking him to get word to her father that she was safe and unharmed? The latter was more than a stretch—'twas a bold-faced lie. Without another word, he opened Coventry's door a second time, and slammed it behind him.

Slipping his arms into his coat sleeves, he rasped, "Guard the lass with yer life, Darby."

"Done."

The acid of his anger roiled in his gut as he tucked his cravat in his pocket, but he didn't let it show on the outside. O'Malley kept his expression neutral as he opened the door to the building and stepped outside.

Masterson was waiting for him. "Are you headed to Bow Street?"

O'Malley shook his head.

"Greenwood's in bad shape," Masterson said. "He's going in and out of consciousness. I'd wait to try to question him."

O'Malley considered the advice. "By the time I get there, he may be able to stay awake long enough to answer a few questions."

The colonel studied him before adding, "If you plan to speak to Lieutenant Cameron as well, you'll need to keep a tight rein on your temper. He's very protective of his new wife and her younger sisters. His father-in-law is on the mend, but needs his rest after being poisoned."

"I will. I do not plan to take up too much of his time. I only need a few minutes."

"From what Tremayne has said of Cameron's wife Eglantine," Masterson said, "she's a handful and liable to try to interfere on the lass's behalf."

"Does she know Michaela?" O'Malley asked.

Masterson shrugged. "I would not be surprised if she does."

For a brief moment, O'Malley thought about confiding in the colonel about his third and final stop, then decided against it. It would be best if no one knew the last person he planned to interrogate.

The colonel locked gazes with him, and it felt as if the man was attempting to read his mind, though O'Malley knew it was not possible. He was still surprised when Masterson drawled, "If you're going where I think you're going, Miss Michaela may never forgive you."

O'Malley shrugged. "I'm doing what she asked, getting word to her father."

Masterson stared at him. "Ye plan on doing more than that."

O'Malley didn't have time for palaver. "Aye. She'll have forgotten about me speaking out of turn to her da by the time we're saying our vows."

The colonel's eyebrows rose. "You asked her to marry you?"

"Not yet. But I will. Sharing me name will add another layer of protection around the lass."

Masterson was silent while O'Malley untied his horse's reins from the hitching post. "Is that the only reason you plan to marry her?" The question wasn't a surprise, as O'Malley had asked it of himself a short time before.

He whispered promises of oats and a carrot or two to his gelding before scratching behind the animal's ears. "'Tis reason enough."

"The angel of the streets deserves a man who will cherish her," Masterson said, "value her good works, and stand beside her through thick and thin. She deserves love, O'Malley."

A slap of jealousy hit O'Malley between the eyes. "I thought she irritated ye?"

"She does, but that does not negate what I've just said. If you do not agree with me, tell me, because I'm half in love with her already and will marry her to protect her."

O'Malley lunged for the colonel, who evaded the blow. "Well?" Masterson demanded.

Fists raised, O'Malley rasped, "Over me dead body! I have worked alongside her, healing a few of the lasses we've rescued. I admire her spirit, her gift of healing, and her ability to calm even the most skittish of those she tends to. There's magic in her small hands." Needing to ensure Masterson knew the truth, he continued, "I didn't know how deep me feelings for the lass went until I'd heard she was missing." He stared down at his clenched fists and opened them, relaxing them. "I'd die for her, Iain."

Masterson slowly nodded. "I believe you would. I'll not challenge you for her love, Emmett."

"'Tis a good thing, because ye'd lose." Feeling as if a heavy weight had been lifted from his shoulders, O'Malley added, "I love the lass to the depths of me soul, and I will love her from this lifetime into the next."

Masterson's lips twitched. "I always wondered if you were as poetic as other Irishmen I've met over the years."

"Count on it. Me da once confided it took his considerable gift with words to charm *his* stubborn lass, me ma Bridget Flynn, into marrying him."

The colonel's snort of laughter had O'Malley grinning before he sobered once again thinking of the conversations and the information he needed to confirm his suspicions. "This may take a while, as the last stop and conversation won't be an easy one."

"Michaela's father will be relieved that she is safe. We'll guard her with our lives, O'Malley."

He should have known the colonel would guess the last stop he would be making. O'Malley mounted his horse and settled onto the animal's back. "I'm counting on it."

AS HE WOUND his way through the streets toward his first stop, he was not surprised to discover that Greenwood was sleeping. O'Malley left word where he could be reached and set out for Cameron's father-in-law Colonel Merriweather's town house on the fringes of Mayfair. He only needed to speak to the former dragoon for a few moments, then he would track down the last man he planned to speak with today. Depending on what he found out, he'd be riding to Bow Street before he returned to the corner of Hart and Lumley.

The dour-faced butler who answered the door had him wondering how the Scot handled living temporarily in his father-in-law's house if the servants all shared a similar disposition. "O'Malley to speak with Cameron."

The servant's eyes widened. "*The* O'Malley?"

A snort of laughter escaped, and O'Malley cleared his throat. "Aye, if ye're meaning meself, Emmett O'Malley, head of the duke's guard in London."

The butler said, "If you require privacy to speak, may I suggest the stables around back? Horses don't talk."

"'Twould be best if no one overheard our conversation. Thank ye…?"

"Hendricks," the butler replied.

"Thank ye, Hendricks." O'Malley inclined his head, untied his horse, and led him to the stables behind the town house.

"We'll get to the bottom of this, laddie," he told his gelding. "You and I know this was well planned, and there is more to the abduction than appears on the surface."

"Aye, O'Malley." The familiar Scots brogue had him looking over his shoulder. "How is she?"

There were few men O'Malley trusted outside of his brothers and cousins, but the hulking Lieutenant Alasdair Cameron, with the slashing scar bisecting one side of his face, was one of them. "Then ye agree with me?"

Cameron frowned. "Are ye deaf?"

O'Malley lifted his hand to scratch behind his gelding's ear. "I have a lot on me mind."

Cameron was silent for a moment before asking, "Ribs or knife wound?"

"A shard of window glass," O'Malley replied. "If ye know the lass was abducted, ye should know how she fares."

The Scotsman's hand shot out, reaching for O'Malley's throat, but O'Malley tilted his head to one side and held up both hands. "Ye didn't know?"

The anger simmering in the former dragoon's gaze intensified. "She never should have settled for one guard, when the angel needs half a dozen."

"How many times did you have that conversation with Michaela?"

Cameron raked a hand through his hair. "Too many to count. Ye know how stubborn the lassie is."

O'Malley snorted. "Aye. King received the information late last night, though her da must have known or suspected sometime yesterday, but did not report it."

"He has never looked after the lassie the way I would have if she were *my* daughter," the Scot rumbled.

O'Malley noted the hint of surprise in the other man's eyes. He should have realized Cameron would see beyond his mask of indifference to the heartache he was trying to hide. "Don't ask."

"I don't have to. I can see how ye feel about her. I've suspected ye'd be the one to fall for Michaela, given her healing ways and dedication to what has become her life's work."

O'Malley shook his head. "I thought I was masking how I felt."

"To any other man, aye, but to one who's only just been granted a second chance with the woman who has held his heart for more than half a decade, 'tis plain as the nose on yer face."

Before Cameron demanded to know the details, O'Malley gave them to him. "King sent for me—that's how I learned she was missing. I used me contact Leach over on the Dark Walk, and then Garahan's, O'Shaughnessy, on the docks." He paused.

"Apparently a woman friend of O'Shaughnessy's noticed a dark carriage pulled by a matched set of grays arriving the night before last. A man alighted with a rug on his shoulder. As she'd seen the like before, she paused to listen and heard the muffled cry for help. She told O'Shaughnessy."

"I'll skin the bloody bugger before I—"

"Get in line, Cameron."

"Finish it, O'Malley."

He nodded. "He returned to the mouth of the alley empty-handed." O'Malley ignored the low growl of anger and continued. "I decided not to wait for Darby to arrive. I made me way down the alley, inspecting the run-down buildings, looking for signs of a forced entry, and found one building with a broken window. I climbed inside to investigate and heard an odd sound…like tapping."

"Someone was trying to get your attention?"

O'Malley shook his head. "I followed the sound past a handful of rooms with open doors. The sound stopped when I stood in front of the only closed door. 'Twas locked."

Cameron clenched his hands into fists, then relaxed them. "Ye broke down the door."

"Aye, but not before the lass shouted that she wouldn't change her mind."

The other man nodded. "That's the brave lassie we both know and ye love…" Cameron's face lost all expression, except for the promise of death in his eyes. O'Malley knew it was the moment the man had come to the same conclusion that he had earlier. "She knows her captor."

O'Malley did not bother to deny it. Reliving what happened carved a hole in his gut, so he got to the point. "She'd been lying on the floor all night, with her hands bound behind her back. She had worked the gag off her mouth, but could not loosen her bonds."

"Why couldn't she roll out of the way when ye broke the door down?"

"She was exhausted and in pain. The bloody blackguard kicked her in the ribs…three times. I saw the bruises meself after Miranda and Aimee washed the filth from the abandoned warehouse away. They were the size of a man's foot."

Emmett had not been expecting the drastic change in the Scotsman. Gone was his calm demeanor, replaced by raw hate burning in the depths of his eyes. Cameron clenched his jaw and raised his hands, closing them into tight fists, as if he were strangling someone.

"Ye've a wife and her family to protect while her father recovers. I'll take care of her kidnapper."

Cameron dropped his hands to his sides, and his expression was neutral once again. "Ye're looking for a name."

"Aye. Someone from her past…before she devoted herself to rescuing others from the streets."

"Because she knew what they suffered, had felt their pain, but they had no one to rescue her," Cameron rasped.

"Do *ye* know who was responsible?" O'Malley could not utter the rest of what he wanted to know—who'd violated her and taken what she had not freely given.

"Nay. I surmised that may have been what led her to dedicate her life to saving others. Every once in a while, there'd be a young woman who told a tale of a bloody lord who forced himself on her. The lassie's expression would change—'twas there for anyone to notice if they looked hard enough."

O'Malley nodded. "You looked, and you knew."

"Aye. If my heart had not been stolen already…" Cameron didn't bother to finish the statement.

"I have been fooling meself," O'Malley said, "believing that the lass hadn't tugged the heart from me breast the first time I looked into moss-green eyes that held compassion laced with pain."

Cameron shook his head. "I'd be lying if I said I had not felt the same the first time I looked into my wife's eyes."

"You'll see what ye can uncover, then?"

"Aye, O'Malley, I will."

"And ye'll be careful not to share any information about who's asking and why?"

"I give ye my word."

Emmett held out his hand to Cameron, who took it. "Thank ye."

"Do ye need the address for Dr. Colborne?"

"Nay," O'Malley replied. "I have it."

"Good luck to ye."

"Thank ye."

Retracing his steps, O'Malley headed in the direction of Colborne's town house. As he neared the building, he sent up a silent prayer that his gift of words would not fail him. 'Twould be his first conversation with his future father-in-law.

Once he'd spoken to Michaela's father, he'd be speaking to the lass. If she was as intelligent as he'd given her credit for, she should be expecting his offer of marriage.

A curl of dread started to unravel in his gut, but his mind was made up—he planned to save the lass from the nameless man. After they were wed, he'd deal with the repercussions of what he feared she still harbored…the touch of a man.

But by then he wouldn't be just any man. God help him, he'd be her *fecking* husband!

CHAPTER SEVEN

MICHAELA WAS TRYING to rest, but every time she closed her eyes, O'Malley's face filled her mind. His jaw set, anger changing the hue of his emerald eyes to a dark forest green as they burned with vengeance. Though she had not known him long, she had observed his tamping down his temper and redirecting his anger where the young women they had rescued were concerned. As he was a member of the Duke of Wyndmere's private guard, she knew he would be doing what the men did best—ferreting out information from the very streets she worked tirelessly to save young women from. Then and only then would he act. If she remembered correctly from overhearing a conversation between Cameron and James Garahan, the men never sought justice alone. The duke would require witnesses should there ever be a question as to a situation involving the duke's guard.

But somehow, she was gutted knowing that O'Malley was searching the streets of London for information that would lead him to the one man she had hoped to never see again. The one man she loathed with ever fiber of her being, the lord who had taken more than her virtue against her will—he had dashed her hopes and destroyed her dreams. She shuddered just imagining how O'Malley would react if he ever knew the truth of what happened to her that long-ago night in the garden. Would he treat her differently? Would it color his respect for her healing abilities? Dear Lord, would he believe what Lord Haversham had spouted after he'd had his way and let her go?

O'Malley could never learn the truth. To lose his friendship after finally admitting that they shared a connection through their conviction that it was their duty to rescue and heal others… He'd all but said he would marry her.

She paused and shook her head. Nay, what he said was that they *would* marry, and she would agree when he was ready to ask her.

She would not tell him, and she prayed he would never find out.

If she had not been hit on the back of the head, she would have stood a chance against her attacker face to face. When Alasdair had worn her down and talked his way into acting as her guard, she did the same, repeatedly asking him to teach her how to fend off an attack. At first the former dragoon had refused, but once he saw the chances she took, and how often danger lurked just outside her door, he showed her that a well-placed punch— or knee—to the groin could double a man over. That and to keep a sharpened knife hidden on her person at all times.

She'd had to employ that tactic only once. It had surprised her attacker and won the loyalty of one of the young women she had given aid, shelter, and the start of a new life to with employment in a household Michaela trusted. She had connections in and around London, far-reaching contacts who felt as she did about what was happening to young women being lured to the city with the promise of employment.

Someone had to protect these women, and she had volunteered for the task. Her dream of becoming a physician would never come to fruition, nor would her father's dream that she would one day marry well and give him grandchildren.

Reacting to what he conceived to be a blow to his pride, and the waste of his precious time, the lecherous lord had used his strength to overpower her, ensuring that she would suffer as he had.

Did the blackguard care that she would be shunned, and her father's very livelihood would be at risk, because of the lord's need to, as he told her, put her in her place? He would curse her for trying to reach higher than her social station.

There were times at night when she would lie awake and ask God if this had been his intention all along, knowing the idea of a studying to become a physician in a male-dominated environment would be unattainable for her. She'd instead put her skills, learned at her father's side, to good use in giving aid and encouragement to those who despaired of ever regaining their self-respect, honor, and pride. A part of that had been confiding in a select few who seemed to need to hear her story in order to begin to heal. Aimee Garahan had been one of those few. And Aimee, along with Miranda, had helped her after she had been abducted.

Have I come full circle, Lord? she silently asked. *Am I supposed to publicly accuse the man responsible for ruining me in order to finally begin to heal myself?* Her belly ached at the very idea. No matter the consequences of speaking up at this point in time, she wondered yet again—would it have been better to tell her father what his choice of husband for her had done?

She hadn't realized she was crying until a pristine white handkerchief appeared in front of her face. Blindly, she reached for it, mopping her tears before blowing her nose.

"Michaela, after all you have helped me through, you know that you can trust me not to tell a soul what happened to you."

She lifted her head. The compassion in Aimee's eyes wrapped around her like a hug. Fear that the *ton* would discover her shame and turn their backs on her father curdled in her stomach. "If I could tell anyone, Aimee, it would be you."

Aimee sat in the chair opposite from her. "You have my word that I will never breathe a word of what you confide in me. But given what the men in the duke's guard have witnessed, and the number of women they have rescued in the last two years, I believe they have a very good *idea* of what happened. Darby guessed what happened to me."

Michaela shook her head. "I never divulged what you shared with me."

"I know you didn't. He and his brothers and cousins have witnessed the cruelty of those with twisted minds and black hearts…and the aftereffects of that cruelty."

"Even Darby and Emmett would shun me and stop lending their aid—"

"Listen to yourself," Aimee chided her. "Do you really believe that, or are you pushing what you feel you deserve onto the thoughts and words of others?"

Michaela's heart clenched painfully, but she knew it was emotion causing the pain. "Why would you…" She bit back the rest of what she had been about to say. "I believe that was the advice I gave to you a few weeks ago."

Aimee nodded. "At the time I did not quite believe it, but with the steadfast love and support of my husband, I have made great strides in actually accepting your words and holding them to my heart."

When Aimee reached for her hand, Michaela felt a soothing comfort in the other woman's firm grip. "Don't push Emmett away. It would have been the biggest mistake of my life if I succeeded in pushing Darby away."

Michaela sighed. "And now it is your turn to help him, as he heals from injuries he sustained in his bid to protect and defend you."

Aimee looked away, then back before whispering, "I blamed myself."

"You were not responsible," Michaela insisted. "The men who tried to beat him to a pulp when they jumped him in that alley are. They are currently being held at Newgate Prison."

Tears welled in Aimee's eyes. "But his sight…"

It was Michaela's turn to soothe. "You know he vowed to give his life protecting the duke and his family."

Aimee nodded. "And the duke's extended family."

"Which now includes the wives, stepchildren, and babes of the men in the duke's private guard who have married."

Miranda walked over to join them. "I hate to interrupt, but I am in desperate need of a strong cup of tea."

"And something sweet to go with it?" Michaela asked.

Miranda smiled. "I just put Emma down for a short nap. Earlier, I baked scones along with the gingerbread Gordon cannot seem to do without on a daily basis."

Aimee smiled and rose to her feet. "Let me help you. Michaela was just about to close her eyes for a few minutes. Weren't you?"

Michaela could not believe Aimee had repeated the very same words Michaela had said to the other women rescued from the boarding house. In hearing her words parroted back to her, Michaela realized she truly had come full circle. "Just for a moment," she said.

"That's all you need," Miranda replied.

A SHORT WHILE later, Michaela opened her eyes. "Forgive me, do you need help with the tea?"

Miranda and Aimee shared a look before Aimee asked, "How do you feel?"

"Like someone bashed me on the back of the head, abraded my wrists until they were raw, and then kicked me in the ribs."

Miranda's look of concern had Michaela feeling as if she had struck the young woman with her harsh reply, when she had only been asking out of concern. "Mayhap I should see if the broth I was preparing for you is ready," Miranda said. "You can have tea another time."

"Forgive me," Michaela replied. "I have not been myself since I woke in that abysmal building. I am rather terrified of rats."

"You were left in a room with *rats*?" Aimee sounded horrified.

"I heard the scratching and scurrying, but did not actually see any vermin. I was told there was a hole at the bottom of one wall, where the rats could come and go as they pleased."

"There is a special place in hell for whoever said that to you," Miranda said. "The blackguard knowingly added to your fear."

Michaela admitted, "I really am quite terrified of the creatures."

"Rats," Aimee whispered. "That would mean that you were near the docks!"

"I must have been, but I confess I was in a state of shock when O'Malley rescued me, and did not notice much of my surroundings. Thank you again for allowing me to stay with your family, Miranda. I am grateful."

"Our home is always open to you," Miranda replied. "You have succeeded in convincing those you aid of their worth. Whereas others have tried their hardest to make the women feel it is somehow *their* fault that they ended up in circumstances beyond their control."

"They desperately need a champion," Aimee said. "You are their savior… You have been mine."

"I know I said it before, but however I can help, please let me know," Miranda said as she rose and walked to the kitchen. "I hope you do not mind, but Aimee and I did not want to rouse you and couldn't wait. We had a cup of tea while you were resting, but we saved the sweets for when you woke up. We can have them now with another pot of tea."

"You did not have to wait," Michaela insisted.

Miranda smiled as she stared at Aimee. "Someone else, aside from my darling husband, has been particularly fond of eating my gingerbread as of late and indulged in a slice or two. I waited to have a bite with you."

Michaela turned to study Aimee and noticed a subtle glow about her, as if she held a wonderful secret to her heart. She slowly smiled. "Have you told Darby your news yet?"

Aimee shook her head. "I have only just realized it today…after Miranda asked me how I was feeling."

"I could tell from the way you turned a bit green when I was preparing the broth for Michaela. The scent of beef boiling always triggered an immediate response from me while I was carrying Michael and Emma."

"It nauseated you," Michaela stated. One noticeable sign of pregnancy was an enhanced sense of smell and a sensitivity to scents.

Miranda agreed, and added, "Aside from that, I had a tendency to become lightheaded and swoon."

"Are you feeling light of head too, Aimee?" Michaela asked.

"A bit, but everything is so new to me. The second chance at life with a man who treats me as if I am to be treasured is so unexpected that I thought it was my constant worry that I would wake up and find myself back at the Underwood boarding house."

Michaela rose to her feet and embraced Aimee. "Congratulations, Aimee. I am so happy for you and Darby." The movement strained her ribs and had her drawing in a sharp breath.

"Sit down," Miranda ordered her. "You won't do anyone any good if you injure your ribs further before they have even had a chance to heal."

Michaela sank back onto her chair. "I believe I have advised more than one of my patients to do the same with similar injuries," she said. "I'm not used to having to follow advice."

Aimee and Miranda shared a look and smiled. "We know," Aimee said. "But if you do follow the advice that you have doled out to others, you will find that you will heal."

"Without running the risk of doing more damage to yourself," Miranda said, "which would require a much longer healing time."

Michaela sighed. "I take it you are speaking from experience with your husband?"

Miranda nodded. "I have come to the conclusion that most men are a trial to a woman's patience, believe themselves to be impervious to injury, and are shocked to the core when they feel pain."

Michaela smiled. "I have not had the same experience as you. You are most fortunate."

"I did not think so when I received the news of my first husband's death. I was in a daze until the day I chanced to hear that Gordon had been badly injured in the same sea battle. I went to the hospital needing to find him. He and my first husband were as close as brothers, and I needed to see for myself that he would recover. I needed that connection, for myself and for my son… Michael had just turned two."

The door opened and Miranda's face transformed from despair to joy. "Here's my son now. Have you come for tea and cake, or to issue orders from the captain?"

Michael smiled. "Father said that I needed to spend half an hour keeping you ladies company."

Miranda frowned. "What is that man up to?"

Michael shrugged. "I am following orders, learning all I can from Father before I follow in his footsteps, and that of Papa's, in the Royal Navy."

"Two of the bravest men I have had the honor of knowing," Miranda remarked. "Your papa would be so proud of the young man you have become. Prouder, because he would know that it is because of Gordon's influence when he stepped into the role of protector to us all those years ago, keeping his promise to your papa."

Michael wrapped his arm around his mother. "I know Papa is smiling down on us, even though it took you and the captain far too long to realize the three of us were meant to be a family." He pressed a kiss to her cheek. "Any chance of the two of you giving me another sibling? I wouldn't mind a little brother, now that I have a little sister."

Miranda's mouth opened and closed, but only a garbled sound escaped. When she managed to regain her voice, she chastised him, "That is not a subject for polite company."

He slowly smiled and said, "If I don't ask with witnesses, you may not remember that I asked."

Aimee's laugh was infectious and had Michaela bracing a hand to her ribs as she joined in the merriment. How wonderful it would be to experience the joy of welcoming a new babe into one's family.

She immediately pushed the thought away. It was not a part of the Lord's plan for her.

Pushing thoughts of an angel-faced babe with blond hair and green eyes from her mind, she watched the others bantering back and forth, wishing that her life had been different. But if it had been, would she still have met the duke's man-at-arms?

She shook her head. Nay, she would not have had the pleasure of meeting and working alongside Emmett O'Malley. For however long he would be in her life.

CHAPTER EIGHT

O'MALLEY KEPT MISSING Michaela's father by five minutes or more at each stop he'd been assured the good doctor would be. Fed up with the chase, after trailing in the physician's wake for the last hour, he changed tactics and rode to Colborne's town house to wait for the man.

Frustration and worry tangled inside of him, as he wondered if Michaela was still listening to reason and resting. Taking a chance that the butler would be as astute as the duke's London butler, O'Malley was ready to demand entrance if necessary.

"O'Malley to see Dr. Colborne."

The older man squinted up at him, frowned at his disheveled state, then asked, "Do you have an appointment?"

"Gavin King sent me."

The butler's expression changed to one of respect. "Of course. One moment, please." The man turned and motioned to one of the footmen hovering behind him. "See to O'Malley's horse."

"Me fine four-footed friend has been waiting to slake his thirst," O'Malley told the footman who walked over to take the bridle from him. He leaned close and pitched his voice low. "Don't listen if this fine gelding demands a shot or two of whiskey—'tis water me horse is needing after being one stop behind the doctor for the last hour."

The footman snorted with laughter. "Water it is."

"Thank ye." O'Malley gave his horse a quick pat and walked over to where the butler waited for him. Raking a hand through his hair, he had to hide his grimace of annoyance from the pull of the threads holding his most recent injury closed. "Please excuse me appearance. I have been on duty for the last twenty-four hours. With what I've just learned, I thought it best to come directly to speak with Dr. Colborne."

The butler held the door for O'Malley and waited until they were inside before asking, "Do you bring news of Miss Colborne?"

O'Malley hesitated, but the hopeful expression on the man's tired face had him going with his gut. "She's safe." The butler's eyes were suspiciously damp with emotion. O'Malley went on to explain, "I can say no more until I speak with the doctor."

"That she is safe is a huge relief. When she did not return home…" The servant straightened his shoulders and cleared his throat. "I beg your pardon. Allow me to show you to Dr. Colborne's study. I do expect him to return at any moment."

"Thank ye…"

"Stark, sir."

"Thank yc, Stark."

Alone, O'Malley scanned the room. He'd heard it said that you could gauge a man's wealth by the number of books he owned. Da always said a man's true wealth was found in his family. Gazing at the books littered about the room, he imagined Colborne was a man of considerable wealth. If this was the physician's study, he could only imagine how many books were housed in the man's library! There were books on shelves, tables, and stacked on the floor beside one of the leather wingback chairs by the fireplace. The desk was a thing of beauty, a huge, dark, scarred piece of furniture that did not look as if it belonged among the other pieces in the room. It had books stacked this way and that on two corners of the large desk.

Aware that he looked as if he'd been either brawling on the

docks or one of the alleys in the stews, he brushed off a bit of dirt from the cuff of his sleeve, still more from his frockcoat. No one usually cared what state he was in when he arrived with urgent news—he generally only stayed long enough to deliver his missive, or verbal message, before leaving.

This time would be different. Now that he had time on his hands, he wondered why he hadn't acquiesced when Michaela asked him to change his shirt.

The door to the study opened, interrupting his thoughts. Stark announced, "Dr. Colborne." With a nod to O'Malley, the butler added, "O'Malley was sent by Mr. King."

The physician paused to stare at him before turning to Stark. "We are not to be disturbed."

"Of course, doctor." The butler closed the door behind him, and Michaela's father walked over to where O'Malley waited.

"Stark blurted out that my daughter is safe. Why didn't you bring her home?"

"Why did ye wait until this morning to report her missing? It would have spared the lass the pain she's suffering."

The man visibly blanched as he grabbed hold of O'Malley's arm. "Take me to her!" O'Malley dropped his gaze to where the man clutched his coat sleeve, but the physician did not remove his hand—he tightened his grip. "Now!"

"Not without her permission."

"I'll have you hauled down to Bow Street, and you can explain to King why you refused."

O'Malley snorted. "King knows full well why I will not be bringing her here."

They stared at one another, not speaking. Just when O'Malley was about to grab the man by his cravat and start shaking him, the doctor capitulated. "My reasons for waiting to report her missing to King are my own."

"How much do ye love yer daughter?"

"What kind of question is that?" the physician demanded.

"What would ye give up to save yer daughter and her reputation?"

The bluster went out of Colborne. "Everything."

O'Malley narrowed his eyes. "You'd give up yer life, yer thriving practice, yer hard-earned reputation?" Colborne blinked and opened his mouth to speak, but O'Malley cut him off. "Because that is what the lass gave up a decade ago to do the only thing that would purge the anguish in her soul." His voice broke when he continued, "To help other women who have been ill used, abused, and violated."

The older man's face flushed as he clenched his jaw and reached again for O'Malley, who stepped back out of reach. "I'll ask ye again, why did ye not report the lass missing yesterday?"

Colborne scrubbed a hand over his face. "It was part of the agreement I have with my daughter. She accepted my insistence that she have a guard and agreed never to divulge her full name, if I allowed her to continue what she told me was her calling without interference."

"Did ye never ask why she felt compelled to answer this particular calling?"

"Before I answer any more questions, tell me how she was injured."

O'Malley looked away for a moment to block out the memory of the lass's pain-filled eyes when he broke the door down and found her trussed up, lying on her side. "Three broken ribs, a lump on the back of her head, and her wrists rubbed raw."

Colborne strode over to the sideboard and the crystal decanter, poured a squat glass half full, and downed the contents. "Has she been seen by a physician?"

"In a way."

"What the bloody hell does that mean?"

"I'm a gifted healer, as is yer daughter. I wrapped her ribs meself, though she was tended to first by two women I'd trust me life with to wash away the filth from the warehouse floor when she'd been dumped."

The doctor's hand trembled as he set the glass on the sideboard. "You will take me to her immediately!"

"Nay."

"I am her father!"

"And fat lot of good ye've done for her while she's been an angel to those in need, suppressing her need for compassion and understanding herself."

A fierce expression settled on Colborne's features. "Michaela is my life!"

"Is she now? I do not think yer daughter is aware of that fact. Though she was worried enough about ye to ask someone to get word to ye that she is safe."

"Why you?"

"She trusts me."

"Why would she?"

"We've worked together more than once, tending to those who have been cast aside by the same Society ye cater to with yer tonics and laudanum. Do ye have any idea how many young women yer daughter has saved?"

Colborne opened his mouth to speak, but a groan emerged. He shook his head. "We used to be close, helped one another grieve after my wife died. All Michaela wanted was to become a doctor like me. She worked tirelessly by my side, learning all that I could teach her. She was a comfort to my patients, who adored her." Colborne frowned. "But there was no future for her. Who would allow a female doctor to tend to them? I told her it was time to give up her dream and urged her to accept a few of the invitations she had received from young men I approved of."

O'Malley listened, though the need to plant his fist in the man's face nearly overwhelmed him. "Men like yourself, or men with a title?"

Michaela's father glared at him. "Both."

"And did she do as ye asked?"

"Aye. But only once or twice before she came down with a virulent fever."

O'Malley wondered if he had been wrong about what he

suspected happened to the lass. "And ye treated her?"

"She would not let me in her bedchamber," the doctor replied. "She feared that I would succumb to the same fever and knew my patients depended on me."

O'Malley had to call on all of his steely control not to go for the man's throat. "So ye don't know if she had a virulent fever or something else was wrong with her."

"What do you know?"

O'Malley didn't answer.

Colborne took another step closer. "By God, you will tell me what you know!

O'Malley crossed his arms in front of him. "'Tisn't what I know—'tis a feeling I have."

"What possible reason would my daughter have for hiding in her room?"

O'Malley glared at Colborne. "Ye might ask yerself why she didn't trust ye enough to confide in ye." He pushed past Michaela's father and strode to the door.

"O'Malley, wait!"

He paused on the threshold.

"What is Michaela to you?"

The despair in Colborne's voice cut through O'Malley's anger. He spun around and locked eyes with the man. 'Twas plain to see the man loved his daughter. O'Malley could not condone the fact that he had waited to tell King his daughter was missing. Putting himself in the other man's place, O'Malley answered, "Everything. I have risked losing her trust and her love by coming here and speaking to you without her knowledge. Yer daughter may never speak to me again, but I love her enough to risk that, because she cannot go on hiding from the bloody bugger who…" He shook his head, turned back around, and strode from the room.

"Wait!"

He ignored the doctor and inclined his head to Stark. "I'll send word as soon as I'm able, but remind yer employer that the lass is safe and well cared for."

"Thank you." Stark opened the door and closed it behind O'Malley.

Emmett vaulted into the saddle and was a few houses away when he heard the doctor bellow his name. He did not give he man the satisfaction of stopping or turning around. 'Twould be a sign of capitulation. He'd cut off his right arm before he gave in to the man.

"Bloody blind, fecking *eedjit!*"

The threads holding the paltry nick in his side itched and felt as if they were on fire. He should be able to ignore the minor wound. *Just like ye should be able to ignore the lass with the moss-green eyes and healing hands.* Calling on his innate ability to block out the pain from injuries and worries in order to concentrate on his duties, he was surprised that the irritation did not immediately disappear.

The heat from the wound spread beyond where the window glass had sliced into his side. Slipping a hand beneath his frockcoat, he unbuttoned his waistcoat. He wanted to see if it was his imagination, or if the wound was putting off heat. "Bloody hell!" Heat radiated through the bandage and his cambric shirt. 'Twas infected.

Torn between the need to add one more stop, to see if Greenwood was conscious and able to speak before returning to the captain's building, and the knowledge that his wound was beginning to fester, he retraced his steps, riding back to the captain. "Well, laddie, change of plans. I need to have another look at me side before we speak to Greenwood and corner King in his office on Bow Street. I'm thinking King knows more about the situation between the doctor and Michaela than he is letting on." The runner had a lot to answer for, the most pressing of which was why he had intentionally kept O'Malley in the dark where Michaela's father was concerned. Surely King knew that O'Malley had added the lass to those he protected.

Mayhap he didn't.

CHAPTER NINE

"Now then, let me serve our tea. Aimee, would you please bring the plate of sliced gingerbread and scones?"

Michaela watched the two women working smoothly beside one another and wished she had someone to share her day-to-day life with. The women had formed a fast friendship, had husbands who loved them, protected them…would lay down their lives for them.

What do I have?

The answer filled her heart: the gift of healing, and the admiration and protection of Emmett O'Malley. She found that she was thinking about his statement that they would marry, and she would accept his offer—when he got around to asking her. She fought the urge to laugh and instead smiled.

"You'll be feeling better in no time, Michaela," the captain's wife assured her. "I happen to keep a small supply of calves' foot jelly on hand. It does wonders for whatever ails you."

Michaela shivered. "But the *taste*."

Aimee and Miranda laughed when they placed the teapot, cups and saucers, plates, and confections on the small table between the settee and the pair of matching wingback chairs. Without asking, Miranda handed Aimee a plate with two large slices of gingerbread. Aimee had eaten half a slice by the time Michaela had taken two small bites of her scone.

Studying the younger woman, Michaela wondered if Aimee had given any thought as to whether she was carrying a boy or girl. Would she want to know that she was carrying a boy? After all, the tales passed down from Michaela's grandmother's time were more often than not based on truth. Women carrying a girl were more apt to temporarily lose their looks, while those carrying a boy appeared radiant. She thought Darby Garahan would welcome the babe, no matter if it be a boy or girl, but would secretly be thrilled to have fathered a son.

Sipping from her tea, Michaela nearly bobbled the cup and saucer when Masterson burst through the door, holding O'Malley up.

"What happened?" Miranda demanded before Michaela could even form the words.

The expression on the colonel's face reflected concern, but only for a moment. "He fell off his horse and is burning with fever." His gaze pinned Michaela's. "Caught him before he smacked his head."

"Didn't fall," O'Malley protested, struggling to keep his balance. "Horse tossed me off."

Michaela had never seen him in such a state. Turning to the colonel, she said, "I watched you cleanse his wound before stitching it closed. There wasn't a speck of dirt in it."

"Aye," Masterson agreed. "But there was quite a bit of time in between when the injury occurred and when you noticed O'Malley was bleeding. Time enough for infection to set in."

Masterson had already stripped the outer layers off O'Malley. He hadn't bothered with the cambric shirt as he helped O'Malley walk toward the kitchen table. Miranda was already clearing the table, while Aimee rushed over with bed linen. As soon as she smoothed it on top of the table, the colonel tried to lift O'Malley onto it.

"I didn't break me legs, Masterson," O'Malley growled. "I don't need yer help."

To Michaela's surprise, the colonel let go of him and stepped back. "As you wish."

She was halfway across the room when the stubborn man swayed a heartbeat before his legs gave out. Breath held, she watched his knees hit the floor. Miraculously, O'Malley braced his hands on the floor and didn't smack his head.

"Bloody stubborn, hardheaded Irishman," Masterson swore. He glared at O'Malley. "Not a word!" Thankfully, O'Malley didn't try to brush the colonel aside a second time.

Michaela wanted to ask the man why he'd let go of O'Malley, but the expression on the colonel's face had her biting her tongue. She walked over to stand beside where O'Malley lay with his eyes closed. Had he slipped into unconsciousness?

"Do not worry about O'Malley," Masterson assured her. "Emmett has the constitution of a warhorse. See that he doesn't roll off the table while I wash my hands."

She nodded and leaned close to O'Malley, calling his name, but he didn't answer. Worry slashed through Michaela. When it was her turn to wash her hands, the colonel stood beside O'Malley, quietly speaking to him, leaving her to wonder why he had been ignoring her.

Miranda poured hot water into two bowls and placed them within Masterson's reach, while Aimee set out a stack of clean linens. Michaela moved to stand beside Masterson, who reminded her, "You should be resting."

She was too tired to argue with the man. "I'm a healer, colonel, I need to do something."

He frowned at her, but just when she thought he would tell her to go sit down, he said, "I would expect no less from the angel of the streets." Masterson's expression changed, and for a heartbeat, the irritation was replaced with a look of longing in his eyes. He blinked and it was gone. Had she imagined it? "Your experience with wound fever is quite a bit different than mine. Given the circumstances, I shall let you take the lead, Michaela. But when I deem it is time for you to let me take over, you will do so without question. Is that clear?"

Incensed that the man thought he could tell her what to do, she replied, "I am not one of the men in your former regiment. I take orders from no one, colonel."

"Listen to him, lass," O'Malley rasped. "Ye cannot afford to have one of yer broken ribs pierce a lung."

She brushed a lock of hair off his forehead. "I'm fine."

"Nay," he grumbled, "ye're not. But ye will be with time and rest. I'm not feeling up to arguing with ye. Please do as Masterson says?" His green eyes locked on hers. "For me?"

How could she refuse his request? "I still think I am fully capable of taking care of you, but—"

"Oh, aye," O'Malley interrupted, reaching up to brush the back of his hand across her cheek. "Just like I didn't need Masterson's help getting on the table." He turned toward the colonel. "I'm sorry, Iain."

The other man shook his head. "Understandable, given that you're Irish."

O'Malley snorted with laughter. For a moment, Michaela wondered if she would have to brace him to keep him from rolling off the table. Relieved when he lay quiet once more, she locked gazes with Masterson, who nodded. "We need to cut the shirt from his body," she said.

Masterson withdrew a wicked-looking blade from a sheath beneath his waistcoat. She reminded O'Malley, "This might not have happened if you had donned a clean shirt when I asked you to."

Masterson answered before O'Malley could. "It's a possibility. Neither of us knows just how dirt encrusted that shard of glass was. Part of the filth may have worked its way in before his shirt rubbed against the wound." The colonel sliced through the black, blood-soaked fabric.

"We'll need to remove the bandage, and check the wound, before we cleanse it again and decide which poultice to use," she said. The hint of irritation in Masterson's gaze was an indication of how far the man was willing to bend and allow her to give him orders.

"I keep a poultice on hand for my husband," Miranda announced. "It has comfrey root in it. Helps with swelling from the objects they repeatedly come in contact with. I also keep herbals on hand to reduce fever."

Michaela nodded. "We seem to have that in common. While you use yours to heal the brave men that work with your husband and the duke, I use mine to treat women who do not deserve the wounds they have sustained." As soon as the words left her lips, she apologized, "Forgive me. I cannot help but worry about who may need me right now, while I'm in hiding. Who will they turn to when they cannot find me? What will happen to those in need of rescuing if I am not there to help them?"

"Ye are known to those who can get word to us," O'Malley said. "Should someone be in need of rescuing, or healing, or know of someone that does. Do I need to remind ye, 'tis what we do on a daily basis, lass?" Michaela shook her head, and she sensed he was satisfied with her response when he added, "Albeit, those we rescue are usually connected to the duke and his family."

"Or destined to be connected to the duke through the men in his private guard," Masterson added.

Michaela had to agree. She had been on hand twice now, and had borne witness when that connection sparked and flared to life between James Garahan and Melinda Waring, and between Darby Garahan and Aimee Anderson. Knowing the duke's men were fiercely protective of their wives, and at the same time unreasonably jealous of their wives being around other men, Michaela said, "I'll apologize to your husbands later, knowing how they feel about the two of you being in the same room when O'Malley is shirtless. Right now, we need your help."

"Tell me what to do," Aimee said. "I can handle Darby."

Michaela was proud of the great strides Aimee had made in the short time she had been married to Garahan. "While the comfrey poultice is soaking in hot water, we need to prepare the herbal for Emmett to drink to combat the fever."

"Not if it tastes like *shite*," O'Malley grumbled, closing his eyes.

"You'll do whatever you need to in order to heal." Masterson's no-nonsense tone had O'Malley shifting as the colonel removed what was left of the shirt.

Michaela sucked in a breath at the sight of the reddened skin surrounding the bandage covering the wound. Ignoring the pain slashing through her ribs, she motioned for Aimee to bring over cloths. "The water is near to scalding—we need it that hot to draw out the infection." Dipping her hands and the cloth in the water, she felt the heat searing her flesh, but did not complain. O'Malley was more important than the slight damage to her hands. She covered his wound with the hot cloth and noticed the way he flinched. "I'm so sorry, Emmett. It is imperative that we draw out the infection with the heat."

When he did not respond, Aimee whispered, "Did he swoon?"

He opened his eyes. "*Bollocks!* I've never swooned in me life. Been unconscious a time or two, though." O'Malley looked at Aimee. "Forgive me for cursing—'twasn't aimed at ye, Aimee lass."

"Nothing to forgive," Aimee said. "Darby uses colorful language all the time."

Michaela frowned at him. "A gentleman shouldn't use that kind of language in the company of ladies." If he was aware enough to curse, she reasoned, O'Malley wasn't as bad off as the signs of infection would indicate. "I hate to cause you any discomfort, but we need to use the hot cloths twice more… We'll add soap this time."

He blinked, and she stared at his impossibly long, dark lashes before noticing that he seemed to be waiting for her to meet his gaze. When she did, he nodded and said, "I trust ye, lass."

Aimee set a bowl of soapy water next to Michaela's elbow. She bit her bottom lip, dipped the cloth in the hot water, and laid the cloth over his wound.

After the third application, he closed his eyes for a moment, then opened them. "That should draw out whatever was inside. Thank ye for noticing I was bleeding, lass. I truly did not feel any pain."

Her hands were shaking as she turned and reached for the bowl with the poultice Miranda had been soaking. Pain sliced through her ribcage.

Her sharp intake of breath had Masterson taking charge. "Enough, Michaela. I'll take over; you can sit here and hold O'Malley's hand to keep him still. If you are in too much pain, you can sit on the settee by the window." His tone was firm and brooked no disagreement.

"I'll sit beside Emmett." She had no intention of agreeing that she had overdone it. Besides, her injuries had already been tended to, and O'Malley needed her.

The colonel thanked her in a quiet, controlled tone. He finished what Michaela started before asking Miranda for the comfrey root poultice.

While he worked, Masterson remarked, "It's a good sign that you aren't out of your head with fever."

"Aye," O'Malley said, trying to sit up. "Me head feels a bit fuzzy."

Michaela braced herself to place her hands on his strong shoulders before gently pushing against him. "You need to lie back down and rest with a cool cloth on your head to bring the fever down."

Masterson disagreed. "Let him sit up. He can drink the herbal with the feverfew in it first, then we'll use the cool cloth."

"If me fever gets any higher, and I'm out of me head, lass," O'Malley began, "don't be holding whatever I say against me. 'Twill be the fever talking."

A moment ago she was desperately worried that he would fall unconscious from the fever, and now she felt her lips begin to twitch as she fought against the urge to smile. "Excellent suggestion to have him drink the herbal while he's able to sit up, colonel."

"Iain," Masterson said. "As we're up to our elbows taking care of the man who all but proposed to you, we should be on a first-name basis."

O'Malley glared at Masterson and nearly choked on the herbal concoction. Before he could speak, Miranda said, "Aimee and I call Iain by his first name. And the other men as well."

The expression on O'Malley's face would have been comical if Michaela were not quite so concerned about him. "Let me help you lie down, while I bathe your face."

"If ye need to bathe more than me face, lass, ye have me permission to ogle me impressive pectoral and abdominal muscles—after all, 'twill be yer right as soon as we wed."

Michaela started to sputter, then began to cough, which quickly turned to a moan of agony.

"Forgive me, lass. I didn't think me words would send ye into a fit of coughing. Easy now," he soothed, rubbing her back. "That's the way—breathe in and out through yer nose, *mo ghrá*."

Shocked at the endearment she had heard both Garahan brothers use when trying to soothe the women they rescued and later married, she met the intensity of O'Malley's gaze and felt herself obeying. When she had her breathing under control, she asked, "Did you mean what you just said?"

"The part about breathing ye in and out through yer nose? Aye." She frowned at him, and he slowly smiled. "Aye, *mo chroí*, ye are *mo ghrá*… Me heart. Ye are me love."

This time when she placed her hands on his shoulders, he lowered himself to the table.

"Close your eyes, Emmett."

"Ye aren't planning on heading to the stews to see if anyone needs ye, are ye, lass?"

"I will not leave your side until the fever breaks and you are sleeping peacefully." The second time she told him to close his eyes, he cooperated. She smoothed the cool, damp cloth over his face and neck before dipping it back in the bowl of water. Her ministrations did not appear to be cooling his face down fast enough to suit her. The quicker his fever broke, the sooner her heart would return to its normal beat. Worry for O'Malley nearly overwhelmed her.

"Ye need to brace yerself not to swoon, and bathe me manly chest, lass."

Masterson chuckled. "I'll leave you to the tender care of the women, O'Malley."

"I'll only be needing the tender attentions of one woman from this day forward." O'Malley opened his red-rimmed, fever-bright eyes and stared at Michaela. "Will ye marry me, lass?"

Shock had her sucking in a breath that had her ribs reacting immediately. Accepting the pain, she stared at him for a few moments without speaking.

"Well?" O'Malley asked. "Will ye?"

"Is it the fever talking?"

His frown was fierce as he struggled to sit up. "Nay! Masterson?"

The colonel paused with his hand on the doorknob and glanced over his shoulder. "Aye?"

"I may need a favor, depending on the lass's answer. Will ye wait a moment?"

"I will."

Michaela glared at O'Malley. "May I remind you that you asked me to ignore whatever you say in your fevered state."

"I meant if I said what's been on me mind, plaguing me, since the first moment I saw ye. Not an important question like the one I just asked ye."

She narrowed her eyes and frowned. "I have plagued you?"

He grunted. "Aye, with the tilt of yer chin when ye're about to say something to irritate the *shite* out of me like ye're doing now. The way ye bite yer plump, rose-tinted bottom lip when ye're feeling uncertain, and the way—"

Masterson chose that moment to interrupt, "I thought you

said it was her gift of healing and the way she is able to calm the most skittish of women she rescues?"

"Aye, that, too," O'Malley agreed. Reaching for her hand, he rasped, "I'm not out of me mind with fever, lass. I'm after giving ye the protection of me name."

Michaela had started to shake her head when the colonel said, "O'Malley, didn't you tell me you love her?"

An emotion deeper, and truer, than want or desire flashed in O'Malley's feverish eyes. Michaela was stunned for a moment before she whispered, "Do you love me, Emmett?"

"With every breath I take, lass. Do ye think ye can love me back?"

Tears welled up and spilled over. Did she have the courage to tell him that if she could ever trust, ever love anyone, it would be him? She hadn't been prepared for him to propose.

There was still the problem she had never thought to face again. Unprepared for the subject to arise, or even be considered, she knew that she feared what would happen in the marriage bed. She believed Haversham's claim that no one would ever marry damaged goods like her, and she had let her girlish dream from when her mum was still alive of a husband and family die along with the dream of becoming a physician.

"Would ye mind if I spoke to the lass without an audience?" When no one moved, O'Malley added, "Ye have me word of honor that I will never take advantage of the lass."

"Please, Miranda?" Michaela asked. "Will you allow us the illusion of privacy, while you and Aimee keep an eye on us from the settee?"

Miranda sighed. "Of course. Gordon has often remarked that if you cut any one of the men in the duke's private guard, they bleed honor. When an O'Malley, Garahan, or Flaherty gives his word, he keeps it."

"Thank ye, Miranda," O'Malley said. "'Tis how we were raised. To go against what Da and Ma instilled in us would be akin to taking a blade through the heart." He nodded to Masterson, who grunted, but walked over to stand guard by the door.

When the women moved to the other side of the apartment, O'Malley lowered his voice and asked, "Have I misread the longing in yer eyes, lass? Look into me eyes now and tell me ye don't have feelings for me. No putting yer hands behind yer back and crossing yer fingers. I'm needing the truth—me heart cannot take less."

How could she possibly love this man more every time she laid eyes on him? Pain and humiliation were what awaited her in the marriage bed. She had to tell him her secret, but how, without telling him the name of the lord responsible?

"I didn't recognize what I was feeling at first," she admitted. "I thought it was merely irritation when you walked into my rooms as if you had every right to be there. The next time I saw you, you were carrying those two little girls you and Darby rescued, snuggled tight against you." Cupping the side of his face in her hand, she lowered her lips to his, feeling every sharp jab of pain that sliced through her broken ribs. She softly pressed her lips to his and drew back so she could stare into his brilliant, fevered emerald eyes.

"I know now that I have loved you from that moment, Emmett O'Malley, but there are things you don't know about me that would have you rescinding your offer of marriage. I cannot let my past tarnish your reputation or that of the duke's guard."

"Masterson, would ye ask Coventry to see about obtaining a special license? I intend to marry Michaela as soon as possible."

"Aye," the colonel agreed as he left the room and closed the door behind him.

"But I just refused," Michaela reminded O'Malley.

"Nay, ye did not refuse me, lass." In a tender voice, he continued, "Ye gave me a reason ye thought would be strong enough to discourage me from marrying ye. I won't take back me offer, no matter what ye think."

"But I'm not—" Tears welled up, and she pushed away from the table.

O'Malley grabbed hold of her hand and gently reeled her back in. "Lass, me brothers, cousins, and I have seen and dealt with more situations than ye could even imagine, even while ye've been rescuing lasses in and around this city. I've surmised what I believe happened to ye. It matters not. Me love for ye will help ye heal from what ye suffered. I'll only ask one thing of ye, lass. Know that I do not say this lightly, but to be truly protected by me name, we must seal our vows after we wed."

Michaela wished she didn't shrink inside from the thought of letting another man do to her what Haversham had. Pushing past what could not be changed, she told him, "If I could trust anyone it would be you…but I'm afraid. What if I cannot do as you ask?"

"No one will know but the two of us. But know this, lass: I don't lie. If I'm asked if we sealed our union, I am bound by my honor to tell the truth. If your father demanded that you return home, and we had not sealed our vows, I would be duty bound to escort ye to him."

Her stomach ached, and her ribs throbbed in time with the pain in her skull. While fear roiled in her belly, the very idea of how freeing it would be to have O'Malley's protection tempered that. His connection to the duke and his family, Captain Coventry, and Gavin King would ensure no one would dare to touch her. But could she willingly allow herself to let another man—

She could not even finish the thought.

"I need to see what ye're thinking. Let me see yer angel's face, lass."

When she looked at him, her heart melted. Everything he said he felt was there in the depths of his eyes.

"If ye truly love me, lass, like I think ye do, then trust me. Once we say the words before the vicar and witnesses, in the eyes of God we'll be wed. Ye'll be stuck with me for the rest of yer life. I vow I will never turn me back on ye, never hold what happened in your past that has ye fearing the future or a man's touch."

Had he guessed what she had not wanted to confess? It was hard to catch her breath. Her mouth opened, but not a sound emerged. He couldn't know her shame, could he?

"Trust me, lass, I'll never lay a hand on ye in anger, nor will I use me body as a weapon to cause ye pain. Love isn't like that, *mo chroí*. After we seal our vows, I will not force you to do anything ye do not wish to, until ye come to me and tell me ye're ready to let me heal your soul-deep hurts." He lifted her hand to his lips and pressed a feather-soft kiss to her knuckles, then another above the bandages covering the abraded skin on her wrists. "I've already given ye me heart, lass. 'Tis yer turn."

Michaela thought her earlier tears had run dry...but she was wrong. She could not hold back the cleansing tears that flowed from her eyes any more than she could hold back the need to wrap her arms around Emmett O'Malley and tell him what he wanted to hear. She bit her bottom lip and leaned toward him. Without asking what she needed, O'Malley gave it to her, wrapping his arms around her. Sheltered and safe in his embrace, she held him tight.

This was a man she could trust, and yes, he was the man who had stolen her heart. She should have accepted and acknowledged it when it happened—it was his tender care of two little moppets who'd been intended for one of the notorious brothels in London. She would tell him what lay heavy on her conscience before they wed. She would trust him with her heart, soul, and body.

She laid her head on his shoulder and felt the thundering beat of his heart against her breast, where hers drummed a rapid beat of its own.

"I'm trusting you with so much more than my heart, Emmett."

"With God as me witness, lass, I know it. Whatever it takes to erase the pain weighing heavy on yer soul, I shall do. We're stronger together, lass. Trust me to protect ye, and love ye the way ye deserve to be loved. With tenderness and compassion while I replace what ye fear with what ye'll come to crave."

His words tempted her, while the entreaty in his eyes swayed her. He was the man she had trusted without question the moment they met. Though she had trusted the Garahans, Tremayne, Coventry, and the others, there was one difference—she had not felt this deep connection and affection with anyone before. Only this man. Only him.

"I trust you, Emmett," Michaela whispered against his lips. "And yes. I would be honored to marry you."

His kiss was gentle and held the promise of more. "Ye won't regret it, lass."

CHAPTER TEN

L ORD HAVERSHAM STOOD in the warehouse hallway staring at the body-sized hole in the door he'd locked behind him hours earlier. "Where in the bloody hell is she?"

"She was here half an hour ago," the man he'd left in charge guarding his prisoner replied.

Haversham rounded on the man, who alternately stared at his feet and the door to the room that had held the one woman who had spurned him. Anger at losing the angel of the streets nearly choked him. Michaela had rejected him because of some ideal and need to follow in her father's footsteps. Her beauty and rumored dowry aside, Miss Michaela Colborne was an abomination who tempted him! No other woman had ever wanted to supplant what was a man's calling—to become a physician and heal others.

Though it had been years since that night when he'd thought to appease her by asking what she dreamed of, mistakenly thinking she'd say *him*. She had slashed his pride, and the very heart of what made him a man, by confessing her desire to become a doctor like her father. Incensed, he'd struck out at her with vicious words. When she absorbed them, ignoring his words, he'd snapped. Overpowering her with his strength, he showed his superiority the only way he could—taking her by force, using her roughly, swiftly, and without emotion. When he was finished, he lashed out at her again, predicting that no one would have her now. She was damaged goods, and everyone would know of her shame. If she ever dared to speak of what happened between them, he promised that her father would be humiliated, made to share in her ruin.

The emptiness in her once-bright eyes had him regretting his ill treatment of her. But in the next breath, she had gathered her composure around her like an impenetrable suit of armor. In that one moment, his heart blazed with hatred for her that consumed him then…as it did now.

"Find her!" he shouted.

His cohort flinched, nodded, and tripped as he rushed off to do his bidding. Haversham wondered how a mere woman like Michaela could find the strength to continue in the face of ruin. When his anger had cooled, he felt certain that she would never show her face again. Supremely confident that he had put her in her place, he'd dismissed her and never thought of her again. That had been his mistake.

He had been slowly cultivating contacts within the *ton*, those who shared his views that women were put on this earth to amuse men and appease their needs. Period. They'd carefully selected individuals to deliver the young women who answered their advertisements for honest work in London, spent time speaking to boarding house owners, until they had a handful that were not above earning more coin training innocent women from the country how to please a gentleman's baser desires.

It wasn't until recently, when one of his partners in their very lucrative business had been exposed and hauled down to Bow Street before being sent to Newgate, that he'd gathered the information pointing to one individual whose name was revered by some, hated by others. This, he thought, curling his hands into fists…this was how Michaela Colborne had managed to go unnoticed for so many years. Hiding in plain sight during the day, while combing the streets searching for women of her own ilk, with tattered reputations, undeserving of a second chance, at night.

How could I have been so blind to believe that I had conquered her? Bloody hell, I thought by taking the one thing all women waved as a prize before a man they hoped to marry that she would realize she no had no value at all.

Haversham slammed the side of his fist against the doorframe. The shaft of pain went unnoticed, as he realized she still prized her unrealistic dream of healing others. She had succeeded where he had failed, thinking he had demeaned her, conquered her, when she in fact survived and still fulfilled her calling.

"I will find her…and I will make her pay!"

He ached with need, remembering how quickly he'd lost control once he'd used his brute strength to overpower her to take her against her will. He slowly smiled. He preferred an unwilling partner—it heightened his pleasure.

He acknowledged his prey was stronger now, no mere virginal chit. His erection hardened to the point of pain as he imagined her fighting the inevitable… He could not wait to take her again!

CHAPTER ELEVEN

"I BEG YOUR pardon?" Michaela must have been letting her mind wander. Surely she had misheard what O'Malley just said. His gaze bored into hers, as if he were sifting through her thoughts. His color was back to normal, and he was sitting upright without aid. His ability to recover so quickly astounded her.

"No need to ask me pardon, lass. Ye said yerself that yer da needed to know that ye had been found and were being taken care of. I delivered the message for ye."

She struggled to keep calm. Losing her temper would only lead to her breathing erratically. She'd end up suffering for it because of the way her ribs had been tightly bound.

"Yer face is turning red, lass. Breathe!" O'Malley ordered her.

With a hand braced against her ribs, she blew out a breath, drew one in, and glared at the stubborn Irishman. "Why didn't you mention it earlier?"

"When Masterson all but dragged me into Coventry's apartment because I wobbled dismounting from me horse?"

"He said you fell out of the saddle," she reminded him.

"Nay, I think he said I *all but* fell out of the saddle. 'Tis a different thing altogether."

"But you were fevered, and the infection—"

"Do ye not remember trying to convince me that ye needed

to clean out me wound a second time, or that ye were struggling to breathe even then?"

Michaela fought the need to shout at him. "Of course I remember. I was not the one in danger of keeling over!"

"Ye're getting yer dander up again, lass, and for no reason, or are ye forgetting that me fever broke? I'm thinking ye were right about donning a clean shirt. Between that and yer undivided attention, I'm thinking both together did the trick. It healed me, lass."

Ignoring the twinges in her side as she gulped in air, she demanded, "Am I not allowed to show emotion?" When he leveled a neutral look at her, she prodded him, "Well?"

He grinned. "God in Heaven, if I haven't fallen into a pile of sweet-smelling *shite*!"

Her mouth dropped open. "Are you comparing me to a pile of horse dung?"

O'Malley snorted with laughter. "That I am. Did ye forget I was raised on a farm? 'Tis part of a farmer's life and essential to the soil."

She was momentarily speechless. He shook his head at her. "Faith, I love the way ye're trying to be proper and not cursing a blue streak at me. Ye'd be mistaken thinking I was insulting ye, lass. 'Twas a compliment. A fine wife ye'll be." He leaned toward her. "Ye're even more beautiful when ye're angry, Michaela-mine."

His words deflated her. How could she stay angry with Emmett when he said lovely things like that? "You do not fight fair."

He swung his legs over the edge of the table, braced a hand on top of it, then pushed to the edge and stood. Placing his hands beneath her elbows, he drew her closer. "I'm not after arguing with ye, lass." He stared at her mouth, then lifted his gaze to meet hers. "I have other things in mind."

She placed her hand in the middle of his chest to stop him, and stifled a moan of pleasure when his muscles shifted beneath her hand. Gathering her composure, she pleaded, "You need to rest, Emmett… Your fever—"

"Were ye not listening? In truth, it broke half an hour ago. I sat as ye asked, to make certain me head was clear. 'Tis clear, lass. I have a job to do, Michaela, and will not get any answers lying on the table or sitting here on me *arse*."

"But the infection—"

"I've had more than one over the years, lass." He traced the curve of her cheek. "Ye said yerself that the redness was fading after the second cleansing and soaking with the poultice."

Michaela wished he did not have such an overwhelming effect on her senses. She felt as if she were being pulled toward him, and at the same time felt the need to shove him away. Why couldn't her heart make up its mind? She had already said she would marry him, and furthermore, she had agreed with him that in order to be truly wed to him, she had to lie with him, let him consummate their union… She shuddered remembering what that entailed, and gasped as sharp shards of pain jabbed into her side.

Before she could gather her wits about her, she was enveloped in the warmth of O'Malley's embrace. His strength was evident by the way he gentled his touch so as not to hurt her. "Easy, *mo chroí*. Ye have to be the most difficult patient I have ever had. Can ye not remember to keep calm and not allow yerself to get riled up? Ye're doing yerself harm taking in great gulps of air, and 'twill do ye no good if ye end up in bed for a fortnight because ye've injured yer lungs as well as yer ribs."

"I did not cause my injury!" Her acidic tone had her immediately apologizing. "Forgive me, O'Malley. You do not deserve the sharp edge of my tongue."

Instead of agreeing with her, he smiled and brushed his lips to her forehead. "A fine and feisty wife ye'll be, lass." His callused fingertips traced the line of her jaw before he cupped her face in his hands and whispered, "Kiss me, lass."

She had already promised to marry him—why would he want to kiss her now, when they would share a kiss after they were wed? Michaela had already shown him a glimpse of her temper. After all he had done on her behalf today, she really shouldn't continue to vex him. So she acquiesced.

Leaning against his powerful chest, she was surprised when his firm, yet pliant, lips molded with hers and immediately pulled at her heartstrings. Michaela had no choice but to respond to his kiss. Sensations she had not experienced before swept her up in a maelstrom of emotions too tangled to pull apart and dissect. A bolt of heat sizzled between them when the tip of his tongue traced the rim of her mouth. She moaned, and he immediately pulled back.

"I did not mean to frighten ye, Michaela."

She stared at his mouth and blinked, unable to believe that the meeting of lips could elicit such a whirlwind of feelings. "I wasn't… You didn't…" She was unsure of how to put into words what she felt because it was new…unexpected.

"Well then, that's fine. I would never want to give ye reason to fear me, lass. But the taste of ye went to me head like three fingers of the Irish on an empty gut."

Michaela was surprised by his response, though she sensed he had felt something, too, when they kissed. With a hand to her belly to ease the fluttery feeling inside of her, she dug deep for the courage to ask, "Is it common to feel so much from the mere meeting of lips?"

His eyes darkened with what she hoped was desire. "Ah, lass, there are so many ways to express yer feelings with a kiss. If ye'll allow it, I'd be happy to demonstrate." His lips were a breath away from hers when the door to Coventry's apartments burst open.

"Kiss yer intended later, O'Malley!" Garahan grumbled. "Coventry's alerted the new recruits to our London guard, and the men on the docks and in the stews, to the situation, instructing them to see what they can uncover. He agrees that there is something more sinister behind yer kidnapping, Michaela. He's waiting to meet with us."

She was not about to tell either man the connection she had to her kidnapper. She'd have to find a way to get word to Lord Haversham. Michaela needed to let the man know that she was willing to pay him to remain silent, if he would leave her father out of his need for revenge. She could save the pin money her father indulgently gave to her for visits to the modiste, hoping it would be enough to pay Haversham. Fortunately, she received anonymous donations of gowns to replace tattered ones for those in need. Michaela would need to seek donations for the time being to maintain her supply of linens, herbs, and tinctures.

"What aren't ye telling us, *mo ghrá*?"

Emmett's tender endearment nearly had her confessing what she feared was behind her abduction. When he pressed his lips to her temple, she wanted to tell him all that she knew and who had orchestrated it.

"Darby!" Aimee rushed over to his side. "I need to speak with you."

"Later, love, we've an important…" Garahan's words trailed off when he looked into Aimee's upturned face. "What is it, lass? Are ye feeling poorly again?"

Instead of answering, she nodded. Without asking, he swept his wife into his arms and carried her over to the settee and gently set her on it. "Rest until I get back. Ye've yet to recover from this morning's stomach upset."

"I'm afraid I won't recover for quite some time," Aimee replied.

Garahan's face lost every ounce of color. He plopped down on the settee beside her, pulled her onto his lap, and pressed her face against his heart. "Michaela, what do ye know about Aimee's illness? Is there no cure for what ails her?"

The entreaty in his voice had tears welling in Michaela's eyes and Garahan shaking his head.

"Nay, I'll not believe there is naught ye can do to ease me Aimee's suffering. She's been sick of a morning for over a week now, and again at odd times during the day. I've told her to rest, but she refuses."

"Aimee is quite fit, Darby, but I agree that she needs to rest often, and nibble on bread or scones to keep something dry in her belly upon rising so that she won't feel nauseated."

"Just what kind of stomach ailment does she have?" Garahan demanded.

Michaela kept her response cryptic at first, hoping Garahan would catch on to the fact that his wife was carrying his child. "The kind that will ease in the next month or so as she gains weight."

"Emmett!" Garahan barked. "What do ye know of this?"

O'Malley grinned. "If ye'd quit yer worrying for a minute and think about what has been described to ye, and what ye've noticed, ye'll put two and two together and get three."

"Three? Are ye daft? Two and two together is four, not three!"

Aimee giggled.

"Ye could be dying, lass. Do ye find this funny?" Garahan glared at everyone. "Have you all gone mad?"

Michaela took pity on the man. He was obviously too concerned for his wife's health to even realize he had all the clues to come up with the answer. "Aimee, tell Darby what he can expect in nine months' time."

Garahan's eyes narrowed. "Nine months?"

Aimee's eyes welled with happy tears that spilled over when she placed a hand on her still-flat belly.

"A babe? Are ye carrying me son?"

She shook her head. "I may be carrying our daughter."

Garahan's shout of joy bounced off the walls. He shot to his feet and twirled Aimee around in circles until she moaned. "Ah, lass. Forgive me, I didn't mean to make ye—"

Miranda rushed over with an empty chamber pot in time to avert disaster, but not Aimee's acute embarrassment at having relieved the contents of her stomach with an audience.

"Don't give it a second thought, lass," O'Malley assured her.

"Me cousins and I have been on hand with a chamber pot, planter, vase…what have ye, whenever the duchess, countess, or viscountess have had need of it."

"Quick on our feet," Garahan said. "I'm so sorry, lass. I wasn't thinking."

Miranda handed Aimee a cloth to wipe her mouth. Michaela urged Garahan to place his wife on the settee. "No sudden movements for the next little while, Darby."

"Ye have me word." He pressed a kiss to the top of Aimee's head and slowly eased his arms from around her. "Rest now, lass."

"We will," she replied.

"We." He grinned. "I'm going to be a da!"

O'Malley walked over and clapped a hand to his cousin's shoulder. "Congratulations, Da."

Suddenly solemn, Garahan rasped, "We're having a babe. 'Tis a big responsibility."

"The biggest," O'Malley agreed. "Now let's be off—we've work before ye can come back and wrap yer wife in cotton batting to keep her safe for the next nine months."

At Garahan's thoughtful expression, Michaela said, "Not a realistic or helpful suggestion, Emmett."

O'Malley smiled, opened the door, and yanked Garahan's arm to get him to follow. When the door closed, Miranda and Michaela sat on either side of Aimee. "It'll take him a while to become accustomed to the fact that sudden movements may upset your equilibrium," Miranda said. "Or that certain scents may bring on a bout of nausea."

"From what I have observed of your darling Darby," Michaela said, "he'll soon catch on and catch up to what you need. He'll be a wonderful father."

Aimee whispered, "After what happened to me, I never thought I'd marry. Not once did I even dream I'd want, or deserve, to be a mum."

"You deserve all the happiness your heart can hold."

Michaela's tone was stern because Aimee's words were the same thoughts she had had ten years ago, and still had on occasion.

"Trust Darby," Miranda urged. "Every man in the duke's guard can be trusted to guard the duke, his family, and the guards' wives and babes. I have never heard one of them pass judgment because of circumstances beyond one's control."

"From what I have noticed," Michaela said, "your husband and his men are cut from the same cloth."

Miranda smiled. "They truly are. All of them appear gruff, hardened. It's a reflexive emotion to protect themselves from years of being treated as if they were half a man because of the injuries they incurred serving king and country."

"Gallant, brave men," Aimee agreed. "One and all."

"Even when they are annoying us," Michaela murmured. "Now then, Miranda what can I do to help with supper?"

"Not a thing. I have the stew simmering, and Aimee and I baked bread first thing this morning."

"I'm a fair hand at making scones," Michaela said. "Though I haven't used that talent since my mum fell ill."

"I lost my mum the year before Michael and I married. We were always in the kitchen together. My favorite job growing up was having a turn on stir-up Sunday. It's been years since I lost the both of them."

"I loved making Christmas pudding." Michaela smiled, remembering happy times in the kitchen with her mum. "I wonder if we could make more than one, so the men could all share in the tradition and have a turn stirring."

Miranda beamed. "I think that is a wonderful idea. Let's put our heads together and see if we need to double or triple the recipe."

Aimee suggested, "It might be easier to just make separate batches—that way, the proportions and ingredients will be correct."

Michaela smiled, thinking that she felt at ease with these two women and had finally found true friends—women who yearned for the same traditions and basic need to have a home and family. Though neither Aimee nor Miranda shared the overwhelming need to heal others as Michaela did, they were adept at caring for all manner of wounds. A necessity, given whom they had married.

By the time the women had the meal ready to be served, Garahan and O'Malley had not returned. The captain had been summoned to Bow Street, leaving Masterson, Tremayne, and Miranda's son to guard the women.

They ate in shifts, little Emma and Michael sitting down for the first serving, Masterson the second, and Tremayne after him.

Michaela's worry increased with each passing hour. Where were Garahan and O'Malley? Why hadn't Captain Coventry returned? After a few hours, her gut was roiling. As if she sensed what was happening, she announced, "We need to prepare for injuries. I need to be able to look Emmett in the eye and tell him that I did not overdo it, so I'll sort and fold the linen strips. Aimee could keep the kettle warm and put on a large pot of water...just in case."

"I'll ready a few poultices and herbals," Miranda added. "That way, we'll be prepared for anything."

The sound of shots fired at close range, and a heavy object hitting the door to their building, had the women freezing for a moment before Miranda jumped into action. "I'll bring Emma out into the kitchen. No one is going to climb in her window again! Aimee, grab one of my heavier pots, and give one to Michaela, too!" With that, she disappeared into her daughter's room.

"Pots?" Michaela asked.

Aimee nodded. "Aim for your attacker's face and throw it as hard as you can."

Michaela nodded as the door burst open, and her nightmare stepped over the threshold. Impeccably dressed, a sneer on his face, and a dueling pistol aimed at her heart. "Aimee, run!"

In answer, Aimee hurled a pot at Haversham's head. He lifted the hand that held the pistol to deflect the pot from bashing him in the face. "Bloody hell!" He leveled the pistol at Aimee, and Michaela threw her body in front of her friend as Haversham fired.

White-hot pain seared through her upper arm as the lead ball grazed her. She stumbled, but did not fall. She had to protect the others…one a mother and the other a mother-to-be. Without thinking of the repercussions to herself and her father, she said, "Lord Haversham, wait. I'll go with you. Please leave the others alone! They have no part in what I have been doing these ten years past."

His chest was heaving, whether from anger or exertion, she did not have the time to discern.

"Please?" She struggled to keep her balance, though her vision was a bit blurry. She walked toward the man responsible for ruining her, shoving those thoughts back into the tiny box she kept at the back of her mind. Now was not the time to ruminate over the past—it was time to take action to save Miranda, Emma, Aimee, and the babe in her belly. She had to get Haversham out of there before he realized Miranda and little Emma were in one of the back rooms, or he decided to take Aimee hostage, too. Michaela would not allow it! She could not let any harm come to her friends!

Digging deep for the strength, she put one foot in front of the other until she stood before the man she detested with every fiber of her being. Meeting his dark and twisted gaze, she did something she never thought she'd do…surrendered herself. "I'll go quietly. I promise not to cause a scene or call for help once we step from this room."

His breathing slowed to normal, and the flush on his face faded. As if it had been his plan all along, he nodded and grabbed hold of her arm, ignoring the fact that it was bleeding from where he'd shot her. "Toss that pile of linen to me!" he ordered a pale-faced Aimee. Garahan's wife quickly did as he asked.

"When we are in the carriage," he told Michaela, "I'll bind

your wound…if you come along quietly."

Michaela nodded and let herself be led. Stepping outside, she gasped in horror. Masterson was lying in a pool of blood on the front steps. *He wasn't moving.* "Please, let me—"

Haversham pointed the gun at Masterson's head. "One more word, and I'll shoot him between the eyes."

Tears welled up and spilled over, but she did not utter another sound. She prayed that the Lord would send help, and soon. There was no sign of Tremayne. Where was he? Where was Miranda's son?

Haversham opened the door to his carriage and prodded her in the middle of her back with his pistol. "Inside."

She obeyed, ignoring the narrowing of her vision as the detestable man shouted to the coachman to drive and the carriage lurched forward. He settled on the seat across from her, still aiming the dueling pistol at her heart. "Now then. Wrap this around your arm and tie it tight." He tossed the strips of linen at her face. She could not imagine he would have willingly bound her wound. She barely had time to react and catch the linen before it landed on the floor. God only knew what he had stepped in before he entered the carriage.

Silently praying for the strength to bind her own wound, she managed to wrap her arm, but could not tie it off. After her third attempt failed, Haversham leaned toward her, roughly tightened the bandage, and tied it.

The pain helped to clear her head. Now that the bleeding was under control and her vision was returning to normal, she felt woozy. Her stomach was nauseated, but she held on to consciousness until he leaned close and rasped, "I'm going to have you again, Michaela. I'm going to take my time with you to see what you've learned about pleasuring a man since the last time I buried my shaft deep inside of you."

Her heart stuttered at his coarse words and the meaning they carried. O'Malley's handsome face filled her mind's eye. She would never submit to Haversham. She was stronger, wiser, and had had lessons in protecting herself from Alasdair.

Lifting her head, she stared into Haversham's soulless black eyes. His look of astonishment when she had not cowered at his threat was all the encouragement she needed. She would not submit without a fight! She was no longer a young miss just out of the schoolroom, and hadn't been for a decade.

Haversham was about to meet the fierce angel of the streets and learn that she was a strong, formidable woman in her own right. She had risen from the ashes of her shattered reputation and life to save herself so that she would be able to save others. Michaela would stand up to him this time. She would fight to save herself, because she would never be taken by force again!

CHAPTER TWELVE

O'MALLEY SHOULD HAVE expected Captain Coventry to be in deep discussion with Gavin King by the time he and Garahan arrived at King's office on Bow Street. He stood in the hallway digging deep for a calm he did not feel, holding himself back from storming into the office when he heard them discussing his cousin's injury and the fact that there had not been any recent improvement. The lid he had clamped down on his irritation ever since Coventry had suggested Darby was not up to par after his recent injury battered at him. Before the lid blew off, he knocked on the doorframe, nodded to King, and glared at Coventry. No time like the present to let the captain know that he'd already warned his cousin of that fact. "Ye don't have to dance around the subject, Coventry. I've already informed Darby here where ye stand on including him in our duties for the next month or so."

He flexed his hands, curled them into fists, and then relaxed them before he turned to meet King's bland expression. Did King hold the same opinion as Coventry? Did no one trust O'Malley's pronouncement that his cousin was back to fighting form?

King lifted his chin in O'Malley's direction and cleared his throat. "As a matter of fact, Lieutenant Sampson has already sent his detailed assessment of Garahan's condition. Coventry and I were just discussing it. Apparently the good captain has an objection that he was about to explain, as I am in full agreement with Sampson."

O'Malley noted a muscle twitching beneath Coventry's eye and the set of the man's jaw. He swallowed a crude comment and felt satisfaction that he wasn't the only one to get a rise out of the unflappable captain. *About bloody time.* He glanced over his shoulder to gauge Garahan's mood before turning back to Coventry and reminding the captain, "Ye aren't the only man to have been severely injured, and had to learn how to compensate for his injury." Satisfied that he now had the captain's full attention, he added, "Michaela knows who kidnapped her."

The shift of subject had Garahan, King, and Coventry simultaneously demanding, "What?"

"I know for a fact not one of ye is deaf. I'm not repeating meself."

"Did she tell you that she knows?" Garahan asked.

"For feck's sake, ye were there when she was dancing around the topic of us searching for her captor. Did ye not see the panic in her eyes? There's more to what happened than the lass is telling us."

"What specifically has you believing she knows her kidnapper?" King asked.

"'Twasn't anything she said," O'Malley replied, "but the faraway look in her eyes…a look laced with pain that changed to one of dogged determination. I know the look, have shared it with me brothers first, me cousins second."

"When Patrick delivered the news yer da was dead," Garahan said.

"Aye." O'Malley swallowed against the lump of emotion that clogged in his throat whenever he thought about the injustice of his da and uncle having been wrongly accused and imprisoned. "There was a bit more added to the look in the angel's eyes… 'Twas fear. She's hiding something. I'm thinking she knows who kidnapped her." The men's gazes were riveted on him when he added, "I'm willing to wager it has to do with the reason she began her mission to rescue lasses off the street."

"And that it interferes with someone's ability to turn a profit," Garahan murmured.

O'Malley met Coventry's look of speculation and said, "Before we go any further, I want to know why ye don't have faith in Garahan."

The captain seemed surprised by the question. "I have the utmost faith in him. He has reflexes like a cat, an intuition that we have depended on more times than I can count, and a strength equal to every last man in the duke's guard."

"Then why exclude him?" O'Malley demanded.

King answered before Coventry could: "Aimee."

Garahan frowned. "What does me wife have to do with me position within the guard?"

Coventry raked a hand through his hair, then swore when it loosened strands from his military-style ribbon-wrapped queue.

King answered O'Malley's question, leaving him to surmise the two men had been discussing his cousin for more than a few minutes. "Suffice it to say, there is more to it than Garahan's mental acuity or his physical readiness for the task."

"Bollocks!" O'Malley growled. "Do ye think I'd trust me cousin to guard me back if I didn't believe he was up to the task?"

Coventry answered, "It's more me than you, Garahan. Miranda and Michael were in my life for a decade, and in all that time, I never thought I was worthy enough to offer marriage. Now that I have been married, I lie awake nights worrying that if something should happen to me, they would be in worse straits than if I had never married Miranda."

O'Malley snorted with derision. "That's a load of *shite*, and ye know it."

Garahan stared at Coventry for a few moments, shook his head, and then said, "His Grace, the earl, the viscount, the baron, and every man in the duke's personal guard would protect Miranda, Michael, and little Emma with their lives. Miranda would have to decide where she wanted to live: Wyndmere Hall,

Lippincott Manor, Chattsworth Manor, Penwith Tower, Summerfield Chase, or the duke's town house on Grosvenor Square. Ye have no worry about yer wife and family—everyone would insist she move in with them."

O'Malley grunted. "Me married brothers and cousins would insist that she live with them." From the identical expressions on the captain's and Garahan's faces, O'Malley sensed it was time to distract them. "Have ye forgotten how devoted yer men are, Coventry?"

"You've already established that your brothers and cousins would open their homes to Miranda."

O'Malley grinned. "*Yer* men, captain. Tremayne, Bayfield, Masterson, and Hennessey… All of whom have plenty of space in their living quarters and would protect yer wife and family with their lives—night and day."

Coventry's expression was priceless, then—to O'Malley's delight—the man growled and lunged for him. "Are you questioning my men's honor?"

O'Malley calmly stepped to one side and asked, "Are ye?"

"Stop taunting him," King ordered O'Malley before glaring at Coventry. "You're letting your emotions interfere with your decisions."

The captain's face paled, and he admitted, "You're right."

Garahan spoke up. "Meaning no disrespect to ye, King, but neither yerself nor me cousin know what it's like to love with yer entire being, all the while worrying something would happen to the woman ye love."

The runner was oddly silent, and for a heartbeat O'Malley saw anguish in the man's eyes before King blinked and it was gone. So the man had had a love at one time, mayhap recently. Time enough later to see what could be found out.

O'Malley turned to stare at Garahan, silently willing him to accept the fact that O'Malley did understand. Just because he had not wed the angel of the streets yet, that did not mean he did not have a fierce love for the lass.

"Well now, gentlemen," Garahan said. "It seems as if I'm wrong… Another of the sainted O'Malleys has fallen."

Coventry's expression changed, and O'Malley relaxed. The man had himself back in hand and under control. The captain nodded at him and said, "I have already seen to your request." He pulled a sealed document from his waistcoat pocket and glanced at King before handing it to O'Malley. "Open it."

O'Malley clenched his jaw to hide his overwhelming need to shout with elation that the captain had received his request and already seen to the task, obtaining the permission he needed. Willing his hands to steady, he broke the wax seal and opened the document. Satisfaction swept up from the soles of his boots. He looked up and noted Coventry's look of understanding.

"I have already secured a vicar known for his discretion in situations like this," Coventry told him. "Highly recommended by Captain Broadbank…er, Viscount Moreland." Coventry shook his head. "We served together in the Royal Navy for years as captains…far longer than he has been a viscount."

King nodded. "Vicar Dalrymple. Excellent choice. Is he available tonight?"

Coventry nodded and said to O'Malley, "Given the situation, I thought you would want to marry immediately."

"Aye, thank ye, Coventry." O'Malley looked at Garahan and waited for his cousin's nod of agreement. "I spoke with Cameron, as Greenwood wasn't in any condition to question, and Dr. Colborne."

"What did you find out?" King asked.

"Cameron suspected Michaela's past influenced her decision to help others. He is going to make discreet inquiries. He's needed at home. His father-in-law is recovering, thanks to Lieutenant Sampson, but the poison took a toll on Colonel Merriweather."

"Of course, Cameron is newly married and responsible for his wife's two younger sisters to protect as well. From what I understand, Cameron's sisters-in-law are more of a handful than his wife," King remarked. "What did you learn from Dr. Colborne?"

O'Malley's anger started to burn. "After pointedly questioning the doctor, I believe he now suspects his daughter was not ill with a virulent fever ten years ago after attending a function with one of the gentlemen he approved of."

"Virulent?" Coventry asked.

"Aye, the lass is cagey and must have used that as a ruse to cover up what happened." O'Malley schooled his features, adopting a neutral expression before continuing, "I'm going to go back and question her da to get the handful of names the men approved of at the time. No doubt the lords are still in London, married by now. One of them is to blame for what happened to my wife-to-be." The need to seek vengeance flared to life and threatened to burn him alive. "When I have the name… I will track him down…"

He bit back the rest of what he was going to say. No point in letting King know his plans. The Bow Street Runner was against premeditated murder. Garahan, Tremayne, or one of the others would probably follow him and try to stop him from actually letting the man bleed to death when O'Malley extracted a pound of flesh.

"What have your contacts reported, men?" Coventry asked.

O'Malley and Garahan filled the others in on what they had heard, adding what they had uncovered speaking with some of the additional men the duke had Coventry hire, expanding the web of protection around the duke's family through additional contacts in the stews and on the docks.

Three quarters of an hour later, the meeting ended. Garahan went in search of Burke, his contact in the bowels of the city, while O'Malley would meet with Leach on the Dark Walk. Garahan agreed that since his contact, O'Shaughnessy, had already been instrumental in aiding O'Malley in finding Michaela that O'Malley should be the one to speak with O'Shaughnessy, too.

O'Malley was determined to have the information he needed by the end of the day. He would take care of the bloody bugger who had gotten away with stealing the lass's virtue, her hopes, and her dreams. *I'll never hear the end of it if I don't take two witnesses with me.* He considered who to take with him as he rode toward the docks.

"Garahan," he said aloud. "He won't talk and may even hold the man while I wield me blade." The second witness was more of a problem. Though he'd worked with Findley recently, he did not know how the man felt about justice or revenge. He finally decided on Tremayne—he'd worked closely with Garahan and his brother James, and O'Malley's brother Finn. Tremayne had argued in favor of leaving Melinda's cousin alive when they had accompanied James to exact retribution with the duke's approval…and conditions not to kill the man.

Mayhap he should ask Masterson. The man had all but admitted that he was half in love with Michaela. Masterson wouldn't think twice if O'Malley told him he planned to take a pound of flesh or geld someone. He'd have to ask Garahan whom he thought would be the better choice, Tremayne or Masterson.

That settled, he was ready to question O'Shaughnessy when he noticed the man's bulk moving toward him at a fast clip as he approached the docks. Before he could speak, O'Shaughnessy called, "He's got her! Ye have to help me get her back!"

O'Malley dismounted, grabbed O'Shaughnessy by the arm, and dragged him toward the alley then let go. "Lower yer voice, man. I'm needing their names."

Ignoring O'Malley, the big man rambled on, "He has the lass… The one I told ye about that I convinced to go into hiding."

"Ah, the one who saw the carriage and the toff carrying a rolled-up rug on his shoulder."

"Aye." Worry bled from the man. "She's got a heart of gold. I don't want ye thinking just because she's—"

O'Malley interrupted, "She's the woman who helped me find Michaela. I will not hear a slight against her. All I'm needing is her name."

"Pretty Mary."

O'Malley felt the man's love pouring out of him. "Does Pretty Mary have a last name?"

The big man shrugged. "I wasn't in the way of asking... Ye'd understand why."

"Aye. Tell me her height and describe her to me. I'll be needing to know so I can find her." O'Shaughnessy's pain was a living, breathing thing. O'Malley had felt the same depth of emotion himself just the day before. "How tall is she?"

"Five foot nothing. She's a curvy lass with black hair, green eyes, and a nose that tips up."

"Any distinguishing birthmarks or scars? Does she have a limp? Anything that would help narrow my search."

"Pretty Mary has a scar that slashes beneath her left cheekbone...from one of her customers a few years back. When she finally tells me his name, I'm going to—"

"Do nothing," O'Malley interrupted for the second time. "If Bow Street got wind that you injured..."

The bold laughter had O'Malley realizing O'Shaughnessy did not intend to *injure* anyone. "*Permanently* injure. No coming back from what I plan to do to the man."

"Don't say another word," O'Malley warned. "If I'm asked, I'll have to confess what I know."

Garahan's contact clamped his mouth shut and folded his arms over his massive chest. "She's been gone for at least four hours."

O'Malley asked, "Anyone else see her leave?"

The man shook his head. "You have to find her, O'Malley."

"I promise ye that I will." They parted company, and O'Malley headed back to Coventry's building and the angel who waited for him there.

CHAPTER THIRTEEN

M ICHAELA HEARD A soft moan and realized there was another person in the carriage with them! "Who—"

Before she could get the question out, Haversham leaned toward her and pressed the barrel of his pistol to her temple. "Do not say another word, or I shall be forced to kill you."

From the tone of his voice, and the illegal trade she surmised that he was involved in, she had no doubt that he would follow through with his threat.

She nodded, and he nudged a lump on the floor with his foot. "You too," he barked, pressing his foot down hard. "One more sound out of you, and I'll be forced to use my fists on you again."

The whispered curse was soft, yet still Michaela heard the wisp of a sound, and she coughed to cover it.

There it was again…another whispered curse. This time she sneezed.

Haversham glared at her. "You'd best not be ill with some wasting disease from those trollops you drag out of the gutter and rehabilitate."

She did not answer until the tip of the pistol dug beneath her chin. *If it be your will, Lord, I am ready to die.* "I am not ill. Something tickled my throat and then my nose."

The barrel was eased away from her face. He grunted, then said, "I hope you will be pleased, Michaela, I have arranged for company for you." In the faint glow of the lantern inside the carriage, she saw his expression change and quickly thanked him before he either threatened her again, or made good on his first threat.

His nod of approval had relief spearing through her. She had no idea who was buried beneath what appeared to be a pile of rags. Michaela would see to it the woman did not suffer at the hands of the loathsome man sitting beside her.

"The two of you can be a comfort to one another while I decide which one of you will have the honor of showing me just what you have learned about pleasuring a man since I took your virtue."

Bile roiled in her belly while Michaela strove to show no emotion, no indication that she was affected by the lord's disgusting words.

Silently, she promised herself that he would never use her ill again. She was strong, wiry, and knew where to punch a man to temporarily put him out of commission. There was no point in praying for O'Malley to rescue her this time. The length of time he had been gone meant that he was likely embroiled in another special assignment for the duke. She doubted he would return for hours, and when he did, she would be long gone with no hint of where she was being taken. This time, Michaela would have to get herself out of this situation on her own.

The pile of rags on the floor shifted, and she remembered…she was no longer alone!

The coach slowed to a stop, and Michaela sensed the hidden woman was poised to escape. But Haversham would never allow that to happen, especially after Michaela had managed to do so with O'Malley's assistance. Risking his ire, hoping the woman beneath the rags was listening, she said, "I know it would be pointless to try to jump out of the carriage now that it has stopped."

Their captor snorted. "So you have got some sense after all. If either of you tries to make a break for it, I would have had no compunction in shooting you in the back."

Michaela knew that would be his response and prayed that Haversham's other captive was listening carefully. *Very* carefully.

"I shall emerge first and hand you off to one of my staff. Do not try to coerce him into setting you free, or it will be the last thing you do on this Earth, Michaela. Nod if you understand."

She immediately did so, wondering if he would keep his word and allow the two women to be locked up together. Not willing to risk challenging him—yet—she waited for Haversham to alight from the carriage and speak to the waiting footman.

Haversham grabbed hold of her arm, cruelly squeezing where his pistol ball had grazed her. The shock and stabbing pain had her gasping for breath. She blinked, desperate to regain control, lest he grab her arm again.

When Michaela opened her eyes, her gaze clashed with that of the footman. He looked far too rough to be on any lord's staff. He had a few days' worth of whiskers on his chin, unkempt dark hair threaded with strands of gray, and a wide smear of dirt on his scarred cheek. The flash of empathy in the man's dark eyes caught her off guard, but was quickly replaced with a look of boredom.

"This way, miss." The hint of a cultured tone in his voice had her wondering just who this man was. From the scar marring his cheek, she wondered if he was a second son who served in the King's Dragoons, or mayhap of one of the king's regiments, and had fallen on hard times. Mayhap he had gambled away his fortune to Haversham. Michaela had no doubt that among other vices, her captor was a card sharp and a cheat. The man had no honor!

When the footman cupped her elbow to steady her, she breathed a sigh of relief that he had not grabbed her injured arm. Whoever this man was, he treated her as if she were a lady and not a captive.

"Watch your step," he murmured low enough that Haversham would not hear.

Grateful for his assistance, she slowly made her way toward what appeared to be a side entrance to a neglected building. Michaela slowed her steps as the urge to look over her shoulder to gauge the condition of the other woman filled her. Certain that her abductor would object, she hesitated for a moment, before tamping down the temptation to keep walking. She would be of no help to the other woman if Haversham shot her between the shoulder blades.

"Best not," the footman quietly warned, confirming her suspicion.

She gave a brief nod that she understood. A moment later they were inside a long, dark hallway. They walked past a few closed doors and entered the only room where the door stood open. He leaned close and urged, "Swoon! I'll catch you."

A tiny inner voice told her to obey, and she was immediately swept into strong arms, held securely against a broad chest. Intent on steadying her heartbeat and breathing, she closed her mouth and inhaled, detecting a hint of sandalwood. "What do you—"

"No time. I'm a friend. You can trust me to help you escape."

Lifting her gaze, she saw the truth of his words in the depths of his eyes and sincere expression. "And the other woman, too?"

"Aye."

"Who are…" Her voice trailed off as she heard footsteps coming toward the room.

"Trust me and pretend you've fainted from being shot."

She wanted to ask if he'd guessed as to her injury or if he knew, but the bombastic, preening voice of her captor drew closer. Michaela met the footman's gaze and recognized the intensity and unspoken promise to protect her with his life. In that moment, she sensed they were somehow connected through her former guard, Cameron. "Were you in the dragoons?"

If she blinked, she would have missed the hint of a smile. His gaze riveted to the door and he called out when Haversham arrived, "She's fainted, your lordship, and her arm is bleeding through the bandage."

"I don't give a bloody damn if she is bleeding. If she's unconscious, she'll be less trouble. Set her on the floor in the corner and put this one next to her."

Michaela heard the scraping of feet…as if the other woman was pulling against being dragged further into the room. It took all of her control to fight against the overwhelming need to open her eyes. But the slight squeeze from the man who held her was his warning to keep up the pretense. She felt herself being lowered with care and wished that she had asked the man's name. Mayhap she would have a chance to ask later.

"Should I try to rouse her?"

"Leave her!" Haversham ordered the man. "And put this one next to Michaela."

She might not be able to see, but Michaela distinctly heard the sharply indrawn breath of the other captive. Had this woman been searching for her? Was she in need of medical assistance and more? Undoubtedly, Haversham would leave soon, and she would be able to find out. The lecherous lord had not seemed to change that much over the years, and she highly doubted his personality had undergone a drastic transformation. The man who had been one of her father's choices as suitor would never soil his hands doing his own dirty work. He would pay his underlings to do so.

"Stand guard outside this door. I want the women secured in this room. Michaela has already escaped from a locked room."

She fought the urge to smile, remembering how she had managed to pull the gag off her mouth. Though she had not been able to free herself, O'Malley had found her and tried to keep her from being harmed when he broke down the door to get to her.

Keeping as still as possible, she opened her eyes the tiniest slits and wished her lashes weren't quite so thick. It was hard to see, but she did manage to see Haversham's footman, their gaoler. The man was tall enough to block her view of Haversham, thank goodness. She had no desire to see the blackguard who had shot her.

Even as she thought of it, insidious pain caught her off guard. She lowered her lashes even more and clamped her jaw shut, able to keep quiet. She could moan later.

"I'm expecting another of Michaela's admirers to attempt to free her."

Stunned, though she shouldn't be, she peered through her eyelashes again. Had Haversham heard that she had a protector who would stop at nothing to rescue her? Did the man have such vast resources and contacts in the underbelly of London? She knew for a fact that O'Malley and Garahan had far more than her contact on Bow Street, Gavin King.

"What if more than one man shows up?"

"Dead men tell no tales," Haversham replied. "Send word immediately after you dispatch any bodies." With that last command, he left without a backward glance. The tall man followed. Stepping over the threshold into the hallway, he closed and locked the door from the outside.

Her eyes shot open. Had she just been duped? Heart racing, breath ragged, she turned to the other woman and had to bite back her cry of dismay. The poor woman's face was badly bruised. She had two black eyes, and one was nearly swollen shut. Michaela was about to ask the woman if she suffered any other injuries, when the captive whispered, "I'm Mary... Are you really the angel of the streets?"

"Aye. Who did this to you?"

"Not the footman—he was the one who helped me into the carriage after his lordship beat me."

"I am so sorry this happened to you. Where else are you injured?" Michaela asked. "I'm hoping to prevail upon our guard to bring some healing supplies." She shifted, and her ribs complained. The reminder had her asking, "Do we need extra lengths of linen to wrap your ribs?" In a bid to straighten and not slump, she bumped her arm against the wall and sucked in a breath.

"I should be asking you that. I only took a beating," Mary

said. "You're bleeding. Did he use a knife on you or shoot you?"

"Grazed by his pistol ball when I leapt in front of my friend. She only just discovered that she's expecting. I could not let him shoot her!"

Mary's less swollen eye widened. "You truly are an angel."

Michaela was having none of that, shaking her head and asking, "Has Haversham hurt you before?"

Mary sighed, and Michaela wondered if the young woman had not heard Haversham's boast about his plans for them. "Aye. He is the reason I was forced into this life. He ruined me and left me with no other way to feed myself." She lifted a hand to the side of her head as if to quell the pain.

Michaela asked, "Is your vision blurry and your stomach nauseated?"

"A bit, but I don't want to talk about that now. I want to find out if you will help me expose him. Only then will there be a chance to stop him for taking out his twisted treatment on some of the other women who ply their trade on the docks like me."

"I will gladly help you. I had thought doing my part to help others who suffered would be enough, but now I know that men like Haversham must be stopped. I have a few men that have helped me before. They will again. Do you know a big man by the name of O'Shaughnessy?"

Tears gathered in Mary's eyes and slowly fell. "He is a good and kind man. Always pays for my time. But sometimes he only wants to feed me, or hold me."

"You're the one who saw Haversham's carriage!" Michaela exclaimed.

"Aye, and the rolled-up rug he carried into the alley. I was hidden in an alcove." Mary reached for Michaela's hand. "That was you! I heard you call for help. I decided then that I would tell my sweet man—"

"O'Shaughnessy?"

Mary nodded. "He has spoken of a connection, he has. Two honest men who work for someone high up in Society, though his connections have feet of clay like the rest of us. Cousins born on a farm in Ireland."

Michaela knew of O'Shaughnessy's connection to the duke's guard, to Darby Garahan and Emmett O'Malley in particular. "You saved my life."

Mary shook her head. "Yet here you are again, in Haversham's clutches. Do you know what he intends to do with us?"

"You heard him threaten to shoot me in the carriage. Did you hear his other threat?"

"Nay. Against you or me?" Mary asked.

"Both of us. I'm not sure how much time we have. He said we can be a comfort to one another while he decides which one of us will have the honor—the bloody bastard—of showing him what we have learned since he took our virtue."

Mary shuddered. "He promised earlier that I would get another beating… He must have changed his mind. Why do you think he wants to kill you?"

Michaela knew she had to confide in the badly beaten woman. Should she not escape with her life this time, mayhap Mary would be able to get word to O'Malley and explain what happened. "He thought he had stolen more than my virtue. I think I somehow injured his pride. After he violated me, he threatened to not only ruin my reputation, but my father's. I could not allow that, nor could I ignore the other women that I came across, those that had suffered as we have. I had no idea that I was interfering with his highly profitable business."

Mary sighed. "It is how most of us end up working the streets. Once we are forced out of our homes due to the shame of what happened to us—"

Michaela interrupted, "We did not ask to be violated."

Mary shrugged. "No one seems to believe that—they are more concerned with their reputations being sullied by association with us."

"I never told my father," Michaela whispered. "Haversham was a gentleman my father approved of. I could not take the chance that my father would call him out… He's a physician to members of the *ton*. It is the only thing that kept him going after we lost my mum."

"Would he have disowned you if he knew?"

Michaela considered Mary's question. "No, but he would be hard pressed to come up with an explanation as to why I suddenly went abroad, when I had been a constant presence in his surgery."

"Do you plan to reveal Haversham's depravity?" Mary wanted to know.

"Not unless I can be assured he will not destroy my father's reputation."

"Then he will never be made to pay for his crimes," Mary whispered. "Haversham has connections to a man who was recently apprehended and sent to Newgate."

Michaela knew immediately whom Mary referred to—she'd been involved in aiding their latest victims. "Lord Ashbrook."

"Yes. That's the name. How did you know?"

"I helped give aid and place a few of their most recent victims in situations where they would be safe and learn a trade. Young women from the country lured to the city for a different purpose altogether. The two youngest ones were eight or nine years old."

"He's even more depraved than I thought," Mary rasped. "And vindictive, if you have interfered with his thriving business. There is only one way he will ever let you go."

Michaela lifted her chin and met Mary's gaze, firm in her belief that O'Malley would hear what happened to her and move Heaven and Earth to find her. "My betrothed will force him to."

"You are to be married?"

"Aye, and I'm quite certain that I am getting the better end of the bargain. I'm not sure if I can bring myself to…" Michaela couldn't finish.

Mary reached for her hand. Instinctively, as if she sensed what Michaela had not been able to say, the young woman told her, "Not all men are rutting beasts. Some are gentle, others forceful, but still manage to restrain themselves from injuring you."

"Really?" Michaela had no experience other than the one time. She shuddered, remembering the pain.

"My sweet man's gentle touch belies his appearance," Mary confided. "While I doubt he would ever offer marriage, in my dreams he does every night."

Michaela clung to Mary's hand. "Why is it that those of us who are the victims are forced to accept the blame for something we never sought and was beyond our strength to control?"

Mary sighed again. "The horrified reactions of those around us shape our thoughts, forcing the blame on us, rather than where it should be, on the perpetrators. For those who steal what is never offered, I believe they continue to prey on the innocent because of a need to feel the power it gives the bloody blackguards who violate us, and the fear that if they are found out, they will be exposed for who and what they truly are."

"Depraved despoilers of the innocent who thrive on taking a woman against her will, and then threatening to expose her to Society if she so much as breathes a word of what happened."

"Does Haversham know that you have been helping others escape from the streets of London as our angel?"

"I don't believe so. He would have sought me out long before now if he had."

Mary nodded. "I agree with you. It must have been when you were involved in rescuing those young women from the boarding house."

The sound of the key turning in the lock alerted them that either their gaoler was ready to help them escape, or Haversham had changed his mind and returned. Michaela prayed it was the former, then could not help but worry what the cost of freedom would be.

Chapter Fourteen

O'MALLEY'S GUT WARNED that the trail would eventually lead back to the docks where he'd found Michaela. God help those who had abducted Mary if one hair on her head was harmed! He would not be able to stop O'Shaughnessy from slowly tearing them limb from limb.

His blood ran cold when he followed the lead right back to where he'd left the lass—at Coventry's apartment under the protection of Coventry's men. "We know the bleeding bastard abducted O'Shaughnessy's woman, and she's the one who helped me find the lass!" As he approached the intersection of Hart and Lumley, O'Malley felt as if his guts were being shredded. "The devil take him if he's nabbed Michaela, too!"

Though the urge to push ahead at full speed had him by the throat, he and Garahan had to slow their horses to navigate around two slower carriages. Garahan leaned close. "We don't know for certain that he has her. Get a hold of yerself!"

O'Malley's heart did not want to listen to his cousin, but his head knew it was essential to verify the facts. The most important being discovering if Michaela had been snatched from the protective web he'd woven around her with the help of Captain Coventry and his men. Knowing his cousin expected it, he nodded and urged his horse toward the building on the corner where he'd left his angel.

Their horses balked as they reined in. "What in the bloody hell…" O'Malley fell silent as the scent and metallic tang in the air reached him. *Blood!* The front steps were awash in it, which spooked the horses. He calmed his gelding and, using hand signals, motioned to Garahan to follow him around back. They could leave their horses in the alley and enter the building without disturbing the evidence out front.

The building was oddly quiet when they entered through the back door. The hallway was paneled in dark wood and dimly lit, hiding their approach. The two men shared a glance before silently making their way toward Coventry's rooms near the front. A door opened and closed, and O'Malley exhaled the breath he'd been holding. Tremayne paused for a heartbeat before his head snapped toward O'Malley and Garahan. He motioned them forward and opened the door he'd just exited. "In here."

Masterson locked gazes with them as he and Garahan stepped into Coventry's apartment. The colonel was standing, jaw tight, hands fisted at his sides. O'Malley sensed Masterson was fighting pain in order to give his report. The colonel's eyes were red-rimmed and slightly dilated.

"I failed…" He shook his head and grimaced. "I was standing guard out front. I heard a woman call for help. When I turned to render aid, I was clubbed on the back of the head."

O'Malley admired the man's strength, but he needed to gather more facts. He had to find Michaela! "'Tis the front of yer head that's bleeding."

"I'm aware," the colonel said.

"Where's me wife?" Garahan growled.

"Safe upstairs with Miranda and little Emma in the captain's office," Tremayne replied. "Bayfield and Michael are guarding them."

"Go to her," O'Malley ordered Garahan. "Ye'll be no help to me until ye see that Aimee's safe." His cousin didn't argue. O'Malley heard the door close and heavy footsteps pound up the staircase. He understood his cousin's urgency to ensure the woman he loved was indeed safe.

Masterson turned and locked gazes with him. "I was focused on the well-sprung, dark carriage that was slowing down out front when I heard the call for help."

O'Malley drew on his ability to separate himself emotionally when dealing with serious wounds. It had worked when he fought to save his cousin Sean's arm. It aided him now. "Did ye see the bugger who clubbed ye on the temple?"

Masterson waited a beat before continuing. "A pair of matched grays had me checking the side of the black coach. No crest. No insignia."

The urge to throttle the colonel for not answering the questions was equal to O'Malley's need to run off in search of Michaela. *Not wise.* He needed whatever facts Masterson had. "Where is the lass?"

"I recall the sound of a pistol being fired, and a searing pain ripping through my arm. Another shot hit my other arm." The colonel paused, then said, "The last shot fired had white-hot pain blazing from the front of my head to the back… Then darkness."

"Ye're certain about the carriage and the team of horses?"

The colonel nodded, and it was clear from his stilted movements and deliberate recounting of the sequence of events that he was hanging on to consciousness by a thread. The blood out front was a testament to how much the man had lost.

"O'Malley… I… Find the angel," Masterson rasped. "Bring her back so I can apologize."

O'Malley nodded. "Ye have me word. And if that bloody bugger touched one hair on her head, I'll—"

"We'll," Masterson interrupted.

"Aye, together," O'Malley said. "Ye'll hold him, while I geld him."

Masterson's eyes blazed with the same emotion that roared through O'Malley, and that had him poised to tear through the streets of London at a gallop. But emotion equaled mistakes and led to narrowed vision, where one missed what was happening peripherally. He tamped down the urge to dive into action. O'Malley would use calculation and caution in order to run Michaela and Mary's captor to the ground.

"I'll have your word on it, O'Malley."

"Ye have it, colonel." He turned and nodded to Tremayne. "Ye know how to find us." Tremayne didn't bother to answer, but O'Malley didn't expect him to.

He walked toward the rear entrance and paused at the sound of someone thundering down the stairs, then glanced over his shoulder and noted the grim expression on Garahan's face. It matched his own. They were both battle ready. Their next move was to get to the docks. Their ultimate goal—finding Michaela and O'Shaughnessy's woman.

They scanned the alley where they'd left their horses, but didn't note anything suspicious. They mounted and rode around the building to the front. "We'll start with the docks and work our way to the heart of the—"

"O'Malley!" A man on horseback rode toward them at too swift a pace for the carriages snarling traffic on Lumley. They rode out to intercept him before the man spooked the next pair of horses pulling a carriage he was about to overtake.

Drawing closer, O'Malley recognized the man as one of the new recruits to the duke's expanded London guard. "Donnelson!"

The man reined in his horse next to O'Malley and Garahan. "We have the connection, and the reason why the angel of the streets has been singled out... Lord Ashbrook."

"The bastard who would not think twice about selling innocents no more than babes," Garahan growled.

O'Malley forced himself not to react—he'd carried those two little poppets out of hell. They'd clung to him and refused to let go even once he delivered them into Michaela's keeping. "Do ye have a name yet?"

Donnelson nodded. "Dr. Colborne gave three names to King. Coventry narrowed it down to a member of the *ton*...Haversham. Lord Haversham."

"We're headed to the docks where we found Miss Michaela," O'Malley explained. "If she is not there—"

"We'll work our way back to the stews," Garahan interrupted.

"He owns a trio of abandoned warehouses slated to be torn down." Donnelson gave the rest of the details to O'Malley and Garahan as they made their way through the streets toward the docks. If O'Shaughnessy was surprised to see them, he gave no indication other than to lift his chin in silent question.

"Donnelson is one of our contacts," O'Malley told O'Shaughnessy, who visibly relaxed. Turning to Donnelson, he added, "O'Shaughnessy's woman has also been abducted. We were fortunate to have a solid lead as to the description of the coach and the direction they were headed. It matches the one from the night Michaela was abducted and delivered here."

"Aye," Garahan said, "it led us to Coventry's building." He waited a beat and said, "Michaela is in Haversham's clutches by design!"

O'Malley grabbed his cousin by the throat. "What did Miranda and Aimee tell ye, and why didn't ye tell *me*?"

"And have you react like this, before we had the information we needed to locate the women?" Garahan demanded.

O'Malley eased his grasp, but did not let go. "What else aren't ye telling me?" Garahan shifted and shoved hard. O'Malley held up his hands in front of him. "I'm not apologizing. Now spit it out."

"Aimee said that Michaela called him Haversham so they could tell us who he was when we arrived." Garahan clenched his jaw and rasped, "Haversham took aim at me wife." His voice broke, but then he shook his head and continued, "Michaela leapt in front of Aimee and was grazed in the arm by the lead ball."

A calm swept over O'Malley, as all emotion shut down and a resolve took hold of him. "I'll kill him."

"Ye cannot," Garahan reminded him.

O'Malley's heart pounded in time with the instinctive need to find Haversham and tear him apart. He met Garahan's determined look with one of promise. "Ye won't stop me."

"Where are they?" O'Shaughnessy demanded. "I've searched through all of the abandoned warehouses."

"Even the ones blocked off, slated to be demolished?" Donnelson asked.

O'Shaughnessy roared in anguish, mounted his horse, and took off. O'Malley and the others spread out behind him as they spurred their mounts toward the group of roped-off, run-down buildings. Two had no doors or windows, and half of the roofs had caved in. The third building was in far better shape. It had most of its roof, a door, and partial windows.

The men dismounted and approached the buildings, splitting up to perform a careful search. O'Shaughnessy and Donnelson began to search the first two buildings.

Garahan and O'Malley approached the other building with caution. "Could be a trap," Garahan murmured.

"I'm counting on it," O'Malley replied. He paused outside the rear door to the building. "Did ye hear that?"

"Aye," Garahan said. "Voices, pitched too low to make them out."

"They must be in the room closest to the door. I'll go in first," O'Malley said.

Garahan nodded. The two men entered the building and jolted to a stop at the sight before them. A tall man was leading Michaela and a woman who had been badly beaten directly toward them.

Michaela wavered on her feet and gasped, "O'Malley?"

He had her in his arms in a heartbeat. "We need to see to yer arm, lass."

"How do you know about my arm?" she asked.

Faith, the lass didn't sound as if she was about to swoon. She sounded irritated as hell. "Garahan told me."

"Put me down."

The man who seemed to be aiding the women spoke up.

"Miss Michaela said she was able to walk. From what little time I have spent with Miss Michaela and Miss Mary, they only say what they mean."

O'Malley grunted, but didn't respond. Instead, he turned to the other woman and said, "O'Shaughnessy's frantic with worry, Pretty Mary."

Her eyes widened, and she shook her head. "He won't call me that anymore after… After…" She bowed her head.

Michaela pinched O'Malley above the wound in his side. He immediately swung his gaze back to stare at her. "What?"

She whispered, "Let me down. Please? Mary needs me."

Reluctantly, he lowered her, bracing her when she wobbled on her feet. He let go when she straightened and walked over to the other woman. Reaching Mary's side, Michaela said, "If O'Shaughnessy is anything like O'Malley and Garahan, he may yell, but not at you—because he is angry."

"I know," Mary replied, leaning against Michaela. "It is how he expresses his fear."

Garahan's loud whistle had the women jolting apart as the sound of running feet, and then a door smashing against the wall echoed through the building. O'Shaughnessy pounded toward them, stopping short of knocking Mary off her feet in his haste to get to her. Lifting his hand to cup her cheek, he stopped a hairsbreadth away and dropped his hand to his side as if he were afraid to touch her battered face. "Tell me who did this to ye, lass."

Mary closed her eyes, and O'Shaughnessy's expression turned deadly. She sighed, and O'Malley watched the other man school his features as she slowly opened her eyes.

O'Shaughnessy's expression was neutral when he slipped an arm around Mary and swept her into his arms. "Let me tend to yer wounds."

"Fitzsimmons already did what he could under the circumstances," Michaela said.

O'Malley noted that the other man watched them closely.

There was something in Fitzsimmons's gaze that reminded him of his brothers and cousins. "Ye were helping the women escape."

"Aye."

"How did ye find them, when others had combed the docks without finding them?" Before the man had a chance to answer, O'Malley stalked over to Fitzsimmons. "Ye were left to guard them… Ye're one of the ones responsible for them being abducted."

"I am."

O'Malley's move to wrap his hands around the other man's neck was blocked. He feinted to the right and again found his move blocked. The men traded blows, half blocked, half landing, accompanied by grunts of surprise, until finally O'Malley said, "Ye fight well for a blackguard. I'll be sorry to have to break yer legs." He grinned when he added, "It'll be a pleasure, seeing as how ye've managed to evade me fists longer than others I've fought."

When O'Malley stepped back from his opponent, O'Shaughnessy stared at the other man. "I know ye."

"You should," Fitzsimmons replied. "We fought in the same regiment—and, since retiring from the military, have passed one another outside of the Prospect of Whitby pub. But you were intent on other business."

O'Shaughnessy stared at him for a few moments before nodding. "Fitzsimmons. I thought that was someone who resembled you."

Fitzsimmons snorted. "You still owe me."

"Bloody hell. I thought ye were dead, and I was free of me promise to save yer bleeding hide one more time."

Fitzsimmons chuckled. "Sorry to disappoint you, O'Shaughnessy. But you still owe me for the *second* time I saved your life."

"Best leave him be, O'Malley," O'Shaughnessy grumbled. "Fitzsimmons is cut from a similar cloth as yerself and yer cousin. Stubborn as the day is long, with a head thicker than mine!"

Garahan snorted with laughter. "No one's head is as hard as yers, O'Shaughnessy."

"I wouldn't want to put that claim to the test," O'Shaughnessy warned. "But I'll gladly hold yer coat if ye want to go a few rounds with Fitzsimmons here."

Garahan and O'Malley shared a look before Garahan shook his head and asked Fitzsimmons, "How soon before Haversham returns?"

"He has other business to attend to, but is unpredictable," Fitzsimmons replied, "and could return at any time. If I encountered either O'Malley or Garahan in my search, I was to remind you that Cameron told you he had connections."

"Cameron?" O'Malley asked. "How do ye know him?"

"A connection through Colonel Merriweather."

"Ye're lying."

"Am I?" Fitzsimmons asked.

"Aye, Cameron's father-in-law was a dragoon," O'Malley said. "Not a foot soldier like O'Shaughnessy."

"True," Fitzsimmons agreed. "And he was nearly poisoned. Save for the keen eye of Cameron, and the efforts of Lieutenant Sampson, the colonel would have died and Cameron's wife would be married to that cur who would poison his future father-in-law to get his hands on her dowry."

"Ye're either working for Haversham," O'Malley murmured, "or ye're telling the truth!"

Fitzsimmons's fist connected with O'Malley's jaw, snapping his head back. Instead of knocking him off his feet, it had O'Malley grinning. Rubbing his jaw, he spat blood. "Faith, ye used me own move on meself. I was about to deliver a right cross."

"Ye would have, too," Garahan said in his cousin's defense, "if ye hadn't been injured."

"Cameron warned that you would test me with your fists," Fitzsimmons said.

Garahan shoved the man out of his way with his shoulder.

"Fall in line. O'Malley's giving the orders today."

Fitzsimmons nodded and stepped back.

Without another word, O'Malley scooped Michaela off her feet and strode toward the door leading to the back of the building. O'Shaughnessy followed, and they both waited while Fitzsimmons took the lead and Garahan fell in line behind them, bringing up the rear.

"If I'm leading the way, I need to know where you are headed," Fitzsimmons said.

"The duke's town house," O'Malley replied.

"Are ye daft?" O'Shaughnessy demanded. "We cannot just ride up to the duke's home as if we'd been invited, especially with the lasses injured."

Garahan shrugged. "'Tis a sound plan. Haversham traced Michaela to her new location, took out Greenwood, and clubbed the lass on the back of the head, broke her ribs—"

Before his cousin could get up a head of steam and list all of the lass's injuries, O'Malley growled, "Haversham managed to track Michaela down at Coventry's apartment. Where else would ye suggest that we would have backup that could easily defend our position while protecting the women?"

"I cannot go with you to the duke's home," Mary protested. "I would never disrespect His Grace by entering his home, even by the back door."

"Poppycock!" Michaela elbowed O'Malley, who jolted to a stop to stare down at her.

"What now?"

Michaela's gaze bored into O'Malley, silently entreating him to answer honestly. "Will the duke's staff treat Mary unkindly?"

"'Tisn't in them to even think to do so. They are kind women who have served three dukes faithfully. No one who enters the duke's doors is ever a stranger. No servant was ever let go without a glowing recommendation."

"Aye," Garahan agreed. "They've patched us up more than once, and have a way with babes. They're gems and have a light hand with making scones."

"Scones?" Fitzsimmons's eyes lit up. "I wouldn't mind lending my expertise in that regard taste testing scones. I am renowned for my good taste."

O'Shaughnessy chuckled. "Do ye not mean renowned for tasting anything and everything sweet?"

Fitzsimmons grinned as they approached their horses where they'd left them. "We'd best be on our way."

Garahan and Fitzsimmons held the reins while O'Malley and O'Shaughnessy mounted the horses with their precious burdens held close to their hearts. Fitzsimmons fetched his horse from the back of one of the derelict buildings and the group rode out, single file, the same way they'd exited the building, with Fitzsimmons in the lead and Garahan bringing up the rear. Given the hour was closing in on teatime, there were fewer carriages as they entered Grosvenor Square. No one was out and about as they rode up to the duke's town house and O'Malley signaled to Findley, who led them to the stables around back.

"Alert Mrs. O'Toole that we have two women who have been injured," Findley told one of the stable lads. "Hurry now!"

The young man took off at a trot, while the others dismounted and turned their mounts over to the other stable hands to care for them. Without asking permission, O'Malley carried Michaela to the back entrance. "I can walk," she protested.

The feeble sound of her voice had worry gnawing at his gut. "Ye're weak from blood loss, exhausted, and could use a hot meal."

She sighed and laid her head in the hollow of his shoulder. "As long as the meal comes with a cup of tea."

"Mrs. O'Toole always has the kettle on."

Michaela's sigh of acceptance was music to O'Malley's ears. "Trust me, lass."

"I do."

CHAPTER FIFTEEN

"**Y**E NEED TO send word to Coventry and King where we are, and what's happened," Garahan said.

O'Malley ignored him in favor of watching Mrs. O'Toole carefully cleanse the wound left by the lead ball that grazed Michaela's arm. It was deeper than he'd thought. Given the length of time it had gone untreated, the chances of the lass developing wound fever were far greater. "Why did ye insist on waiting for Mary's injuries to be tended before yours?" When she did not answer fast enough, he asked, "And why in the bloody hell did ye not tell me how deep the wound was, lass?"

Michaela kept her gaze on Mrs. O'Toole's ministrations when she answered, "I was concerned that Mary had suffered a concussion, given how many times she was struck in the face and head. Besides, I did not have time to inspect the wound. I had a pistol against my temple at the time."

O'Malley's entire being absorbed her words like blows from Declan McNamara—his first bare-knuckle opponent, a mountain of a man. He could not have heard right. "Did ye say ye had a pistol to yer head?"

She turned to look at him and met the intensity of his gaze. "Yes."

He was torn between the need to chase down Haversham, geld him, hobble him, and then beat him within an inch of his life, and the need to stay with Michaela and Mary until the threat of the lass suffering from wound fever had passed, and the worry of Mary being concussed had been ruled out. Time was not on O'Malley's side.

"No," Michaela rasped. Her shocked expression surprised him.

"No, what?" He would see that justice was served. Haversham would pay for everything he had done to this brave, strong, resilient, willful woman glaring at him.

"You are not going to chase after him and do whatever it is that turned your eyes a hard yellow green." Michaela flinched when Mrs. O'Toole removed another bit of cloth from her wound.

"Ye'd best understand, lass, that no man, nor woman, tells me what to do."

"I will say whatever I want, whenever I want," Michaela replied.

"Faith, but I admire yer spirit, lass. A fine bride ye'll be. Have I mentioned that Coventry has arranged everything?" She shook her head, and O'Malley took her silence to mean she was too overcome with gratitude to speak. "I have the special license, and Vicar Dalrymple will be marrying us tonight."

He looked over his shoulder at his cousin. "We need to get word to the vicar that we've relocated to Grosvenor Square."

Garahan shook his head. "With the number of connections King and Coventry have on the streets, they'll have heard what happened. By now Coventry will be ensconced in his apartment with his family. Do ye think his family is safe there?"

O'Malley removed his frockcoat, rolled up his sleeves, and washed his hands. Considering his cousin's question, he replied, "Given the amount of traffic going past the building he lives in at all hours of the day, the chances of someone trying to sneak past the guard the captain has posted are high."

Mrs. O'Toole straightened and said, "There, all ready for you to close the wound, O'Malley. I'll just go down the hall and check on Mary."

"Thank ye, Mrs. O'Toole. Make certain O'Shaughnessy hasn't let her fall asleep."

"Of course," the duke's cook replied.

He walked over to stand beside his intended. Because of who she was, and the bond of trust he was working to build, he confessed what he would normally keep to himself. "I do not normally have to tend pistol ball wounds on women, nor have I ever done so for my bride-to-be."

Michaela slowly smiled. "How many brides-to-be have you had, O'Malley?"

He chuckled. "Tell her, Darby."

Garahan frowned. "Well now, are ye wanting the long list of women pining for ye back home in Cork, or the ones in—"

"Blithering *eedjit!*" O'Malley interrupted. "Do not listen to me cousin. I should have realized he would be no help to me. Ye're the only woman I have asked to be me wife. Ye're the only woman for me, lass."

Her smile added a sparkle to her moss-green eyes. That she held affection for him was evident, but would she trust him with her body as well as her heart? Time would tell. The need to show her that not all men are rutting beasts filled him. He needed to show her that she could trust him, or else he'd never be able to help her heal from the horror he suspected she still held inside of her.

O'Malley was the man she needed. He would be the man who would gently show her, teach her, that she could trust him to keep his word and not hurt her. He would show her with an open and loving heart, tender touches, and feather-soft kisses that her heart and body would be safe within his arms.

"What are you thinking, O'Malley?"

"Thoughts best saved for later, lass, after I've taken care of ye." He glanced over his shoulder. "Garahan, I could use a hand."

Michaela grimaced. As a healer, she would know what was to come.

"If there was a way I could stitch ye without causing ye pain, lass, know that I would."

She sighed. "I have never had a wound deep enough to require threads," she confessed. "I know from having taken care of a number of patients who suffered through the mending that it will be painful, no matter how sharp the needle or how carefully and quickly I work."

"Well now, mayhap ye can tell me a tale of yer most difficult patient while I thread this needle and close up yer wound." He locked gazes with Garahan. "Hold her arm, steady…gently."

"I'm wanting to hear about yer most difficult patient too," Garahan said. "Was it me sister-in-law, Melinda?"

Michaela laughed softly, then gasped as O'Malley began to close the wound with the sharp needle and boiled threads.

"I'm thinking it was yer pain-in-the-arse eldest brother," O'Malley said. "Didn't he get slashed or shot rescuing Melinda?"

"James?" Garahan asked. "Oh aye, didn't he refuse to let ye sew him back together, Michaela?"

She drew in a breath, flinched, and exhaled as O'Malley worked carefully closing the wound. "Up until meeting O'Malley, I thought James was the most stubborn man I had ever encountered."

"Stubborn is a compliment, lass," O'Malley murmured. "Almost done. Ye're a brave woman, *mo chroí.*"

"I'm grateful that you have a firm but gentle touch, O'Malley," Michaela rasped as he tied off the thread. "Thank you for tending to my wound."

"Hold still while I apply the healing salve." She watched him tend to her, and a feeling of rightness settled around O'Malley. Knowing she trusted him, he said, "I don't believe you mentioned when or who shot you."

Michaela did not answer right away. Giving her the time he thought she needed, O'Malley said, "Garahan, hand me a few of those linen squares, would ye?" His cousin complied, and O'Malley instructed her, "Hold the edges carefully, now. I'm going to wrap a length of linen around them to hold them in place."

His mind was racing with possibilities. The one that kept coming back to him was that Michaela for some reason was protecting the person who shot her. Why would she? Who was Haversham to her?

Mrs. Wigglesworth, the housekeeper, walked into the kitchen and smiled at Michaela. "I just wanted to tell you how grateful we are that you were instrumental in lending aid to Melinda and Aimee when they needed it most. His Grace sent a missive recently. He wanted to convey his thanks. The duke and duchess value every man in his private guard, and their wives as well."

O'Malley let the lass be distracted by the engaging housekeeper. There would be time enough to ask the lass again who shot her.

Letting Michaela think that he would not remember she had yet to answer his question, he said, "The duke and duchess have been instrumental in lending their aid to those sailors and soldiers who have been injured serving king and country, as well as the widows and orphans of those who have given the ultimate sacrifice." He paused, then said, "Coventry once confided that it was His Grace's father, the fourth Duke of Wyndmere, that met and befriended him when he'd returned after the Battle of Trafalgar so badly injured and lying in that hospital bed."

"They are some of the rare few," Garahan said, "that see where help is needed and do whatever they can to lend their aid. Whether it be His Grace standing up in the House of Lords pushing for reforms, or opening his town house to the lasses we rescue who steal our hearts and fall in love with us."

Michaela's eyes welled with tears. "I have felt the same calling, and have devoted my life and skills that I learned at my father's elbow to help others." She turned and smiled at Garahan and then O'Malley. "It *is* my calling, something I know Emmett understands and shares—the need to heal others to the best of his ability." Tears spilled over as she confided, "It warms my heart and reaffirms my hope that there are still others in this life who judge not and lend aid to whomever needs it."

Mrs. Wigglesworth handed her a handkerchief from her sleeve. "You need not worry about Mary—not one of us on His Grace's staff judges others. She needs us right now, and we are more than up to the task. With O'Shaughnessy as her protector, you can be certain she will be safe and well cared for."

O'Malley finished clearing away the supplies he'd used, and set the ointments, salves, and herbs back in the basket Mrs. O'Toole kept them in. Washing up again, he experienced something that never happened before. As he stared at Michaela's blood on his hands, her words ripped through him… *I had a pistol against my temple.*

A delayed reaction set in, and his hands trembled. He willed them to stop, confident that no one would see, as his back was turned to everyone. He regained control of his hands, but not his racing heart. He had been up to his elbows in blood more than once when called upon to heal others, but this was the blood of the woman he loved.

"And that makes all the difference," he murmured. He accepted the visual proof—the lass's blood on his hands. His head was finally in accord with his heart, and O'Malley silently vowed to share his love, the hope of the family they could make between them with his life-giving seed. God help him, he would be half a man without Michaela by his side.

"Did ye say something, O'Malley?"

He shook his head at Garahan. "We'd best ensure the vicar knows to come to Grosvenor Square tonight."

"I'll speak to Jenkins," Garahan said.

"Before ye do, Darby," O'Malley said, "I'm thinking ye need to bring Aimee here and insist Coventry bring his family—and his men. Even though Masterson is injured, he's still an excellent shot. With Hennessey, Bayfield, and Tremayne added to our numbers, we'll be better able to defend the women and little Emma."

Gratitude shone in Garahan's eyes. "I was going to suggest it, and am glad ye agree. 'Tis a sound plan and a much easier location to defend. I'll advise Jenkins and Findley of our plan. Ye can speak to Mrs. Wigglesworth and Mrs. O'Toole."

"I'll stay here to keep watch over the women, until ye return with yer wife and the others in tow. The next few hours are critical—for their healing and for waiting for Haversham to make his next move."

O'Malley turned to the woman who would be his wife, and still could not believe his good fortune that she had said yes to him. "We've had a bit of a change in plans, *mo ghrá*. Ye'll soon have the company of Aimee, Miranda, and little Emma." When she smiled at him, he repeated his question. "Now then, lass, I've let ye avoid answering me long enough. Who shot ye? Was it Haversham?"

MICHAELA FELT EVERY ounce of blood rush from her head to her feet. Her stomach roiled as her head began to pound, her ribs ached, and her arm... She bit down on her lip to ignore the slashing pain from the stitches O'Malley had used to close the wound. Thoughts of the precious, tiny babe growing in Aimee's belly, and the thought of how close the young woman had come to losing not just the babe but her life, had bile surging up Michaela's throat. Haversham had taken so much from her, but would have taken far more from Aimee and Darby if she hadn't reacted so quickly.

Dear God—if O'Malley knew about Haversham, then he must know what had happened to her that night... He would have no choice but to rescind his offer of marriage! There was no way a proud man like Emmett O'Malley would marry a shell of a woman like her. Ruined, her reputation in shreds. Beyond redemption.

Doubled over in pain, fearful of being sick in front of O'Malley, she fought the urge to cast up her accounts. When she could no longer control it, she glanced up in time to see O'Malley holding a pot in front of her. Her eyes watered as she heaved until she relieved the meager contents of her stomach. It had been hours since she'd had tea, a scone, and a bite of gingerbread.

"Easy now, lass. I did not mean to upset ye to the point where you'd vomit."

Mrs. Wigglesworth handed him a cloth, and he gently wiped her mouth before handing it back to the housekeeper, who had a damp cloth ready this time. When he gently bathed Michaela's face with the cloth, as if she were as fragile as her mother's bone china teacups, she felt her composure begin to crack.

When he held out a cup of water to rinse out her mouth, she accepted it, surprised that he'd added a bit of mint to the water to wash away the vile taste. O'Malley was a thoughtful, caring man who would have valued her—if she had not been tainted.

Unable to hold back the tears, she gave in and cried, remembering the fear that slashed through her when Haversham pointed his dueling pistol at Aimee. She cried for the terrible beating Mary had suffered at Haversham's hands. And lastly, she cried for the love of the man who offered another dream that would now be snatched away from her.

She didn't realize she'd curled into a ball until she was gently lifted off her feet and wrapped in the strong embrace she would dream of for the rest of her life. It was the only place she felt safe…and now that too would be taken from her. Being unable to protect her virtue from the man who stole it from her rendered her unworthy of being in the same Society as others who had not suffered the same fate. Where would she go now? What would she do if Papa found out what had happened ten years ago?

Gradually, she regained control and felt acutely embarrassed. She eased back to look at O'Malley's face. "Forgive me," she rasped.

He brushed a lock of hair from her eyes with the tip of one

finger. "Nothing to forgive, lass. Ye've been through more than I have in one day. Rescued after being abducted and held against yer will. Bound and gagged, suffering from broken ribs and a good-sized knot on the back of yer head. Then shot at and held captive a second time. Ye're due for a good cry."

She stared at the man who'd blithely announced his intention to wed her this evening—without asking if she was ready, mind you. Now that she knew she would only feel safe with O'Malley, she was absolutely positive that he would change his mind and want to have nothing to do with her.

Such had been her luck for the last decade—to be forgotten, to feel as if the only way she could atone for what happened to her was to give aid to others who had suffered as she had. She had had a purpose rescuing others and helping them rebuild their lives. Now, when the gift of this man's love had been offered, the man who'd taken her virtue had resurfaced and tainted her beyond redemption for the second time. *O'Malley will never marry her now.*

Michaela pressed a hand to her forehead and closed her eyes, just for a moment. She needed to apologize again. Maybe then he would not come to revile her. "Please forgive me, O'Malley. I never mean to bring trouble to Captain Coventry's door. If I thought my nightmare would reappear and try to wreak havoc on those that I have come to care deeply for, I would have refused your offer of help."

He grunted. "As if I'd leave ye in that rat-infested room I found ye, hands bound behind yer back, lying in the filth he placed ye in."

"If I had refused to go with you, Aimee, Miranda, and little Emma would never have been in danger. You should have left me in that abandoned warehouse."

He nudged her chin up with a knuckle and stared into her eyes. "I will always come for ye, lass. Ye have me heart. I'll be damned if I'll take it back because ye're afraid of repercussions from the actions of a dishonorable man. One who earns coin by selling young women and girls to the highest bidder."

Shock arrowed through her at the intensity and determination in the depths of his brilliant green eyes. "But you don't know what he took from me..." She couldn't say any more than that. Surely O'Malley would not make her confess to *everything* that happened.

"I guessed, lass. It was what ye didn't say and the path ye've taken. Ye are a woman of great strength. A woman who gives hope back to those who have lost it. Ye're the woman I am proud to marry."

He lifted her hand to his lips and brushed a kiss across her knuckles. "Yer hands heal others, a calling that echoes me own. We're *meant*, lass. Best get used to the idea that we'll marry tonight." Cupping her chin in his callused hand, he said, "I'm going to kiss ye, lass. Will ye let me?"

She couldn't seem to find her voice to reply. O'Malley had turned her world upside down with his heartfelt declaration. He knew what happened to her and yet did not blame her for it. He admired her for putting her past behind her by helping others.

She licked her lips and met his gaze, surprised by the desire swirling in his eyes.

She knew what happened in the marriage bed. He'd already told her that in order to keep her safe once they were wed, they had to seal their vows. In the next breath, he'd said once they had, they would be safe in the eyes of God and man. He would be patient and wait for her to come to him when she was ready to do more than seal their vows. She would be a fool to throw away a chance that she would feel whole again and regain a bit of her self-respect.

She cleared her throat. "Please."

O'Malley bent his head and kissed her gently, reverently. "Ah, lass, yer lips are sweet as honey. I'm needing another sip."

He waited, and she sighed. "All right."

This time when his lips met hers, she felt tingles of awareness shooting from her lips to her fingertips, and could not feel the top of her head. Her heart beat a frantic rhythm in her breast as O'Malley staked his claim to her heart with a drugging kiss. When he eased back, she whimpered, then opened her eyes to find him staring at her.

"I have much to teach ye, lass, once I've gained yer trust. Know that I would never willingly hurt ye."

"I believe you, Emmett."

"'Tis a start, lass. Now then, I'd best let ye rest while I speak to Findley and Jenkins about adding some of His Grace's footmen to our guard."

She prayed she was wrong, but she had the feeling O'Malley expected Haversham to show up on the duke's doorstep...or climb in through one of the windows. "You truly believe he'll have discerned where I am and come after me here?"

"Aye. But know that he'll never breach our guard. I'll be introducing yerself and Mary to the rest of the men when they arrive."

She'd just noticed that they were alone and Fitzsimmons was nowhere to be found. "Did you ask Fitzsimmons to leave after he was instrumental in freeing Mary and me?"

"Nay, he had an appointment to keep and will be luring Haversham here."

Her heart lodged in her throat.

"Fear not, lass. We'll be ready and waiting for the bloody bastard. He'll not escape justice this time!" O'Malley promised.

CHAPTER SIXTEEN

HAVERSHAM GLARED AT Fitzsimmons. "I should put a lead ball between your eyes! Do you realize what you have cost me?"

"Do you realize," Fitzsimmons said in a calm, clear voice, "that I will lead you to the angel of the streets, and those who have been protecting her...those who were instrumental in arresting Ashbrook and Anderson, destroying a part of your enterprise that impacts the ready income from one of your sources?"

Haversham's eyes widened. "How many men do we need?"

"A handful, no more. They have sought refuge in the Duke of Wyndmere's town house on Grosvenor Square."

"Will they be expecting us?"

"Aye," Fitzsimmons replied. "But they will only have the duke's footmen and two of his private guard in place." With a confidence he felt in his bones, Fitzsimmons added, "You'll crush them and take back what they've taken from you—twice in twenty-four hours."

Hatred was exactly the emotion Fitzsimmons hoped to see, not the bloodless look of indifference. Haversham was about to make a mistake underestimating O'Malley, O'Shaughnessy, and the men who would stand beside them and fight to protect the women Haversham had violated.

Fitzsimmons could not wait for the rest of O'Malley's trap to spring shut on the devil spawn who preyed on young women and, God help him, little girls. Haversham would pay for his crimes.

CHAPTER SEVENTEEN

"M RS. O'TOOLE! MRS. Wigglesworth!" Aimee and Miranda greeted the duke's cook and housekeeper with warmth.

"And is this little Emma?" Mrs. Wigglesworth beamed at the captain and Miranda's little girl.

"My how you have grown," Mrs. O'Toole said. "I have a batch of teacakes that need to be frosted, Emma. Would you like to help me?"

"Cakes?" The little girl bounced in her mother's arms. "Please, Mum?"

Miranda's soft laughter filtered down the hallway from the kitchen to the room next to the pantry, where Michaela and Mary were quietly waiting for the latest arrivals to settle in. Michaela reached for Mary's hand and shook her head at the uncertainty in the other woman's eyes. "You have nothing to fear. Aimee suffered a fate similar to ours."

"Isn't she married to Darby Garahan now?" Mary asked. "I am not married. I chose a different path…"

Michaela patted the back of her hand. "We each chose the only path available to us at the time. Without Aimee's permission, I will not share her story, but know that it echoes yours and mine."

"Men pay for my favors," Mary whispered. "It was either

that…starve…or throw myself into the Thames."

Michaela scooted her chair closer to the cot where Mary had been sitting silent for the last hour. "I pretended to have a virulent fever to keep my father from discovering what happened to me. I could not take the chance that if word got out, every one of his patients would give him the cut direct. He would be ruined."

Mary stared at Michaela for a moment, then said, "Haversham lured me into the garden after dancing and then forced himself on me. When I arrived home in such a state, my parents blamed me, saying that no one would believe it of Lord Haversham." Her eyes filled with tears. "They disowned me and cast me out."

"And you had nowhere else to go?"

Mary shook her head. "Word quickly spread of what happened, I think by Haversham. He delighted in ruining me, and then he shredded my reputation."

"My father's worry that I would die from the fever was what may have kept Haversham from doing more damage than he could have. When I finally emerged from my room, Papa could see that I had recovered. I never told him what happened. After losing Mum, he gave everything he had to his practice and healing his patients. He had little time for anything else, let alone his only child. The only way I could spend time with him was to learn all that he knew about healing."

"And because of that, you became the angel of the streets. Rescuing others because you understood what they were feeling…what they were facing, and what it felt like to be ostracized for something that was never your fault."

"With each woman I helped to heal, I knew it would never be enough. That's when I began to search for kindred souls who saw another need as I did…to help those I healed to find employment. These trusting people helped me by hiring these women and teaching them a skill so that they would be able to forge a new path. Live their lives. Some have been fortunate to have found a man who would love them for who they are despite their shattered past."

Mary whispered, "O'Shaughnessy has never said the words, but I know that he cares deeply for me."

"If you could have seen his face when he raced down the hallway toward you, Mary… The man loves you."

Mary shook her head. "He loves the surcease and release I am able to give him." She sighed. "I have tried not to, but my battered heart didn't listen, and I fell in love with him."

"Did ye now?" a deep voice rumbled from the doorway.

Mary and Michaela both jolted in surprise. While Mary stared at O'Shaughnessy, Michaela rose and walked over to him. "Why don't you sit down for a few minutes with Mary? Her headache is subsiding, but I did not want to leave her alone for the next twenty-four hours." The stark expression on his face was all Michaela had to see to know that she was leaving Mary in the hands of the man who truly loved her. "Please excuse me—I need to speak to Mrs. O'Toole."

When he didn't move, she slipped her arm through his and gave a slight tug. He glanced down at her and nodded. "I would be honored to sit with Mary. I'll give a shout if we need you."

Michaela smiled at the look of adoration on Mary's face—it mirrored the expression on O'Shaughnessy's. She stepped over the threshold and closed the door partway, to afford the couple a bit of privacy.

"Nicely done, lass." O'Malley reached for her hand and tugged her into his arms. "Ye have a caring, romantic heart. 'Tis one of the many things I love about ye."

Michaela stared into eyes that reflected the depth of his affection for her. "But what about what happened—"

His lips cut off her question. At first she tried to resist, needing him to understand, but was soon lost in the wonder of his desire for her. When he ended the kiss and eased back, she blinked, then whispered, "Emmett, I cannot in good conscience marry you without your knowing the truth and understanding that I am not a virtuous woman."

His eyes faded from emerald to yellow green. "If by that ye mean that yer virtue was stolen from ye, I'm aware."

She nodded. "I have no reputation… It was shredded a decade ago."

"By the man you protected then, and are protecting now." His voice had a dangerous edge to it. She flinched as if he had struck her. Seeing her distress, O'Malley drew in a breath and softened his tone. "Why did ye not tell yer da what happened? Were ye afraid he would have ordered ye out of yer home?"

She shook her head, anger bubbling bright and hot inside of her at the inference that she was afraid of her father, when that could not be further from the truth. "I am not protecting the man who did this to me!"

He dropped his hands to his sides and took a step back from her. "'Tisn't how I see it. Ye had no intention of telling me his name, did ye?" When she could not answer him, he fairly growled at her, "Ye're still trying to protect him." A wounded expression flashed across his handsome features before it disappeared and the neutral look she was accustomed to returned. "Do ye love him, then?"

Tears slowly trickled from her eyes as the full force of his question hit her like a blow to the solar plexus. She wrapped her arm around her battered ribs to steady herself, looked him in the eye, and rasped, "The truth would ruin my father! He lost everything when Mum died, and he buried himself in his medical practice. The only way I could feel that I had not lost him too was to work alongside him, learning what he knew to help heal others. Without that connection, I would have lost my father, too."

The light of understanding shone in O'Malley's eyes. "Yer da failed ye when he shut ye out of his life after ye lost yer mum. Me ma pulled me and me three brothers closer after we lost our da. He was wrongly accused and died in prison, hours before he was due to be released. Exonerated for a trumped-up crime that was never committed. Ma did not push us away—she needed us. Kept us close, speaking of Da often. Reminding us of his laughter, his words, and his deeds until the four of us could see Da in our mind's eye. He'll always be in our hearts. Yer ma will always be in yours, lass."

"With the number of patients that flocked to him after he healed an earl's ailing mother, Papa needed me, as he did not trust anyone new to help care for his patients. He praised my skill, was proud of me. We worked alongside one another for a few years more, before he began to take note of the fact that time had passed, and I was of marriageable age. That is when he encouraged me to attend a handful of entertainments with the few men he approved of."

"And how many did ye attend before the unthinkable happened to ye?"

"Just the one."

He glanced away and then into her eyes. "And then ye hid the truth from yer da."

"I could not risk his losing the only thing…" Her voice broke. She closed her eyes for a moment, then opened them and finished, "The only thing that mattered to him."

She was crushed against O'Malley's chest. His big hand cradled her head, holding it to his heart. "Ye cannot know that, lass. Sure and ye matter more to yer da than his patients."

Michaela did not bother to answer. She'd already told O'Malley the truth, and he did not believe her. "Where would my father go if his reputation were smeared?"

"Is this what Haversham did to ye after he stole from ye? Threatened ye so ye would not seek reprisal?"

Unable to speak past the emotion clogging her throat, she nodded.

"*Mo chroí, mo ghrá*," he whispered. "Ye can no longer hide this from yer da. He deserves to know what his retreating from yer life has done to ye. Ye matter to him, lass. Mayhap not in the way ye need him to, but I know that ye matter more to him than ye realize."

Her eyes burned from crying, adding to the list of all of the other aches and pains bombarding her heart and body right now.

"'Tis why I've sent word to yer da," O'Malley said. "He's aware that I intend to marry ye tonight. Whether or not he agrees matters not."

She stared up at him in time to see the tense set of his jaw, the hard look in his eyes. "And if he doesn't agree and give his blessing?"

"Ye've already devoted a decade to saving his reputation by keeping what happened from him. Don't let his lack of blessing us have ye spending another decade devoting yerself to a man who cares more about himself than he does his only child. The daughter he should have moved heaven and earth to protect."

All of the fight went out of her. The reason for protecting her father's reputation, along with the need to keep the name of the man who violated her secret, vanished along with the need to fight to continue to hide the truth from him. O'Malley was right. She should confide what happened, beginning with the two recent abductions.

Then there was the fact that the man who rescued her had already captured her heart when he entered her lodging with an armful of petticoats and two pint-sized moppets clinging to his neck.

The man who stole her virtue had continued stealing far more from innocents than could ever be replaced, while she thought she was doing her part by rescuing other women who'd been cast aside. The crushing knowledge that she may have been able to stop him from continuing to destroy others' reputations and lives ate at her like a cancer. "I'm to blame—"

"Bloody hell, woman! Ye're not to blame for Haversham's twisted proclivities, nor his need to take what was never willingly offered. Ye'll stop blaming yerself right now!"

Footsteps rapidly approaching had her hiding in O'Malley's arms. She did not want to face whoever had overheard the Irishman's rant. Just when she thought the person would leave without speaking, other footsteps echoed down the hall.

"Her head's as hard as yers," Garahan grumbled.

Somehow she'd known Garahan would manage to arrive when she was about to deliver a blistering reply to O'Malley. She lifted her head to respond, and could not believe her eyes. Garahan wasn't alone. The men who enabled her to continue rescuing other young women were standing in a semicircle around them.

Masterson nodded his bandaged head to her and said, "Ah, but her heart is a pure as the angel we know her to be."

"At times demanding," Gavin King gruffly added, "but I have long admired her dedication to her cause."

"As have I," Captain Coventry said. "You have a gift, Michaela. We are all proud to have had a hand in lending our resources and strength when you have asked for it."

O'Malley shifted her in his arms until she was tucked tight against his side before he turned so that they were now facing the men.

"'Tis her willingness to walk into danger, despite trying to keep her safe, which is only eclipsed by me wife." Alasdair Cameron's eyes were alight with mischief when he asked, "Have ye thought of gagging her, O'Malley?"

Michaela's mouth hung open, and for a moment she wondered how much longer the men intended to torment her with their compliments. All the while she wondered if they would begin to list her shortcomings next.

O'Malley slid his arm around her waist, steadying her. His support gave her the strength to say, "I cannot help but wonder if my error in judgment is responsible for his—"

"I'm warning ye, wife—" O'Malley growled.

Garahan burst into laughter. "Ye may have asked her to marry ye, but ye aren't wed yet, boy-o! I came to tell ye the vicar will be arriving in an hour's time." He stared at O'Malley and added, "I'm thinking ye'll want to put on a clean shirt at the very least."

O'Malley shook his head at his cousin's jibe and turned to the others. "And the rest of you?"

"We're here to lend our aid in protecting Michaela," Masterson said.

"And Aimee," Garahan added.

"And my wife and our daughter," Coventry said.

"Hear, hear!" King and Cameron added.

O'Malley shook his head. "Thank ye, men. In return, ye've but to ask, and I'll do whatever ye need. No matter what… No matter where. No matter when."

"Tremayne and the others are forming the exterior guard, surrounding the town house," Coventry advised him.

"Findley and Jenkins have already gone over our interior plans with the footmen," Garahan said.

"The rest of us will be waiting for the bloody bastard to make his move," King said. "And when he does…"

"We'll see that he regrets ever laying one finger on me wife," O'Malley growled.

Garahan smacked a hand to his forehead. "Faith, haven't I already reminded ye that ye're not married yet?"

The laughter of the men surrounding her, protecting her, and the other women warmed Michaela's heart. "I will never be able to thank you enough. Each and every one of you has been instrumental in lending your expertise and aid." She blinked away her tears. "I can never repay you."

Cameron stepped forward and placed a hand on her shoulder. "Ye already have, lass."

"I need another moment to speak with Michaela," O'Malley told the men. "I'll join you in the entryway in a moment."

Michaela sagged in his arms and said, "If I had told my father what happened years ago, I never would have met and been befriended by the men who have stood beside and behind me in my quest." Her eyes met O'Malley's, and she let him see what was in her heart. "I never would have met you. The man who will teach me how to trust with more than my mind… With my heart and my body. Will you promise to be patient with me?"

Desire changed the hue of his eyes to a deep forest green. "Ye have me word, lass."

CHAPTER EIGHTEEN

M RS. WIGGLESWORTH SMILED as she entered the largest of
the duke's guest rooms, where the women had gathered
to help Michaela get ready to marry O'Malley. "Just what this
house has been missing, ladies." She glanced around at the
smiling faces as they were sipping tea and enjoying the teacakes
Mrs. O'Toole and Emma had frosted. "Where is Mary?"

Michaela's heart sighed with relief at the concern evident in
the housekeeper's tone. "Emmett agreed with me that Mary
needed quiet and rest and someone to sit with her to ensure she
was awakened every few hours."

Miranda nodded as she used one of the linen napkins to gently wipe her daughter's tiny fingers after Emma had licked the
frosting off them. "Head injuries are always serious."

"We all would rather have Mary here with us, drinking tea
and offering our advice"—Aimee smiled at Emma and winked—
"when Emma is otherwise occupied."

"Emmett and I were in complete agreement, but it was
O'Shaughnessy who was adamant that he would not be leaving
Mary's side until we were satisfied that she was not concussed,"
Michaela said.

Mrs. Wigglesworth nodded. "Always best to err on the side of
caution." She slowly smiled at the women and confided, "It is so
much easier when the patient in question is *not* one of the duke's

guard."

Michaela burst into giggles. Aimee and Miranda were soon laughing with her, while little Emma clapped delightedly before she dove across the table, reaching for another frosted teacake.

"That is absolutely your last cake, Emma."

Michaela bit her lip to keep from laughing at the little one's fierce frown. She did not want Emma to think she was laughing at her. That was not the case at all—it was how closely Emma's fierce frown matched her father's. More often than not, Captain Coventry frowned.

"Please join us, Mrs. Wigglesworth," Michaela invited as she filled a teacup. "Cream? Sugar?"

"Neither, thank you," the housekeeper said as she sat on the empty chair and accepted the proffered teacup. "I really only just stopped in to advise that the vicar has arrived. Garahan wanted me to tell you that O'Malley has been wearing a hole in the library's carpet."

Michaela flushed, but could not keep from smiling. "Is he really?"

The housekeeper nodded, then sipped from her cup. "Mrs. O'Toole and I are both of a mind when it comes to O'Malley. He is a fierce and formidable warrior with a heart of pure gold. You have nothing to fear marrying him, Michaela. He will guard you with his life, as will the rest of the men in the duke's guard." She turned and beamed at Miranda, adding, "And of course the man who oversees everything from London…Captain Coventry."

Mrs. Wigglesworth set her teacup on its saucer and smiled at Michaela. "Are you ready to dress, now that you have soaked in a hot tub and soothed the rest of your nerves with tea and cake?"

Michaela sighed. "It is not nerves, exactly." She did not how to put into words what she was feeling, so she fell silent.

"We understand," Aimee said with a glance at Miranda. "You trust O'Malley, don't you?"

"With all my heart," Michaela answered.

"Then do as Aimee and I have done," Miranda said. "Remember that as you dress, and we accompany you down to where your husband-to-be is pacing, worried sick that you will have changed your mind."

Michaela shot to her feet. "I promised to marry Emmett. I would never go back on my word."

Mrs. Wigglesworth rose and reached for Michaela's hands. "Best hurry now. I overheard the vicar confiding he missed afternoon tea and is quite famished. We need to feed him soon." With that, the duke's housekeeper nodded and left the room, closing the door behind her.

Miranda and Aimee rose and slipped their arms through Michaela's, escorting her behind the dressing screen. Miranda chatted until Emma got tangled in the damp drying cloth draped across the back of the fainting couch and started to cry when she discovered she was stuck. Aimee took over the chatting and fastening the buttons on the back of Michaela's borrowed gown.

"Please remind me whose gown I'm wearing? I'd like to send a note of thanks."

Aimee was quick to respond, "I believe it is one of Lady Aurelia's gowns. All of the duke's relatives keep gowns on hand so they need not pack so many when they come to London. Her Grace's gowns would be several inches too long for you. Lady Phoebe and Lady Calliope's gowns would only be a few inches too long." Fussing and smoothing the pale cream gown, she stepped back to admire her handiwork. "You look stunning, Michaela, and are so fortunate that Lady Aurelia is the same height and of a similar build."

"Are you certain she will not mind my borrowing it?"

"I am quite sure. Mrs. O'Toole confided that the duke's sister-in-law has had a new wardrobe made to accommodate her new figure. Poor Lady Aurelia is beside herself that she doesn't appear to be able to regain the figure she had before giving birth."

"It seems to be the nature of things, from what I have observed," Michaela said. "I hope the earl has reassured her that she looks as lovely as ever. Women who have recently given birth need reassurance that they are loved and needed by their husband as well as their babe."

"I haven't had any experience with babes or new mothers," Aimee added.

"I would be happy to invite one or two that are quite good friends who would be happy to share their experiences with you. Just say the word, Aimee."

"Thank you, Michaela. I think that would ease my mind. Oh, I nearly forgot—O'Malley sent one of his cravats for you to wear."

"Odd," Michaela said. "Why would I want to do that?"

"He insisted that you listen to someone who has been shot in the arm and knows that the healing time is slowed considerably if you do not keep it immobile and elevated in a sling."

"But if my arm is in a sling, I cannot use it," Michaela protested.

Aimee smiled, folded the black square in half diagonally, and held it up in front of Michaela. "I do believe that is what I just said. Please do this, if not for Emmett, then for me?"

Michaela grumbled, but complied. She knew it was the proper treatment, but had balked because it would leave her with one useless arm, if she had to defend herself.

As if she understood and recognized what worried Michaela, Aimee reminded her, "You have O'Malley to protect you."

"He is often on assignment," Michaela countered.

Aimee nodded. "There will always be one of the other members of the guard, or one of Coventry's men, who will step in to protect you. You are part of the duke's extended family now, and therefore added to the growing list of those the men in the duke's guard have vowed to protect with their lives."

"I had no idea," Michaela whispered.

"Neither did I, until the day came when I needed protection, and Darby was on the other side of the city."

"Gordon's men rotate their duties, leaving one man to stand guard at all times," Miranda said, holding a now sleepy-eyed

Emma in her arms. "If there is a threat, the number of men standing guard increases. If there is a need, Gavin King has a select few who are first choice to fill in for the duke's guard and my husband's men."

Michaela felt the worry leaving her. "Thank you for explaining that to me. I am so sorry that I brought danger to your door, Miranda. You, Emma, and Aimee should not have had to be terrorized by Haversham. Please say you can find it in your hearts to forgive me."

Miranda shook her head, and Michaela's heart sank.

"Of course I forgive you," Miranda rushed to assure her. "I was shaking my head at the idea that you would feel responsible for the actions of a dishonorable man, taking them on as your own."

Aimee added her assurances to Miranda's, then said, "Give me a few moments, and I can pin up your hair. You will look fashionable and O'Malley will thank me later."

Michaela laughed softly. "He's seen me covered in filth, battered, and disheveled. I doubt he cares what my hair looks like."

Aimee shared a glance with Miranda before holding up three hairpins. Michaela frowned. "I use three times as many pins to hold my hair in place."

"Pay attention," Aimee said as she quickly fashioned a flattering updo that required just three pins to fasten it.

"Thank you, Aimee. It's lovely."

"*You're* lovely, Michaela," Miranda and Aimee said simultaneously. "Don't forget to tell us what O'Malley thinks of your coiffure," Aimee added.

Though she wondered at the merriment in the other women's eyes, Michaela didn't ask why, simply agreed.

The loud knock that Michaela had been waiting for, and dreading at the same time, came a few moments later.

Aimee rushed over and opened the door to greet her husband.

Garahan smiled at his wife, pulled her into his arms, and

kissed the breath out of her before stepping over the threshold. "Ye're a vision, Michaela." He cleared his throat and said, "I've been tasked with collecting the bride and escorting ye to me *eedjit* cousin… Er…yer husband-to-be."

Michaela was smiling as she walked over to Garahan and slipped her arm through his. "Thank you, Darby. I'm so happy that you are the one to escort me."

"'Tis the Garahan curse to be wanted by every female in God's creation, when our hearts love but one."

"I have heard that sentiment before, you know," Michaela said. "From your brother James."

"He's always stealing me best lines," Garahan murmured before changing the subject. "We'd best not tarry, lass. O'Malley's temper is on the rise."

"We'll be down in a moment," Aimee said. "I'll make certain Miranda doesn't rush, as she's carrying Emma."

Garahan smiled at his wife and said, "Himself expected ye a quarter of an hour ago and fears the worst."

Michaela lifted the hem of her gown and tugged on Garahan's arm. "Hurry!"

⫸⫷

O'MALLEY WANTED TO stalk out of the library, take the stairs two at a time, and bang on the door his bride-to-be was hiding behind. "What is keeping her? Does she not know the vicar's arrived?"

Cameron smiled. "I dinna think I've ever seen a man so far gone over a lassie before." O'Malley curled his hands into fists. Cameron noticed and laughed. "Michaela is stout of heart and afraid of nothing. She's taking her time. It cannot be easy with one arm out of commission."

At the reminder, O'Malley's gut roiled. "Ye're right. How could I forget?"

The Scot shrugged. "She rarely tells anyone how she feels. It's like pulling teeth to get her to confide when something is worrying her. My wife is the same way."

"I've just extracted vital information that I knew she'd been keeping from me."

Cameron stared at O'Malley, waiting for him to share what Michaela had told him. O'Malley decided that Cameron knew her best, having guarded the lass closely. "She knew the name of her abductor. The man who had her bound, gagged, and delivered to an abandoned warehouse on the docks rolled up in a rug."

Cameron narrowed his eyes. "What of the other man, the one who shot her?"

"Same man." The shock on Cameron's face had O'Malley nodding. "Before ye ask, 'tis the same bloody bugger who stole her virtue."

Cameron's eyes flashed with anger as he clenched his jaw. Relief flowed through O'Malley. Here was a man who would not hold him back. He would insist Cameron accompany him to exact revenge against the man who had tried to crush the life out of the brightest of earthbound angels, his Michaela. "I couldn't understand why she'd keep the name from me. Why she would protect the man who'd taken so much from her."

Cameron relaxed his hands and said, "You thought she was in love with her tormentor."

"Briefly," O'Malley admitted. "She finally confessed that she was protecting—"

Cameron swore and interrupted, "Her father. I was tempted more than once to have a discussion with Dr. Colborne. If he had eyes in his head, he would have seen her turmoil, her need for his assurances."

"Aye, that she was not alone. She was valued… She was loved," O'Malley rasped.

"Michaela is a gem among women, with a healing touch and a pure heart," Cameron said.

"And if she doesn't hurry up and get here in the next few minutes," O'Malley barked, "I'm going to go fetch her meself, toss her over me shoulder, and demand the vicar marry us before I set her back on her feet!"

"Is that really necessary, Emmett?"

O'Malley turned, and every ounce of spit dried up in his mouth. The vision standing in the doorway, her arm linked with his cousin's, was a beauty beyond compare. The gown she wore was the color of freshly churned butter. It accentuated her soft brown hair that had been swept up onto the top of her head, adding to her small stature. Tendrils had escaped their pins and caressed the sides of her face, calling his attention to her full lips and moss-green eyes. There was a hint of worry in the depths of them. Worry for what?

Instead of asking, he immediately sought to soothe her. "Ye're a vision of loveliness, lass, from the top of yer head to yer toes."

The worry faded as a hint of embarrassed pleasure took its place. O'Malley strode over to her and held out his hand. "Careful now—I don't want ye losing yer balance now that ye've finally listened to me instructions and are using the sling to elevate yer injured arm."

She glared, and he grinned. "By God, lass, the temper in yer eyes only adds to yer beauty. I'll have to be careful not to anger ye too much, else ye'll constantly be getting whatever ye ask."

Michaela's lilting laughter filled the room. "I would be a fool to forget that I have a weapon to hold over your head, O'Malley."

He closed the distance between them. The toes of his boots touched the toes of her serviceable footwear. The incongruity of his wife-to-be wearing her worn boots and a gown that had to have belonged to Lady Aurelia, given their respective heights, bothered him. Did the lass not own more than one pair of half boots? What of gowns? Did she only own the trio that he had seen her wear—dark brown, dark blue, and dark gray?

He would see to it that Madame Beaudoine created a gown just for her. In the meantime, he would send word to the modiste that his new wife was in need of a few new gowns immediately.

He knew from what the Garahans had said that the modiste had a supply of ready-made dresses on hand that could easily be altered to fit at a moment's notice.

"I'm sorry for the urgency, lass, else we could have waited to marry and mayhap asked Earl Lippincott if we could be married in his garden."

Garahan nodded when O'Malley held out his arm to Michaela. He let her go and bowed to her. "It was me pleasure to escort ye, Michaela. Have ye noticed that me cousin seems a bit impatient and possessive today?"

Michaela pressed a kiss to Garahan's cheek before placing her hand on O'Malley's arm. He placed his much larger hand atop hers. The chill surprised him. "Lass, are ye unwell? Yer hand is cold to the touch."

She licked her lips and shook her head. Leaning close, she whispered, "I never thought to marry, O'Malley. I confess to worrying that I would disappoint you. We share common ground with our calling to heal. We work to do something about the injustices we encounter… But my past—"

He bent and brushed a kiss to her lips to silence her. "Yer past is part of what has made you such an admirable woman, Michaela. Knowing what obstacles ye have faced and beaten back to enrich the lives of others is more irresistible than yer faerie eyes, the sunshine of yer smile, and the beauty that shines from yer heart."

Tears welled in her eyes, and he immediately eased a step back, though he did not release her hand. "I didn't mean to make ye sad, lass. I'm after explaining the reasons why I love ye."

"Ah," a raspy voice said from behind them. "I see the bride and groom are ready at last."

O'Malley wished the vicar to perdition for interrupting when he was about to kiss Michaela again, while at the same time was relieved the man was here. "Thank ye for coming on such short notice, Vicar Dalrymple."

"I am honored to be asked, O'Malley. Viscount Moreland is a

longtime friend, as are Gavin King and Captain Coventry."

O'Malley noticed the others had begun to file into the room. Garahan escorted his wife, and the captain escorted his. Little Emma must be visiting with Mrs. O'Toole in the kitchen. He frowned, and was about to ask where O'Shaughnessy and Mary were, when they entered the room—walking slowly, given Mary's injuries.

O'Shaughnessy frowned. "The lass wouldn't let me carry her."

The incredulity of the statement surprised those gathered, with the exception of the captain, Garahan, and O'Malley. They knew the sway the women they loved held over them. O'Malley would walk over burning coals if Michaela asked him to.

The vicar beamed at the latecomers. "I am so happy that you feel well enough to join in the ceremony," Dalrymple said. "Miss Michaela and O'Malley expressly asked that the two of you join them."

The vicar's words surprised O'Malley. Very few of the clergymen that he had met since coming to London would be this kind to the couple who had obviously followed a path that led away from the church's teachings. Then he remembered his cousin James singing Viscount Moreland's praises. Mayhap all those within the former naval captain's sphere were men with strong convictions and a giving nature.

Mary's face flushed beneath her bruises, and O'Shaughnessy straightened his shoulders.

O'Malley was ready for the vicar to begin, and was surprised when the man continued speaking to the other couple. "Your act of bravery, Mary, when you knew that there was a distinct possibility of retaliation and injury, saved Miss Michaela's life and weighs heavily in your favor. God has heard your plea, and that of the man standing beside you."

The vicar turned to O'Malley and Michaela. "With your permission, O'Shaughnessy has asked me to marry them after you have said your vows."

Garahan's wide grin had O'Malley smiling in return. He squeezed Michaela's hand. "We do not mind at all, do we, *mo chroi?*"

Michaela's happiness for her newfound friend was evident. "I think, given Mary's condition, and her need to rest, that you should marry O'Shaughnessy and Mary first—if you do not mind, Vicar Dalrymple."

The vicar's wrinkled face shone with pleasure. "This is a most auspicious occasion for all gathered here, for two of God's children who have atoned and returned to the fold. Aloysious, would you and Mary please come stand in front of me?"

"*Aloysious?* No wonder he never told us his first name," O'Malley whispered in Michaela's ear. She pinched his side, and he smiled at the feisty woman he would soon marry.

The vicar cleared his throat to begin, and a few moments later Mary and O'Shaughnessy were man and wife. "Thank ye," O'Shaughnessy said. "Especially Captain Coventry for applying for the special license on me behalf so I could marry the lass without having the banns read. 'Tis imperative that I protect her from harm. She has suffered enough. And a special thanks to Gavin King for offering me a position with the Bow Street Runners."

King smiled. "We need more men like you, O'Shaughnessy. Those that break the law will think twice when faced with the choice of running or accompanying you to Bow Street."

When the congratulations died down, O'Shaughnessy swept his wife into his arms and nodded. "Thank ye from the bottom of me heart."

"And mine," Mary rasped.

"We'll have a tray sent down shortly," O'Malley said. "We wouldn't want you to miss out on our wedding supper."

O'Shaughnessy's eyes were suspiciously bright as he thanked them again. "Thank ye, O'Malley. Me wife is exhausted, and I'm needing to stand vigil waking her every few hours."

After they left, O'Malley turned to Michaela and pulled her

closer, anchoring her to his side. "'Tis our turn, *mo ghrá*."

A short while later they were married and following the others toward the dining room. Instead of following them inside, O'Malley led Michaela toward the main staircase, lifted her into his arms, and carried her up the stairs and down the hallway to the room at the end. The door stood open, and the room was aglow from the fire burning brightly and the candles set out.

A small table was set for two with covered dishes. "'Tis for later, lass."

Michaela laid her head on his shoulder and sighed. "I have been blessed from the day you frowned at me."

"Frowned, was it?"

"You were contradicting me at the time."

"Ah." He pressed his lips to her cheek. "I don't recall that part, but I do remember being drawn in by your eyes and the way ye stuck yer stubborn chin out at me."

"I did no such thing."

O'Malley laughed delightedly. "Ye're doing it now." Shock had her pressing her lips together, and O'Malley apologizing. "I did not mean to upset ye, lass. Just explaining the reasons ye captured me interest from the start."

"It sounds more like I irritated you from the start," she murmured. As soon as she noticed the turned-down bed, she started to tremble.

"Kiss me, lass." He waited for her to meet his gaze. "I'll do me best not to hurt ye, lass. But we must—"

"We have had this conversation before," Michaela interrupted. "I trust you, Emmett, but ask that you please be patient with me."

"I am, lass."

"It doesn't appear that way."

"That's because I'm fighting the need that has a hold of me bollocks. Ye're a rare beauty, Michaela-mine, and I finally have ye all to meself for the night. For all of the nights, the rest of our lives. I promise to go slowly, but if ye don't kiss me soon, I'll go out of me mind."

She cupped the side of his face, and her lips found his. It was the kiss of an angel. *His* angel. Love for the lass filled him to overflowing. O'Malley dug deep for the control to temper his desire and show the other half of his heart that he was a man of his word. He kissed her gently, reverently. "Are ye hungry, lass?"

She pressed her lips to his in answer.

He took control of the kiss, keeping a tight rein on his passion. "The food is getting cold."

"I don't want to wait, Emmett. The sooner we get this over with, the better."

He ignored the hurt that she would brush away their joining as if it were of no great importance. The two of them becoming one, mayhap creating a babe, was not to be tossed aside as if it didn't matter. 'Twas a gift.

"Ah, lass, a real man takes his time. There's so much more to making love than the act. I'm after teaching ye what pleasure there is to be had between a man and his wife."

She shook her head. "There is pain—"

"Mayhap for our first time together, but before that, I intend to drive ye mad kissing every inch of ye…from yer nose to yer toes…and lingering in between. Ye'll be so hot for me, ye'll be begging me to make ye mine."

Michaela narrowed her eyes at him, then nodded. "Your challenge is accepted."

O'Malley gave a whoop of joy and kissed the breath out of his wife. While she was still trying to get a hold of herself, he removed her sling and waited for her to catch her breath before he suggested helping her undress. He could not wait to teach her the silent language of love with his lips and his fingertips.

CHAPTER NINETEEN

RAISED VOICES ECHOED from the entryway as O'Malley helped Michaela remove her sling. He recognized that voice. "Bloody hell!"

"Michaela!"

She blinked and then frowned. "What in the world is my father doing here?"

"I told ye that I sent word to him that we planned to marry, but he did not reply, nor did he arrive in time to give you away."

"Lower your voice, Colborne!"

Relief filled O'Malley. "Coventry's handling the problem."

"I demand to see my daughter!"

Michaela sighed. "Why on earth would he want to see me now, when he has spent the better part of a decade ignoring me?"

"You missed the ceremony," they heard another voice claim. "But are welcome to return to greet the happy couple at teatime tomorrow."

Michaela's eyes were filled with merriment. "That sounds like Gavin King."

"Aye. He's a good man and friend to His Grace."

Other low voices rumbled, and O'Malley knew that Michaela's father was being handled by his cousin, Coventry, King, and Cameron. In the silence that followed, he sighed. "We will need to be ready to present a united front tomorrow at teatime, unless yer father plans to return in the morning."

Michaela lifted her shoulder and winced. "How long does it take to remember that I was grazed by a lead ball and to not move that arm or shoulder?"

"A bit more time, lass. Now then, shall I undo yer buttons?"

Michaela turned her back to him. "If you would, please." He quickly handled the task and bent to ask, "I can help lift it over yer head. 'Tis best if ye wait a few days before attempting to do so."

"I normally don't require help undressing. My maid is used to my coming and going at all hours and not requiring much more than her bringing my morning tea and breakfast tray."

"'Tisn't help I'm offering—'tis part of what a man and his wife share, lass. The uncovering of one another is a gift."

His words shocked her, as he'd intended. He didn't want her to start thinking of everything that would happen, bracing herself to expect a repeat of her other experience. O'Malley planned to obliterate that deeply entrenched memory.

"A gift?" she whispered.

"Aye, lass. Me face and manly form have caused more than one lass to swoon. And that was with me clothes on."

Her gasp was followed by her lilting laughter. He went down on one knee and removed her half boots one at a time. Carefully running his hand from her ankle to her knee, he smiled up at her. "I'm thinking ye should keep yer stockings and garters on, lass."

She bit her bottom lip, studying him, then said, "Let me help you undress. I think we should unwrap you first."

"After I help ye off with yer gown." He carefully lifted it over her head without jarring her injured arm. As she stood before him in her shift, he wondered just how he would navigate her broken ribs.

"At least let me help you with your boots," she said.

"Nay, that will require ye bending at the waist, lass." He took care of removing his boots and socks.

Michaela was staring at his feet as if fascinated by the fact that they were bare. To distract her, he said, "I'll go slowly, lass. I'll not put any of me considerable weight on ye. Ye've enough injuries without me adding to them."

When she stood before him, he sighed. His wife, his heart, his *love* was a beauty beyond compare. He slipped out of his frockcoat, and she surprised him by brushing his hands to his sides while she undid the buttons to his waistcoat and helped him remove one sleeve. He took care of the other. When she dropped her hands to her sides, he removed his cambric shirt, delighting in her innocent reaction. "I'm thinking ye're partial to me broad chest."

She licked her lips, and he chuckled. At the look in her eyes, and the frown that settled on her face, he knew she was recalling what he needed to wipe from her memory. "Will ye do me a favor, Michaela?"

"I will try."

"Remember where ye are...Grosvenor Square, about to lie down on a feathered mattress and soft bed linens. And who ye are with...the man who loves ye, values ye, and will for the rest of our lives." A lone tear slid from the corner of her eye. He captured it with the tip of his forefinger. "Think of the pleasure I'm about to share with ye." She gasped when he ran his hands from beneath her arms to her hips and back again. "Kiss me."

He bent his head and pressed his lips to hers, urgently, possessively, heady with the knowledge that she responded with an ardor that matched his own. Mindful of her injuries, but not focusing solely on them—else he'd never be able to seal their vows—he traced the tip of his tongue from beneath her ear, along her collarbone, to the hollow at the base of her throat. "Ye taste of sunshine, lavender, and roses." His lips followed the same path, nibbling and kissing a path once more to the hollow of her throat. "We need to get rid of yer shift, lass. May I?"

Her moan of pleasure nearly had him on his knees.

"I'll take that to mean *aye*."

His wife was lost in the sensations he aroused with his lips and tongue—'twas time to add his hands. Though they were callused, he'd never had complaints before. Striking that thought from his addled brain, he cupped her face in his hands and took her lips in a kiss, laced with his desperate desire to claim her.

She was wide-eyed and panting when he lifted her chemise up over her uninjured shoulder, then her head, and gently maneuvered it off her injured arm. He let his gaze follow the line of her throat, to the bounty of her breasts, to her stocking-clad legs and back again. "God in heaven, lass, ye're perfect. I need to caress and kiss your breasts." He lifted her chin so he could look into her eyes. "May I? I promise to stop whenever you ask me to."

She stared at him for a few moments before giving a brief nod. He gently lifted her in his arms and laid her on the bed. "Because of our height difference, the only way to properly kiss yer breasts, without putting any weight on ye, is to straddle ye. Yer ribs are still healing, and I don't want ye to feel caged in."

"I trust you, Emmett."

He knelt on the bed, one knee on either side of her, and brushed his palms over her breasts. He felt her nipples pebble at his touch. "I can feel yer body reacting to me touch, lass. How does it feel to ye?" She sighed his name, and he asked again. "Does it pain ye, lass? Should I stop?"

"Don't stop."

"I'm going to taste ye before I kiss ye. May I?"

The guttural sound she made hit him like a ton of bricks. The need to plunge into her had him by the throat, but he tightened the rein on his need. "First I'll use me tongue to test the skin beneath yer breasts. Then I'll work me way up to yer nipples and suckle ye."

Her gasp was not one of pleasure, but shock.

"Aye or nay, lass?"

"Aye."

Brave lass. Her passion simmered just beneath the surface, begging him to set it free. He bent his head and poured himself into the task of sampling and testing the weight of first one breast and then the other. "Brace yerself—I'm going to suckle ye, and if

I'm doing it right, ye'll feel a pulling sensation low in yer belly that will add to the need screaming through ye."

He licked around her nipples, pleased by the moans and intermittent gasps as she started to relax and give herself over to him. Pulling her breast into his mouth, he suckled her as if he were starving. She writhed beneath him, lost in the sensations his lips coaxed from her body. Brushing the tips of his fingers over her other breast, she bucked and locked gazes with him.

He stopped, and she whimpered, "Don't stop."

"Ye feel it building inside ye. Let me give ye more." He worshipped her other breast and teased the one he lavishly kissed with his fingertips. He knew she had to feel the bulge hardening where he was pressed against her core, but she did not demand he move—she lifted her hips and brushed herself against him.

It was the sweetest torture. "Lass, I don't know how much more I can take."

Her eyes met his. "Are you in pain?"

"Aye, lass."

"How long have you been in pain?"

He answered honestly, "A few weeks now."

"Weeks, but we… That is, I haven't…"

"Ye're a beautiful woman inside and out, Michaela-mine. If ye think ye're ready, I need to stretch ye. It'll lessen the pain, and yer body will accept all of me."

She bit her bottom lip and stared at the bulge pushing against the placket of his trousers. When she licked her lips, he moaned and she whispered, "I'm ready."

"Ye're a brave lass, wife of mine. I'll go as slowly as I'm able."

HER HUSBAND STOOD, swiftly divested himself of his trousers, and climbed back onto the bed. His hands skimmed from her ankles up to her knees. The silk stockings must have added to what he was feeling, because he locked gazes with her, desire darkening his gaze. He smoothed a hand from her knees to her thighs and then to the very heart of her. Gently, pausing when she couldn't catch her breath from the combination of fear and pleasure, he waited, then asked her permission. Finally, she relaxed and gave herself fully to his ministrations.

O'Malley's hands were magic. His callused fingertips and palms elicited a response from deep inside of her—no matter where he touched, she could not help but respond. It was the same with his beautifully sculpted lips and talented tongue. The things he did, and made her feel, had her body on fire for more…even though she knew the end result would be the tearing pain of his invasion into her body.

He trailed one finger up the inside of her thigh and beyond, brushing against her core. Instead of revulsion, she felt a heat so intense, she wondered if he felt the burn. And then he was inside of her, testing her inner walls with one, and then two fingers, as he claimed her lips in a devasting kiss that had her panting for more. Lifting her hips, she felt his fingers plunging inside her as he drove her to the edge of reason. Then she flew off into the unknown.

"Emmett!"

"That's it, lass—trust me and let go."

Unable to do otherwise, she relaxed, and sensation after sensation bombarded her until she felt as if she were spiraling up to the heavens. His mouth found hers, and he drank in her cries of ecstasy, shifting until he was settled between her legs, poised at the entrance to her warmth.

"Michaela, open yer eyes."

She struggled, but managed to obey. The need in his eyes called to her, and she knew in that moment that she would do whatever he asked—to alleviate the pain *he* was in. "Let me ease your pain, Emmett."

"I'll try not to hurt ye." He slid inside of her, pausing when she stiffened. "Ye need to trust me and relax, lass." His kiss was all it took for her to respond and relax. As soon as she did, he began to move slowly at first, then increased the tempo until he was plunging in and slowly withdrawing. Arms locked, holding his weight off her, he drove her back to the edge. Wanting, no, *needing* to fly again, she lifted her hips and met him thrust for thrust. As the tension and lure of what she'd experienced moments before drove her higher, he filled her to the hilt and they leapt off the edge together. Spiraling higher, she felt liquid warmth as he emptied his life-giving seed inside of her and they slowly drifted back to earth.

She drifted awake and felt the warmth of her husband's big body wrapped around her, sheltering her, cocooning her with his love and protection. She drew in a breath and slowly exhaled. Shifting, she was caught off guard, as her ribs reminded her they were far from healed.

O'Malley moved so that she was lying on her back and he was brushing a tangle of hair out of her eyes. "Easy, lass. Ye need to remember yer ribs are healing."

She met his worried gaze and could not keep the truth from him. "You made it beautiful for me, Emmett. I will never forget the time you took to make it so. I've never felt like that before." Cupping the side of his face in her hand, she smiled. "Thank you."

He grinned. "'Twas a pleasure, lass, as we both shared in the giving and the taking. Equal partners in the marriage bed." His smile faded as he reminded her, "I'll be keeping me word. And as much as it will pain me, I will not press ye to make love until ye ask me to. I will never forget the gift ye've given me today, *mo ghrá*."

She marveled that the man who had taken her to the stars would be able to put off taking her there again because of his promise to wait until she was ready…until she asked him to.

"Are ye hungry, lass?"

Michaela sighed and trailed the tips of her fingers along the breadth of his shoulders, dipping down to skim them over his pectorals down to his abdomen. "I am."

As he eased away from her, she slipped her good arm around his neck. "I think I'd like to taste you this time, Emmett. Is that permissible?"

His eyes glazed over as he choked out his reply. "Aye, though it just may be the death of me, lass."

She bit her bottom lip and stared at his broad chest and small nipples, planning just where she wanted to taste him first. Her gaze dipped low and his shaft twitched in response. Marveling at what the human body could do, she asked, "How did you do that?"

"'Twas the look in yer eyes. I'm thinking maybe we should wait a bit longer before I let ye fully explore me. Ye need to heal first."

"Are you saying no to me, O'Malley?"

He rolled his eyes and groaned. "Faith, I knew ye were going to be a trial. Aye, that is what I just said… 'Tis nay for now."

"What about what we just did?"

"'Tis called making love, *mo chroí*."

"Do we have to wait until my ribs are healed before we make love again?"

His smile soothed her ire. "Nay, lass. But until yer ribs and yer arm have healed, we won't be able to try other positions."

"Positions?" Images of her beautifully muscled husband, naked, poised to make love to her, had her licking her lips. "What other positions are there?"

O'Malley smacked the palm of his hand to the middle of his forehead. "I'll tell ye while ye feed me. I'm feeling weak from satisfying yer needs, lass."

Michaela was laughing as she let her husband lift her into his arms and carry her over to the table. "Aren't we going to put our clothes back on?"

He tilted his head to one side and asked, "Why would we, when we're going to get right back in bed?"

She tilted her head back and stared into his brilliant green eyes. "Will you make love to me again?"

His deep laugh rumbled, settling around her like a hug. "Aye. Food now. Loving later."

IT WAS LATE when Emmett shifted Michaela until she was in a position that would not put weight on her ribs or wounded arm. He pressed a kiss to the top of her head and slipped his arm across her belly. As she drifted off to sleep, she wondered if the Lord would grant her a second miracle. Emmett O'Malley was the first miracle in her life, and the possibility of a babe with blond hair and green eyes would be the second.

CHAPTER TWENTY

O'MALLEY WAS AWAKE at dawn. The overpowering need to cradle the angel sleeping next to him for another hour nearly had him giving in, but he had no choice. Duty called.

He slipped out of bed without disturbing his wife. The lass had given her trust, her heart, and, last night, her body to him. Then the lass had turned the tables and rendered him speechless when she woke up a few hours ago asking for another lesson as the first faint streams of dawn caressed her face. He'd never given up control to a woman before, but he could not resist the mix of uncertainty and shimmering passion in her eyes.

He stood at the edge of the bed, staring down at her sleeping form, marveling that the woman who had had so much of her life stripped from her had given the gift of her innocent heart wrapped in passion to him. It had been agony to go so slowly, but he'd wanted her to experience pleasure in his arms, not pain. Lord, how he had reaped the rewards.

He washed quickly with the cold water in the pitcher and dressed, then stood halfway between the bed and the door, unsure if he should wake her to tell her he was leaving, or just leave. "Bollocks! Marriage is harder than I thought it would be."

Muffled laughter had him looking over his shoulder.

"Are ye laughing at me, wife of mine?"

Michaela sat up, winced, but then slowly smiled. "I could not help but find your predicament amusing, husband of mine. I woke when you left our bed, but couldn't decide if I should greet you when you obviously did not want to be disturbed. Marriage is harder than I imagined."

He walked over to sit on the side of the bed and leaned close to brush a lock of soft brown from her eyes. "I didn't want to wake you, *mo chroi*. It was not that I did not want to be disturbed."

"In that case, I believe I shall accompany you downstairs, if you wouldn't mind helping me dress." She grabbed the bed linen and wrapped it around her as she slid off the bed.

"I've seen and kissed every inch of your delectable body— why are you hiding it?"

She frowned as another lock of hair slid into her eyes. She blew it out of the way and reminded him, "That was last night."

"Aye, and what difference does that make?"

"It was dark." She splashed cold water on her face and shivered, then attempted to use one of the linen cloths to wash, but couldn't hold the bed linen up and wash at the same time.

"Michaela, let me help." She shook her head and stared at the floor, but it did not deter him. He walked over to where she stood and tilted her chin up, then rubbed his thumb over her plump bottom lip. "What happened to the passionate woman who stole my breath last night?"

"It was dark."

He coughed to cover his snort of laughter, tucked the sheet around her, and used the cloth in her hand to blot her face dry. "Ah, I can see I will have to arrange someone to cover me midday shift and convince you to come back to bed. I'll teach you how satisfying it is to make love in the light of day."

Her eyes were round with shock. "During the day?"

He laughed and pulled her into his arms. "Aye, wife. While you are a vision by firelight and candleflame, I cannot wait to see you lying back on that bed with the sun's rays glinting off your warm brown hair. Caressing the cream of your throat, and the satin of your beautiful breasts."

He eased back and stared down at the fascinating woman he'd married. Such a refreshing combination of sharp intellect, healing hands, and innocence wrapped up in a beautiful package that he planned to unwrap one layer at a time. He would take her to the stars every night, and after her ribs and arms healed, every morning, too.

"If you stand still, you can hold the bed linens to preserve your modesty, while I wash your arms and torso for you." She nodded, and he tenderly performed the task, deftly but gently. "I need to check yer ribs."

Michaela nodded. "After that one twinge last night, they haven't bothered me."

He grunted.

"And what is that sound supposed to signify?"

He smiled at her autocratic tone. "'Tis best if we let it go for the moment." He scooped her into his arms and placed her on the edge of the bed. Unwrapping her ribs, he frowned, but admitted, "The bruising isn't quite as deep."

"The comfrey root poultice relieves the worst of the bruising. Why are you frowning?"

He had to clear his throat as emotions he had not felt before bombarded him at the thought of what this brave woman had suffered. He would see to it that she was never at risk again. "The boot print." O'Malley motioned for her to sit while he returned to the pitcher and bowl.

He dipped the cloth in the water, rubbed it with the round of rose-scented soap, and returned to her side. His ministrations were gentle as he bathed then dried her and rewrapped her torso with the clean length of linen he'd added to the washstand last night. The boot print got beneath his calm like a splinter, making it difficult to ignore. O'Malley swept his eyes over her, taking in other fading bruises, landing on the bandage he'd wrapped around her upper arm. He hoped to God she never suffered such an injury again, but it was a distinct possibility given the cause she'd taken up. He would tend to her, but it had left his gut raw and bleeding having to repair the damage a lead ball left behind.

The bloody blackguard had broken her ribs when he'd kicked her three times. Abducted her twice. Held a pistol to her temple. But the worst of his crimes was a decade old… He'd stolen her virtue, hopes, and dreams when she was but a lass of seven and ten.

Swallowing his anger, he retrieved her chemise, helped her to stand, and slipped it over her head. Unable to leave with such dark thoughts crowding his brain, he dug deep for the control he was well known for as the duke's man-at-arms.

O'Malley hid his anger and worry that he wouldn't be able to make the bastard pay for what he'd done to Michaela and asked, "Now then, *mo ghrá*, anywhere else I can wash? Somewhere you cannot reach yourself at the moment?"

A delightful shade of rose swept from the neckline of the soft cotton garment to her forehead. He fought the urge to grin as he watched her fight and conquer her embarrassment to remind him, "You washed me there early this morning. Do you not remember?"

"Aye, lass. I remember every curve, every inch." Pride filled him. This strong and compassionate woman, who'd given so much of her life to others and taken little for herself, had agreed to marry him. Despite what she'd suffered at the hands of a monster, she had bravely put herself into his hands last night, knowing that there would be pain, but trusting him not to intentionally hurt her.

If possible, her cheeks flushed an even deeper rose. Her embarrassment endeared her to him. He would not have minded washing all of her again this morning. Of course, he would have to strip out of his clothes or take the chance he would get them wet.

Pulling her close, he rested his chin on top of her head. "Have I told ye how much I admire yer courage and the gift ye gave me last night?"

"Mayhap you should tell me again," she whispered.

"Yer courage puts Boadicea to shame. I'm humbled by yer trust and will never forget the way ye held nothing back. 'Tis a heavy weight, holding yer tender heart in me hands. I'll guard it, and ye, with me life."

He bent to press his lips to hers, sipping from them, then pressed more fully, tasting her, committing her flavor to memory. When he could bear to end the kiss, he confided, "I had hoped we would have had time for another lesson this morning, but duty calls."

"I hope I have not unwittingly brought trouble to the duke's town house and those who have sought safety within its walls. I know how to wield a knife, though mine is too small to do much damage to a heartless blackguard like the one after me."

"Your fierce determination adds fire to the green of yer eyes and a delightful rose to yer cheeks."

She blinked. "Are you serious?"

"Aye, lass. Did ye not hear me tell ye that ye're even more beautiful when angry?" He raised his eyes to the ceiling and rasped, "Ye'll be the death of me."

"I doubt that, O'Malley. Do not forget that you aren't the only one with the knowledge of healing. I will use all of my skill to heal you, Emmett. You will not die!"

He held her to his heart. Feeling the rapid beat of hers calmed his. "Ah, lass. If yer vow is all it takes to ensure that I wouldn't, then the two of us will live forever, healing one another constantly. But a long life isn't a given—me da's untimely death is proof of that. But the love me ma, me brothers, and I have for him lives on. The love he had for us will never die—it lives on as we remember his words and deeds and hold them in our hearts."

He kissed her deeply, promising, "Should the Lord call me home, I'll go valiantly, fighting to ensure ye, and any babes we make between us, are safe with me brothers and cousins guarding yer lives, protecting yer heart."

O'Malley kissed the tears from her face and in that moment

wondered what it would feel like to live forever with this woman. Knowing it wasn't a possibility, he silently thanked God for the gift of her love, and asked Him to take him first. Patrick, Finn, and Dermott would protect Michaela and any children the couple made between them with their lives. He ended his prayer with another, asking that he be the one to bring Haversham to justice, and if it meant he would forfeit his life to do so, he would willingly give it to keep Michaela safe.

Unaware of the turmoil in his heart, she asked, "Where were you headed before I interrupted?"

"Given the current circumstances, I am expected to report to me post. We have a number of women to protect, especially one who is infinitely precious to me." She sighed when he again kissed her tenderly. "Shall I help ye dress? I'm expecting a knock on the door any moment to ensure I'm up and ready to take me shift."

"Please." She let him help her don her gown and then turned around so he could do up her buttons. That simple act, turning her back to him, knowing she could trust him, had him wishing he had the time to caress every inch of her this morning.

It took great effort to push that thought aside. He needed to keep his mind on his duties. With the threat of Haversham and his lackeys hanging over their heads, he could not afford to let his mind wander.

"Do you really think Papa will arrive this morning?" Michaela smoothed her stockings into place and tied the silk garters.

"Aye."

"I'm not an invalid," she protested while he assisted her with her half boots.

"True, but bending is on your list of what not to do for at least a sennight."

"How am I expected to dress myself, then?"

He slowly smiled and urged her chin up with the tips of his fingers. "Ah, lass. 'Twill be me pleasure—and me agony—to help ye wash and dress each morning." His gaze locked on hers. "And me distinct pleasure to undress ye every night, even after yer ribs are healed."

"Emmett, I—"

The loud knock interrupted what she had been about to say. "That'll be Garahan."

"Open up, O'Malley. 'Tis time to man yer shift."

"I'm not out of bed yet." He was smiling as he kissed Michaela with all of the love in his heart and bade her goodbye. "I'll check on ye in between shifts." He walked over to the door and yanked it open.

"Bloody hell, Emmett! If I have to be up and leaving me wife all soft and warm in our bed, then—" His cousin frowned. "Ye're dressed."

"Aye."

"Ye're a bloody bugger, O'Malley."

"Good morning, Darby."

Garahan stopped frowning and turned to greet Michaela. "Good morning, Michaela. I didn't expect ye to be awake."

"There is work to be done, if we are to be staying here for a few days. Mrs. O'Toole cannot be expected to take care of all of us without assistance. Besides, I fully expect my father to call anytime now. I will have to remind him that I am well above the age of consent and do not need his approval to marry."

"If me da was still alive," O'Malley said, "and if me sisters hadn't already been married, he would have raised the roof with his shouts if any of me brothers-in-law did not ask permission before marrying me sisters."

Michaela sighed. "You and your brothers aren't in Ireland, O'Malley."

"Aye, that we're not, but still, I should have made the time to speak to yer da again and tell him me intentions toward ye."

"And those intentions would be?" she asked.

"Marrying ye to not only protect ye with me strength, but with me name."

"When would you have had the time? When you were out

on the duke's business earlier yesterday? Mayhap afterward, when you were searching for Mary and me."

"She's got ye dead to rights there, O'Malley," Garahan said. "Give it up and realize that yer father-in-law will have to accept what is. Ye can always ask His Grace to write a letter of recommendation to Dr. Colborne listing yer many fine qualities."

O'Malley shoved his cousin aside with his shoulder. "Feck off, Garahan."

Garahan laughed like a loon. "Language, O'Malley."

Michaela was smiling as she followed the men down the servants' staircase to the kitchen. Hand on the rail, O'Malley right in front of her, her stomach rumbled. The echo in the narrow staircase mortified her.

"Ye'd best feed yer wife, O'Malley. I'll let Findley know that ye'll relieve him in a quarter of an hour."

They parted, with Garahan going out of the rear entrance to the town house, and O'Malley putting his hand to Michaela's waist, guiding her down the long hallway to the kitchen. As they passed the room with the cot where Mary was recuperating, the door opened and O'Shaughnessy nodded to them. "I'm to report for duty midday."

"King is lucky to have ye as one of his runners."

"Thank ye, O'Malley. Never thought I'd be working for the law."

"Ye're a married man now, with a wife and maybe someday soon a family to feed."

O'Shaughnessy's head snapped around. "I need to speak to me wife. I just wanted to thank ye again for helping me find her, and yer wife as well. Count on me to help take down Haversham."

"I will."

The door closed behind O'Shaughnessy, and they made their way to the kitchen. "I smell fresh-baked scones!" O'Malley said.

Michaela was laughing as they entered the kitchen. "Now that is what I love to see in the morning," Mrs. O'Toole said. "A happily married couple laughing, sniffing around for a plate of scones, freshly whipped cream, and berry jam."

"Don't be forgetting the pot of tea," O'Malley added, snitching a still-warm scone from the cooling rack. He bit into it and sighed. "Heaven, Mrs. O'Toole."

"You forgot to feed your wife first," the cook reminded him.

O'Malley immediately reached for another scone and offered it to Michaela. "You don't need the cream and jam…but it does add a bit of sweetness to the scone." He met Mrs. O'Toole's steady look and asked, "Would it be all right if I left Michaela in your care while I relieve Findley? Garahan gave me a quarter hour, but I'll have used it up by the time I reach me post."

"Of course. Have a seat, Michaela, while I pour you a cup of tea."

"I'm grateful, Mrs. O'Toole," Michaela replied.

"O'Malley, wait!" The cook wrapped four scones in a linen napkin and handed it to him. "Put these in your pocket, and please tell Findley that I have scones and breakfast waiting for him."

"Don't I get breakfast?" he asked.

"After your first shift, same as always."

"I'm half starved," O'Malley complained.

"And you have four scones in your pocket," Mrs. O'Toole reminded him.

"That I do. Thank ye, Mrs. O'Toole." He leaned toward her and pressed a kiss to her cheek. "Ye're a darling woman and wonderful cook."

"Kissing another woman the morning after we wed?" Michaela asked, though he knew she was teasing him from the devilish glint in her eyes.

"Please excuse me, Mrs. O'Toole—I forgot to kiss me wife goodbye." He bent and kissed the breath out of his wife, then had to steady her so she didn't fall off her chair. O'Malley was whistling when he strode along the hallway toward the back door.

After the night he'd spent in his wife's arms, he was ready to face down anyone…anything!

CHAPTER TWENTY-ONE

"WELL NOW, I'D say that was a man who was quite pleased with himself."

Michaela felt her face flush. "I, uh… I believe so."

Mrs. O'Toole filled Michaela's cup and one for herself and sat beside her. "I know O'Malley treated you well, and from the blush on your cheeks, he treated you as the precious woman you are. He did not hurt you, did he?"

Michaela was not certain why the other woman was so concerned, and immediately worried that her past was not as secret as she had thought it to be.

Before she would ask, the cook said, "When a woman waits until she is well above marriageable age to wed, there are a number of reasons. But no matter her age or status in life, I have always been ready to lend an ear and mayhap a tidbit or two of advice from the years I was fortunate enough to be married to Mr. O'Toole. So, I'll ask again, and not because I am prying, but because I can see from the glow on your face that you are happy. Is there anything you would like to ask me about this morning?"

As she sipped, Michaela did think of one question. "I never expected to marry, and was wondering if it is common for a husband to take his time, with…er…*things?*"

Mrs. O'Toole patted her hand. "Any man worth his salt will. A marriage is stronger when you and your husband have trusted three things into one another's care."

Michaela set her teacup on its saucer. "What would those be?"

"Your heart, your mind, and your body."

"My mum died long before she could talk to me about what happens in the marriage bed…or marriage itself, for that matter."

"I know O'Malley better than I know the others, all of whom who have been stationed here when the duke's guard formed— but he has been stationed here longer than them. I can promise that if you have opened your heart to him, he will guard it with his life, always. His Grace was fortunate the day he asked Patrick O'Malley if he had any family, or knew of any other trustworthy men looking for work in London."

"I haven't met Emmett's brothers yet," Michaela told her. "I have met two of his cousins, James and Darby Garahan."

"All of the men in the duke's guard are strong, trustworthy, and would give their lives to protect the duke and his family. Once the men marry, they have vowed to do the same for their wives."

"Mrs. O'Toole?" Miranda said, entering.

"Good morning, Miranda, good morning, Emma. Is some- thing wrong with Aimee?"

"Just a little morning sickness. Do you have a bit of day-old bread that I could bring up to her? I made Aimee promise to lie in bed until I could bring her something to sop up the bile in her belly."

Mrs. O'Toole beamed with pleasure. "Of course. I always keep it on hand for upset stomachs, and for those times when their ladyships were expecting, and going to be staying in London." She rose from the table and began to prepare a tray.

"Good morning, Michaela," Miranda said. "Did you sleep well?"

Michaela choked on the sip of tea she had just swallowed and noticed Miranda's eyes danced with merriment.

"I'll take that as a yes and trust that all is well. Was that

O'Malley I heard whistling earlier?"

Michaela felt it was better to keep her thoughts to herself while little ears were present. "I have had two cups of tea already," she said. "Why don't I bring Aimee something to settle her stomach while you and Emma sit with Mrs. O'Toole and have a bite to eat?"

"Have you had experience with expectant mothers?"

"A number of them," Michaela replied. She did not bother to add that most had been victims, like herself and Aimee. "Enjoy a chat with Mrs. O'Toole. I'll return after I've ensured Aimee is feeling well enough to rise."

"Thank you." Miranda sighed. "I remember those first few months quite well, and do not envy Aimee just entering that time when all manner of odors, at any given time, could cause a stomach upset."

Michaela had no idea if that was true—not one of the few friends she had had would have anything to do with her once she began devoting her time to working alongside her father in his surgery. After what happened the one time she bowed to her father's edict and attended that ball, they did not give her the cut direct, but something far worse—they cut her out of their lives completely, as if she never existed.

"My experience is limited to the few patients I have had over the years. Not all of them were in as good a situation as Aimee."

"Here you are, Michaela." Mrs. O'Toole handed her a small tray. "Instead of a pot, I have a cup of weak tea for Aimee—no cream, no sugar—and two pieces of dry bread. Be careful going up the stairs carrying that, and be sure she eats both pieces slowly and chews thoroughly."

"I will. Thank you, Mrs. O'Toole. I shall return to help in the kitchen. After all, you have many more mouths to feed."

Taking the tray to Aimee, Michaela could hear feminine voices and little-girl squeals of pleasure and wondered if one of the duke's guard, or mayhap one of Coventry's men, had walked into the kitchen from the main part of the house. From what she observed, Emma reacted like that when some of her favorite guards stopped in on their rounds.

Setting those thoughts aside, Michaela continued toward the stairs—after all, she had a patient waiting for her. A woman who would understand what she was feeling and thinking the morning after she'd wed O'Malley. Though Aimee had not spent the last decade of her life never expecting to marry at all… Michaela recalled it had been at least five years since Aimee's intended unceremoniously deposited her at an inn—without her portmanteau, shawl, or reticule.

She took her time ascending the stairs, and realized she had completely forgotten—and so had Emmett—to immobilize her arm using the sling. She would stop by the room she was sharing with her husband on her way back down to the kitchen.

She knocked on the door and heard a soft moan. "Aimee? It's Michaela—may I come in?"

Her friend mumbled a reply that Michaela could not quite hear, so she carefully opened the door and stuck her head into the room in time to hear Aimee ask, "Why did no one tell me carrying a babe would have my stomach turn upside down every morning?"

"Whom did you ask?" Michaela didn't wait for Aimee to invite her inside. It was clear the woman felt poorly and wouldn't think to do so. She closed the door behind her and set the small tray on a table by the window.

Aimee blew out a breath. "No one. There wasn't anyone to ask."

"What about Miranda? Did you ask her?"

"I have only known her for a few weeks, and though we have become friends, our circumstances are very different from what you and I share."

"That is true, and why I offered to bring your tray up. I was hoping I could speak to you and ask your advice." She handed Aimee the small plate with a day-old bread on it. "Mrs. O'Toole said she always keeps dried bread on hand for upset stomachs, and their ladyships when they were expecting. Nibble it slowly, and chew carefully."

Aimee did as she was told and sighed after a few bites. "What would you like to know?"

"Were you er…hesitant when you knew you had to seal your vows?"

Aimee nodded and took another small bite, chewing slowly. "I believe *terrified* would be a better description."

"And was Darby patient with you?"

"Very. I'm a lucky woman, Michaela. I never thought to have the chance to marry, nor was I certain I wanted to…until Darby rescued me. I certainly never gave a thought to having a family. I'm still growing accustomed to being married." Aimee stared off in the distance. "There is so much I could say about Darby and the challenges and changes I have experienced. If I had to put it into a few words… He saved me."

Tears pricked the back of Michaela's eyes. "That is the heart of what our husbands have done for us, isn't it? I've been holding my fear inside of me for longer than you have, and I confess, I was not quite certain how else to keep the nightmares from happening during the day, taking over my life. It was so hard to be brave last night. But Emmett…"

The understanding in Aimee's gaze gave Michaela the courage to continue discussing a topic that would be frowned upon in normal circles. But she and Aimee were different. They had suffered greatly at the hands of a monster who took something precious from them and then tried to destroy them. "Emmett took his time and explained what he was going to do."

Aimee nodded, then asked, "Did he promise to stop if you needed him to?"

"He did, but once he started…"

"You did not need or want him to."

"I do not deserve him, Aimee." Tears welled in Michaela's eyes and she blinked, but a few escaped before she could hold the rest of them at bay.

Aimee patted the bed next to her. When Michaela sat down, her friend asked, "Where is your sling?"

"I forgot about it this morning."

"I would have, too," Aimee admitted. "But I am sure Darby has a spare cravat lying around. I can fix you up. Now then, we'll need to get you something else to wear so you do not get any food stains on your lovely gown. Mrs. Wigglesworth showed me the closet in the dressing room next to Their Graces' bedchamber, knowing you would need to change."

"Thank you, and thank Mrs. Wigglesworth. After you eat, you can show me and help me fasten the buttons." Michaela waited a beat and asked, "How did you know I offered to help Mrs. O'Toole?"

"Darby mentioned it when he came to check up on me after he made sure O'Malley wasn't still lying abed."

"I noticed that he did seem a bit insistent and grumpy."

Aimee's smile broadened. "I think he would stay abed until midmorning if he could. Darby also mentioned that Miranda and Emma were planning to help, too. I think we'll need to divide our duties between helping with the cooking and mayhap even the bedchambers until the two additional maids arrive."

"I didn't realize His Grace was hiring on two maids."

"Darby said it is what they do whenever Lady Aurelia or Lady Calliope arrive for a visit."

"That would make sense," Michaela replied.

"In the meantime, we can divide and conquer," Aimee said. "With your arm and rib injuries, you should not do any heavy lifting until you heal."

Michaela harumphed. "And you are not to lift anything heavy until after your babe is born."

"Do not be ridiculous," Aimee grumbled.

"You do want a healthy babe, don't you?"

"Yes, of course."

"Then you will take my advice and rest when you feel tired, and put your feet up when you are resting."

"Anything else?" Aimee asked.

"Let your husband coddle you. Eat when you are hungry, and don't hold in any fears or worries. It isn't good for you or the babe you are carrying."

Aimee frowned. "That is an awful lot to remember, Michaela."

"I'll let Darby know, too. That way, he can remember what you need, and do the worrying for you, while you concentrate on eating when you are hungry, putting your feet up when you are resting, and resting whenever you are tired."

Aimee smiled. "Have I told you lately how very grateful I am for your friendship and helping me put my past behind me?"

"A time or two. You have helped me begin to make peace with my own past. I had not realized how much of it I carried with me until you shared your story, which is so close to my own. When Haversham abducted me, it swept me back into the darkness I needed to let go of."

"How did we ever find ourselves married to such honorable, stubborn, strong, handsome, hardheaded men?"

Michaela laughed. "Because the good Lord heard our prayers and gave us a second chance." Seeing that Aimee's plate was empty, she said, "If you are up to it, I'll help you dress and then you can show me where the dressing room is. I'd like to change out of this lovely gown. I'd hate to spill anything on it."

Aimee smiled, got out of bed, and chatted companionably while Michaela helped her to dress. It took little time to settle on an appropriate gown to wear. By the time she had changed, raised voices once again echoed up from the entryway.

Michaela sighed. "That will be my father." She draped the cream-colored gown over the fainting couch as Aimee put a hand to her arm.

"Let Jenkins handle the situation. One of the guards will have alerted O'Malley, if he didn't already see your father step down from his carriage."

"I suppose, but you see…"

"You are a married woman now, Michaela. Let O'Malley protect you. I can guarantee after he speaks to your father, he will have calmed down and be ready to see reason and rein in his temper."

"I would not count on it."

By the time they returned to the room Aimee and Darby were staying in to retrieve the tray, Aimee appeared steadier.

The heavy knock on the door meant it was either Garahan or O'Malley.

"Aimee, 'tis O'Malley—is me wife still visiting with ye?"

"Yes. Please come in."

The door opened slowly, and the frown lines on O'Malley's face disappeared as he smiled. "Well now, don't the two of ye look thick as thieves? What have ye been plotting while the rest of us have been protecting the perimeter and soothing a worried father-in-law's fears?"

"I've been explaining a bit of what Aimee can expect to be feeling in the months ahead and cautioning her to rest and eat well, among other things. I have a list of things Garahan needs to be aware of. Mayhap I should write it down for him."

O'Malley agreed. "Ye might want to make two lists—he's been distracted as of late and may misplace the one ye give him."

When her husband smiled at her, Michaela felt butterflies in her belly. "Er, yes. That is a fine idea."

O'Malley turned and studied Aimee. "Are ye still feeling poorly?"

"I feel much better. Michaela brought up Mrs. O'Toole's cure."

"And what would that be?" O'Malley asked the question of Aimee but was staring at Michaela.

Aimee answered, but Michaela was not certain her husband had heard. She prodded him. "Was there something you wished to ask me, husband?"

He grinned. "Aye, but we aren't alone, so it will have to wait."

Michaela's face flamed and Aimee laughed delightedly. "It looks so good on the two of you."

"What does?" O'Malley asked.

"Love," Aimee answered.

The look of pride on O'Malley's face had Michaela wondering what he was thinking. He distracted her by saying, "Yer da stopped by."

"We heard. I'd best go and speak to him." Michaela moved to walk around her husband, but he held up a hand to stop her.

"No need. He'll be back to speak with ye at teatime, as was suggested to him last night by Coventry...or mayhap it was King."

"I see—and did he have anything to say to you?"

O'Malley grinned. "Aye, but once I explained his error in judgment..." He did not need to say another word. Michaela knew he referred to her father's urging her to accept an invitation from Lord Haversham and the disastrous events that followed.

"Thank you, Emmett."

"Ye're welcome, lass. Why don't the two of ye stay put for the next half an hour? It's a bit chaotic in the kitchen right now."

"Why didn't Mrs. O'Toole send for me?" Michaela asked. "I offered to help her."

"I'm thinking she has far too much help at the moment, and all from a pint-sized female with a smile that would melt even the coldest heart."

Michaela's warmed at her husband's description of little Emma Coventry. So grown up for her age, with her father's temperament and frown, and her mother's smile. "I think we'd best stay put for a little longer, then."

O'Malley slipped his arm around her waist, led her over to the bed, and pressed a kiss to her forehead. "I'm thinking Mrs. O'Toole will be needing a pot of tea, a few of her scones, and mayhap someone to slice vegetables to add to the stock pot on the stovetop. She's promised a hearty stew for supper."

"What about teatime?" Aimee asked, then fell silent.

"'Tis a good thing that yer appetite has returned, lass. It'll ease Darby's mind when I tell him."

"Did you hear anything about what she plans to bake for teatime?" Michaela asked, understanding that Aimee really did need to know.

"There are two pans of gingerbread cooling on the sideboard and two more batches of scones that are all different shapes and sizes. Emma helped with the baking and they're, surprisingly, cooked to perfection. I sampled one or two meself just now."

"How is Miranda holding up?" Aimee asked.

"She was all smiles and delighted to be discussing meal ideas with Mrs. O'Toole just now."

"What about Emma?" Michaela asked.

"Mrs. Wigglesworth took her into the cozy sitting room that overlooks the gardens. They were going to read stories."

"Mrs. O'Toole and Mrs. Wigglesworth are treasures," Michaela said. "They remind me of my mum."

"Both women would be fast friends with me own ma," O'Malley said. His gaze locked on hers. "She'll love ye, lass. Why don't ye write Ma a letter? I'll add it to the one I'm sending home in a fortnight."

"Are you certain you don't want to send it sooner?"

"Nay, I'll be including a portion of me pay in with our letters."

"Do you do that often?" Michaela asked.

"Write home? Aye."

"And send your pay?" Michaela asked.

"Aye, all of us send equal amounts home. We almost lost the farm a number of years ago. 'Tis why the four of us left to seek employment in London."

"But then who keeps the farm running? It must be a lot of work for your mum," Aimee said, asking the question Michaela was about to.

"Our three younger sisters married and stayed on the farm. Over the last few years they've added a cottage or two on the property so the lot of them aren't living on top of one another."

Michaela could just imagine how wonderful it would be living on a farm with sisters and brothers-in-law…if she had had sisters. "It sounds wonderful."

"Aye, it can be. But me brothers and I have grown accustomed to serving the duke and his family. We're able to use our skills. We've talked about going home to visit Ma in shifts. We'll have to arrange the time carefully so His Grace and his family are well protected."

Miranda smiled. "I think your mum would love that."

"Aye, that she would, lass. She has four granddaughters now."

Michaela said, "Well then, you and your brothers ought to start making plans to bring them to visit your mum."

"That we will…after we settle the current issue we're dealing with." One more kiss, one that stole her breath, then O'Malley reminded them to wait half an hour before heading down to the kitchen, nodded, and left.

"Do Darby's married brothers have any children?" Michaela asked.

Aimee smiled. "James and Melinda have twins, a boy and a girl. Ryan and Prudence are expecting, and soon, if I'm remembering correctly."

A short while later, Aimee and Michaela walked toward the servants' staircase. This time, Aimee carried the tray, since she'd found a cravat and fashioned a sling for Michaela.

"I won't be as much help with my arm in a sling," Michaela grumbled.

"How else will you heal if you do not follow O'Malley's orders? If I were the one injured, would you insist I keep my arm in a sling?"

Michaela fell silent as they descended the stairs to the lower level.

"Well?" Aimee prodded.

"Yes," Michaela admitted. "I would."

"I thought so. Now let's see what we can accomplish before teatime, when your father comes back to speak to you."

Michaela dreaded that meeting, but did not say so out loud. There was work to be done beforehand, and she intended to help as much as she was able.

CHAPTER TWENTY-TWO

O'MALLEY FELT AS if he were on tenterhooks waiting for Haversham to deliver a message…or show up at the duke's town house. "Where is the bugger? What is he waiting for?"

He scanned the garden and the wall behind it. It was rather large for being in the city, but small compared to his parents' farm. Nothing caught his eye, so he continued on his rounds of the third-floor interior.

Anxious to get the meeting with his father-in-law over with, he could not help but wonder just how angry the man would be at not having any say in his daughter's marriage. O'Malley stopped to look out of the window at one end of the long hallway, and watched a well-sprung carriage with a fine pair of geldings slowing down as it approached the duke's residence.

He heard his relief coming up the servants' staircase and went to meet Findley. "Take as much time as you need," Findley offered. "The rest of us have the exterior and interior well guarded."

"Thank ye—this should not take too long."

"Will Michaela be joining you?"

"Aye."

Findley snorted with laughter. "Then it might take longer than you think."

With that troubling thought in mind, O'Malley descended to

the first floor, stopping in the kitchen to fetch his wife. "There ye are, lass." He held out his hand, and she brushed hers on the apron she wore. Her cheeks were flushed and more than a few soft brown tendrils had come loose from the knot she'd fashioned on the top of her head.

Tempted to twirl the tendril brushing against the hollow of her throat around his finger, he stared into her eyes. "Ye look lovely, lass."

She smiled up at him, and he was tempted to do more than kiss her.

After clearing his throat, he added, "Yer da has arrived. Are ye ready to speak with him?"

A frown wasn't the reaction he was expecting. "Will you be escorting me and leaving, or staying?"

What kind of a man would leave her to face her father's ire alone? "I'll be by yer side, lass. We'll face yer da together. Ye have nothing to worry about."

Michaela didn't reply as she turned her back to him and asked him to untie her apron. He settled his hands around her waist for a moment, marveling at the strength in the petite woman he'd married, before untying the knot.

She spun around, but did not lose her balance, obviously accustomed to having her arm in a sling, then tucked in a few loose hairpins. "Do I have any flour on my face?"

He brushed the tips of his fingers along the curve of her cheek...not because she had flour on her face, but because he needed to touch her. "There."

"Thank you, Emmett." She lifted to her toes and kissed his cheek. "We'd best not keep him waiting—it grates on Papa's nerves, and then he becomes quite surly."

"I'll keep that in mind, *mo chroí.*"

He held out his arm and felt a rush of warmth as she slipped hers through it. He led them to the door to the main part of the town house, and he heard her breathing change. She was inhaling and exhaling short, sharp breaths.

He closed the door behind him and gently turned her to face him. "Lass, what has ye fretting?" When she did not answer right away, he frowned, wondering if it had to do with last night. "Did I exhaust ye? Are ye suffering any ill effects from our—"

Michaela put her hand over his mouth and shook her head. "Nay. I was trying to remember the last time my father and I had a conversation."

"How long ago was it?"

"I honestly do not recall. A year ago, mayhap longer."

The lass was trembling. "Why don't I speak to yer da alone? That way ye don't have to concern yerself with whatever ye're worrying about. He'll ask me a few questions, and I'll respond. Nothing to cause ye worry."

"I am not afraid, nor am I a coward."

O'Malley tilted his head to one side and stared at her. He watched the wealth of emotions manifesting themselves on her pretty face. "I did not say that ye were." When she fell silent, he offered, "I can escort ye to our bedchamber if ye need to rest."

She drew in a deep breath and slowly exhaled. "I will not hide ever again."

O'Malley's gut warned him that he was not going to like the direction his wife planned to take the conversation with her da. With a nod, he held out his arm for the second time, and once more, she linked hers with it. "Best tell me what ye're planning to say before ye pick up a teacup."

Her gasp had him shrugging.

"I needed to warn ye ahead of time. I cannot tell from yer frown whether ye plan to lob a full cup of tea at yer da's head or whack him with a saucer to get his attention." When she didn't say anything, he sighed. "The tea set belonged to His Grace's grandmother. 'Tis of sentimental value, especially to Her Grace."

Michaela started to laugh, a musical sound that warmed his heart.

"There's the woman I love. Ye had me worried, lass. Now then, let's get this conversation over with so we can move past it." He paused outside the door to the library, leaned close, and whispered, "I cannot wait for out next lesson in loving."

Michaela's eyes widened. "What do you have in mind?"

"Lips and tongues will be involved."

Her face flushed a lovely shade of rose. He decided to do her a favor and touch the tip of his finger beneath her chin, silently letting her know that her mouth was open.

O'Malley knocked and was bade to enter. He opened the door and waited for Michaela to precede him.

"Michaela!" Her father immediately frowned, taking in her sling and stiff posture. "What were you thinking marrying a man you hardly know?"

Without missing a beat, she replied, "I trust Emmett with my life, Papa."

"Trust isn't a reason to marry, daughter."

"It is essential in the man I marry."

Colborne glared at O'Malley, who did not deign to respond to the challenge his father-in-law silently threw down.

"Why would my daughter marry a man with no connections to the *ton*, and a farmer from Ireland to boot?"

O'Malley bit down on the need to blast the irritating man with his reasons. Before he could verbalize what he wanted to say—without cursing—Michaela replied, "I love him."

"You only accepted one offer of escort to a ball a dozen years ago. How—"

"Ten years."

Colborne locked gazes with Michaela. "Love will not feed and clothe you."

O'Malley's guts were churning as the tension built inside of him. But again, Michaela was quick to respond. "Emmett can more than provide clothing and food for us, Papa. If you have nothing more to impart, I am needed elsewhere."

"With your arm in a sling? What possible help could you be to anyone? I blame O'Malley for your current condition and demand that you return home with me at once!"

With a nod worthy of a queen, Michaela turned to O'Malley. "I'm ready to return to the kitchen, Emmett."

"How do you expect me to grant my blessing on your marriage when O'Malley has already banished you to the kitchen?"

The lass spun around so fast, O'Malley had to move quickly so she did not fall on her face without having both arms to balance her. "Have a care, lass."

"Her name is Michaela," Colborne said.

"I followed your advice once before, Papa, and it cost me everything!"

When Michaela sagged against his side, O'Malley cradled her against him and kissed her temple. "Now is not the time, Dr. Colborne. Yer daughter is past the age of consent. We exchanged vows last night. I would think you would wish us well."

Colborne refused to look at him. Instead he glared at Michaela and growled, "I will not let you throw away your life on this...this *Irishman!*"

Michaela locked gazes with her father. "I paid a heavy price for listening to your advice once before. Lord Haversham lured me into the garden during Lord and Lady Andrew's ball. He asked about my hopes and dreams...then mocked me when I shared them with him."

Before her father could utter another word, Michaela rasped, "He brutally violated me. When he was through, he vowed to destroy my reputation and yours if I ever spoke of what he did." Tears filled her eyes and spilled over. "I never uttered a word against him, nor mentioned what happened, to save your reputation because I knew in my heart it was the only thing you valued after Mum died."

O'Malley watched the doctor's posture change, his shoulders slumping forward. The man looked as if he'd suffered a blow. The urge to plant his fist in the man's face had O'Malley clenching his jaw and fisting his hands. His wife had suffered at her father's hands as well as what she endured from her attacker. Her da had failed her, too.

"Why did ye not demand that yer daughter speak with ye?"

"She had a virulent fever, and I was afraid…"

"Ye were not the one attacked. Ye suffered nothing but the inconvenience of not having yer supremely gifted daughter at yer side in yer blasted surgery! She heals with her hands, her heart, and her words. And by all that is holy, if ye raise yer voice to me wife again, I'll wrap me hands around yer throat."

The doctor held his gaze, and O'Malley sensed the man was thinking about accepting the challenge. But at the last moment, Colborne inclined his head. "I still believe you should return home with me, daughter."

"If you have nothing else to say to me, Father, I'll bid you good day."

Shock had the older man's mouth opening, but no sound emerging.

"Well now, I'll escort ye, lass." O'Malley glanced over his shoulder and said, "I'll send Jenkins to ye. He will show ye out."

"What about tea?" Colborne sputtered.

"Mayhap another time, Father," Michaela replied.

O'Malley slipped his arm around his wife when she wavered on her feet. He sensed that she would not want him to carry her, though the urge to do so was hard to ignore. He leaned close and said, "Lean on me, lass, till we're on the other side of the door."

She seemed to steady once his arm was around her and she gave him a brief nod.

Satisfied she would not falter before they reached the door to the servants' side of the house, he walked toward the duke's butler at his station in the entryway. He was about to speak when Michaela said, "Jenkins, I believe my father is ready to leave. Would you mind showing him out?"

"It would be a pleasure, Mrs. O'Malley."

"Thank you, Jenkins."

O'Malley sensed his wife's strength was flagging. He urged her through the door, closed it behind him, and swept her into his arms. "I'm putting ye to bed, lass." Incensed that her da would treat her without care or concern, he urged, "Close yer eyes and rest yer head on me. I've got ye, and I won't be letting ye go."

"I love you, O'Malley."

"I'm a fortunate man, Michaela, and love ye too." He carried her past the kitchen and the startled expressions on the women's faces as he shook his head and kept walking. When he reached the other end of the hallway, one of the footmen filling in as a member of the duke's guard opened the door for them, closing it quietly behind O'Malley.

"'Tis safe to give in to yer tears, *mo ghrá*—no one is watching."

She placed her hand over his heart. "I have no intention of wasting any tears on my father. I need to rally my strength to heal so I can be of use to those who need me."

They reached the top of the stairs, and O'Malley shouldered the door open. "*I have great need of ye, lass.*"

Her soft laughter wrapped around his heart like a hug. "That is not quite what I meant."

He paused outside of their bedchamber. "Ah, but ye're thinking ye wouldn't mind testing me idea of making love by the light of day."

Her face flamed, and he felt the tension that had built up in her waiting for the confrontation with her father slowly dissipate. He shifted Michaela in his arms to open the door. Closing it behind him, he said, "What I wouldn't give to spend the rest of the afternoon getting to know ye more intimately." His frustration ramped up at the thought of making love to his wife, knowing she was exhausted and needed to rest. "Ye need to close yer eyes and rest. I'll send someone up to check on ye in an hour's time."

Gently laying her on the bed, he brushed a lock of hair out of her eyes and bent to capture her lips. Her taste went to his head like a cup of *poitín*. With a groan, he broke the kiss and straightened. "I'd best go now, or Garahan'll come looking for me."

"Emmett?"

He looked over his shoulder. "Aye?"

"Thank you."

"Me pleasure, lass. I'll always stand for ye. Right or wrong, no matter the cause. I'll be there to protect and support ye." Her eyes were already closing when he told her, "Rest now."

"I only need a few minutes."

"Take them, *mo chroí*." He stepped into the hall, quietly closed the door, and nodded to another footman who'd be standing guard until O'Malley returned. "She's sleeping. See that she isn't disturbed."

"Aye, O'Malley."

Satisfied his orders would be obeyed—especially by the lass—he took the staircase to the third floor to return to his shift. Making his rounds, he prayed for an uneventful afternoon.

All hell broke loose a quarter of an hour later.

CHAPTER TWENTY-THREE

O'MALLEY HEARD THE whistle and his mind immediately went into warrior mode. Within minutes, he was bounding down the servants' staircase, issuing orders. Confident they would be followed, and the women would be protected, he burst through the back door, rounded the corner of the town house, and froze. Six armed behemoths stood shoulder to shoulder at the entrance to the alley on the north side of the building. Two were armed with clubs, one had a lead pipe, and two others had blunderbusses—one aimed at his gut, the other at his head. The last man held a wicked looking knife.

O'Malley dove to the side as the knife flew through the air toward him, missing his throat but catching him in the shoulder. He ignored the injury, pulled the knife free, and returned it to its owner. The man's high-pitched scream took the edge off the raw pain in O'Malley's shoulder.

He didn't have time to plan, didn't need to. In a crisis the men banded together, working like a well-oiled machine, to do what they did best—fight! Garahan took out the man with the pipe with the butt end of his rifle. Tremayne shot the blunderbuss out of another's hands. While Garahan and Tremayne tied their prisoners' hands behind their backs, Findley shot the other attacker wielding a blunderbuss in the arm, then tied him up and walked over to stand beside O'Malley. "Ye take the one on the right—I've got the other bugger." They advanced on the pair of men armed with clubs.

"Who are you calling a bugger?" one of the man mountains shouted.

O'Malley laughed and shot the club out of the man's hands. The man howled when a large splinter embedded itself in his arm. "Finish it, Findley."

"Aye." Findley stalked toward the last man standing. "Toss down your club, and I won't shoot you."

"I'm a dead man if I don't kill O'Malley while he goes after the angel."

"Shut your trap!" one of the prisoners roared. "You'll get us all killed!"

O'Malley's blood ran cold. "Where's Haversham?" No one answered, and he knew the blackguard was inside the duke's town house! "Garahan, with me!" He ran like a man possessed. "Michaela's in the kitchen," he said as they raced to the back door and into the building.

"Aimee was upstairs with Miranda and Emma," Garahan ground out.

As soon as they were inside, they heard Haversham's plea. "If you kill me, you'll hang."

"Then I'll die knowing I have avenged the other women you violated. How many was it? Did you keep track? Was I the first or the twentieth?"

O'Malley and Garahan stood on the threshold, mouths open in disbelief. The angel of the streets had her back to the door and the tip of the blade in her hand pressed against Haversham's throat. "Lower yer arm, lass," O'Malley ordered her.

"No."

"Michaela, ye don't want to kill the man," Garahan said.

"Oh, but I do. I really do. He deserves killing."

O'Malley's mind raced. Fear that the lass had finally decided to confront the man who violated her—abducted her, beat her— filled him. He had seconds to decide how to handle the rapidly deteriorating situation.

He hated the man to the depths of his soul, had had plans to use his blade on him before beating him within an inch of his life, but now knew he wouldn't...couldn't. He'd taken a vow and would never go back on his word to His Grace. But he could not let his wife bury the knife she held into Haversham's throat—she'd hang!

He signaled to Haversham not to move. Unable to do otherwise, the man blinked as if he understood. O'Malley turned to Garahan and lifted his chin to the right. Garahan crept in that direction, while O'Malley moved to the left. Keeping his eyes on his wife, and the point of the blade against Haversham's throat, he whispered, *"Mo chroi*...don't!"

"He deserves to be punished," Michaela said.

"Aye," he agreed, moving closer. O'Malley could feel his wife trembling with the force of her anger. She was almost beyond reason...almost. He closed the small gap between them and prayed she would listen. "Drop yer arm. I won't watch ye hang if ye kill him. It would gut me, lass. Ye'll not die on me watch for taking a life...even if I agree that his is not a life that deserves to be saved."

"I don't want to hang," she whispered.

"The lower yer arm."

"But he's guilty," she wailed.

"We both know it, and if ye put the why of it into writing, then King will be able to do something about it. We'll pool our resources with his and collect the names of other women he attacked, and those he threatened. Once we do, he will stand trial and answer for his crimes."

Haversham sounded as if he were choking. O'Malley knew that he wasn't. It was anger that he would finally answer for his crimes.

The sound seemed to snap Michaela back to her senses. She lowered her arm, turned around, and handed O'Malley the knife. Her tear-filled eyes beseeched him to understand. He nodded, and she rasped, "Thank you."

O'Malley saw movement out of the corner of his eye, pulled Michaela close, and spun them around so that his body was between Haversham and his wife. Haversham's roar of anger was punctuated by the gut-wrenching pain O'Malley felt as a blade was buried deep in his back. Where in the bloody hell had the man gotten a knife?

"No!" Michaela's voice sounded far away as he struggled to catch his breath.

The sound of a fist slamming into flesh reminded him that he had planned to punch the blackguard in the face. Garahan must have beaten him to it.

"Hold on, Emmett!" his wife pleaded with him.

Voices mingled with his wife's orders to fetch the stack of clean linen. Why she'd be thinking about setting out napkins at a time like this was beyond him. He shook his head to clear it. They had to subdue Haversham!

"Don't you dare die on me!"

His gentle wife's roared command had him opening his eyes to stare at her. "Ye won't hang, lass. But Haversham might." The pain was excruciating. He needed to call on his control, but couldn't. Insidious shards of pain took hold of him. A numbness crept up from his toes to his knees and...God help him, his bollocks! He wanted to ask Michaela if something had happened to his lower extremities, but his mouth wouldn't work.

O'Malley's vision grayed around the edges and slowly darkened. He no longer heard the frantic tones of his wife's orders, nor Garahan's insistence that he stop being an *eedjit* and fight to stay alive. Everything faded away until all that was left was a blessed silence.

THE AIR CHANGED, and the sweet scent of new-mown hay filled his nostrils. He inhaled and sighed. Recognizing the scents of hay and horse, he realized he was home—in Cork on the family farm.

"'Tis about time ye showed up," his da grumbled. "Though

I'd rather ye stayed where ye were and enjoy life, I could use a hand baling the hay."

The tall, broad man with the crooked grin and emerald eyes—the mirror image of Emmett—was standing right in front of him. His mind had to be playing tricks on him. How could he be in the kitchen at the duke's town house one moment, and back home on the family farm talking with father the next?

He closed his eyes and opened them again, but the man did not disappear. "Da? When? How? Why?"

His father rubbed his chin. "Well now, the when of it is just now. The how of it is that all things are possible with God. The why of it is that ye gave yer life to save yer wife from hanging. Though, in me opinion, it would have been justified. By the by, she didn't kill Haversham."

O'Malley frowned. He could not be speaking to his da, unless *he* was dead, too…

He struggled to sort through the morass of emotions and questions in his mind until finally he asked, "Am I dead, then?"

"So it would seem, if ye're here at the farm to help. Yer grandda's in the barn milking Siobhan."

"That milk cow died years ago… So did Grandda."

"Aye, lad. Come inside. Yer grandma always has the kettle on and was baking scones earlier. She knew ye were coming."

O'Malley forced himself to swallow past the lump of emotion in his throat. "But Michaela… We were wed just yesterday." His heart felt as if it were being ripped from his chest. The ache nearly drove him to his knees.

"Faith, it was a rushed affair," his da said. "Without the banns being read. But we understood 'twas the matter of her safety. She's a brave lass, with healing hands and a heart of gold. Yer ma will love her. Have no fear, Emmett—yer brothers will take care of her."

O'Malley's steps faltered, because he still had trouble feeling his legs. "I don't suppose there's a chance I can go back?"

"'Tisn't up to me, lad. That would be up to a far higher power. I'm in charge of watching over yer ma and yerself, yer brothers and their wives and children, and yer sisters and their husbands and their children."

"Did ye blink and that's why I'm dead?" His father's snort of laughter had O'Malley rushing to add, "Ye know I didn't ask by way of disparaging ye, Da. Nor did I doubt for a moment that ye were taking good care of me."

"I know it, lad."

"God, I've missed ye, Da. So have Patrick, Finn, and Dermott. We had no choice but to leave the farm to make enough coin in order to save it."

His father nodded. "Ye were the youngest, but the only one with the gift of healing." Patrick O'Malley placed his wide-palmed, callused hand on his son's shoulder. "Ye've done well, Emmett, and lived a good life. Ye have always stood for yer brothers, yer ma, and cousins. Ye gave yer all protecting the duke and his family. Ye rescued then married the other half of yer heart. I'm proud of ye, lad. Yer son will be the spitting image of ye."

Emmett's legs went out from beneath him, but his da caught him, holding him up. "Michaela's carrying me babe?"

"Aye," his da replied. "Ye treated yer wife like the treasure she is. Ye healed the tearing pain she still held in her soul. Where there is love, lad, there's life."

O'Malley's voice broke. "Who will raise him? Will Michaela marry another so Patrick will have a da?"

His father grinned. "Ye planned to name yer son Patrick?"

"Aye. Not one of us forgot ye. Ma told us new stories every day, used some of yer favorite expressions so we would remember them and pass them on to our children."

"Even the one I used the most?" his da asked. "'Work until yer bollocks turn blue'?"

O'Malley laughed. "Aye, especially that one."

"She didn't say that to yer wee sisters, did she?"

O'Malley's snort of laughter had his da smiling. "A time or

two," O'Malley admitted. "But that was right before each one of them married. We did our duty as their elder brothers. The four of us took their measure and approved of the men our sisters married. Just as you would have."

"Grainne, Maeve, and Roisin must have had something to say about that. Strong-willed lasses."

"Aye. But they married good men, who took over working the farm, so that we were able to leave and find work in London. Between us, we ensured no one would ever take the O'Malley farm."

"Well now, ye had a bit of help from yer relations up here as well. The seven of ye have done yer ma and me proud, son. Remember that."

The reality that he would not be sharing that information with his brothers or sisters or ma anytime soon was an arrow through the heart. But nothing compared to what he felt knowing he'd never see Michaela again...nor brush his hands across her cheek...press his lips to hers... "How will I live without her, da?"

"Ye'll have a new duty, lad. We'll be adding ye to our ranks to help watch over our ever-growing family. As yer duty to the duke and his made ye part of his family, we'll be adding himself and his family to those we guard from above. Ye won't have time to miss her, lad."

Patrick nudged his son toward the cottage. "Let's go have a cup of tea and a few scones, or yer grandma will be coming after me with her cast iron frying pan. Oh, I'd best let yer grandda know 'tis time for tea as well." He paused and whistled. A short, sharp sound that lanced through O'Malley.

He grabbed both sides of his head and felt himself falling...

CHAPTER TWENTY-FOUR

"D o. Not. Die on me!" Michaela pressed down on her husband's chest with both hands and paused to listen for the sound of his breathing, but could not hear past the roaring in her ears. She pressed on his chest again as her father's voice echoed in her head. *Keep up the rhythm, then force air into his lungs.* She wasn't going to use ash-covered bellows to force air into Emmett's mouth. Michaela fitted her mouth to her husband's and blew what she hoped would be life-saving breath.

"Lass, what in God's name are ye doing?" Garahan demanded.

"Keep the pressure on Emmett's back! We have to stop the bleeding!" Strong hands settled on her shoulders, but she jerked them away. "He needs air to breathe and his heart to keep beating."

"Ye can't—"

Michaela interrupted, "I can. If my father were here, he'd explain while he would do exactly what I'm doing." As she pressed on O'Malley's chest, she asked, "Did you send for my father? He could not have gotten far in his carriage this time of day."

Garahan sighed. "Tremayne left as soon as ye shouted at him to."

Michaela concentrated on her ministrations, though she

feared that the man she loved more than life—the man who gave his own protecting her—was beyond saving.

"Will ye stop beating on me cousin's chest when yer da gets here?"

"How long has it been since he fell unconscious?" Garahan grunted, and she ignored him. "There's a slim chance we can save him. I just need to blow more air into his lungs and shock his heart into beating."

"Doesn't he need to breathe?" Tremayne's deep voice nearly distracted her.

"Where is my son-in-law?"

Hope filled her—if anyone could save O'Malley, it was her father. "Papa! In here. I've been keeping up the chest compressions, but not the bellows method. I've been giving him my air." A sob caught her off guard. "He isn't breathing." She felt the tears pouring from her eyes, but couldn't stop them. "I refuse to let him die!"

Her father knelt beside her. "How much blood has he lost?"

"Too much," Garahan answered.

"Can you quantify that?" Colborne asked, lifting O'Malley's eyelids.

"Nay," Garahan replied.

Michaela watched her father and prayed while he placed his hand close to O'Malley's mouth and slowly smiled. "He's breathing."

Michaela's heart began to pound as hope tangled with the fear that had her by the throat. "He wasn't a moment ago."

She felt her father's hands covering hers. "You can stop now, Michaela."

Though she'd felt more than one of her stitches snap while she was pressing on Emmett's chest, she ignored them. It didn't matter. Nothing mattered if she lost him. "I cannot. He'll die. If he dies, Papa, I have no reason to live."

Aimee knelt on the other side of her and placed a hand to her shoulder. "What if you're carrying his babe?"

Michaela froze. "Babe? But I… We…"

"It is quite common for a woman to conceive on her wedding night, Michaela," her father reminded her. "I thought you paid attention all of those times I counseled mothers-to-be."

"Aye, but—"

"Did you seal your vows?"

"Papa!"

"Forget your embarrassment, Michaela, and answer the question."

"More than once."

The deep voice had to have been Garahan's, though how he would know, she could not imagine. She turned to glare at her cousin-in-law. "This is nothing to jest about!"

Garahan raised his hands, protesting, "I haven't said a word."

She was half leaning on O'Malley when she felt him move. "Emmett?"

"I told you he was breathing," her father said. "You were concentrating so hard on what you had to do to save him that you failed to notice his shallow breathing."

"Ye're carrying me son, lass," O'Malley rasped, calling her attention back to him. "We'll name him Patrick for me da."

"Emmett!" Michaela threw herself on her husband's chest and sobbed. He wasn't insensate now and wrapped his arms around her. The terror from moments before began to fade.

"We thought ye dead," Garahan said. "Ye weren't breathing."

"There are times when our bodies defy the laws of nature," Colborne said. "I noticed his eyes were not dilated. His color was still normal… Not blue around the lips from lack of air. Not pale as flour, or turning waxen as one does when one passes."

Michaela shivered, and O'Malley dropped one arm to push himself into a sitting position. "You should be lying down." She looked into his eyes and saw what her father had—they appeared normal. "I thought you weren't breathing." She could not keep her voice from breaking when she added, "I couldn't detect your heartbeat."

⤛⤜

UPRIGHT, O'MALLEY SHIFTED and slid Michaela closer. "Me chest is a bit sore. Faith, but I thought I was stabbed in me back."

Michaela shook her head, and Garahan chuckled. "Yer wife was pounding on ye something fierce, determined that she was going to restart yer heart."

"Were ye now?" O'Malley asked, locking gazes with his wife. "Do I matter that much to ye, then?"

Tears welled in her eyes and spilled over. "You are my life," she rasped. "*Mo chroí.* My soul, my reason for living."

"As ye are mine, *mo ghrá.* Me da, grandda, and grandma all agree what a fine lass ye are, and are over the moon that ye agreed to wed an *eedjit* like meself. Even Siobhan agreed."

Confused, she asked, "Who is Siobhan?"

Garahan laughed like a loon. "Their old milk cow."

"Are your grandparents still living?" Michaela asked.

"Nay, lass. They passed on some time before me da."

"How is Uncle Patrick?" Garahan asked.

"Hale, hearty, and relieved I was there to help him bale the hay. Me grandma was baking scones…" O'Malley paused, shook his head, and continued, "He whistled, but it sounded more like yerself. And I felt meself falling…" He paused when he felt something warm and wet against his side. "Lass, ye're bleeding." With a groan, he shifted to one knee and shakily got to his feet with her in his arms. "I'm thinking yer hardheaded daughter must have torn her stitches," he told Colborne.

"I'll carry Michaela," Garahan insisted. "Ye need time to recover from yer imitation of Lazarus."

O'Malley wavered, grunted, but knew his cousin was right. He passed Michaela to Garahan's waiting arms, then stared at his wife and wondered if she was even aware that she was still crying.

With a fresh stack of linen squares pressed to O'Malley's back, Colborne nodded to Tremayne. "He should not lose any more blood. Can you manage to—"

"I've got him." Tremayne hoisted O'Malley over his shoulder and pressed the thick pile of linen to his wound. "I'll set him on the cot in the room off the pantry. Garahan and I will help hold him still while you sew him back together."

"Thank you, Tremayne." Colborne followed the men out of the kitchen. "By the by, O'Malley, it may take you longer to forgive me than it took my daughter, but when you do, you may call me Father or Robert, whichever you prefer."

Tremayne bent to set O'Malley on his feet. As O'Malley straightened to standing, his groan of agony had everyone moving quickly. Colborne washed in the basin of water while Tremayne helped him sit on the cot beside Michaela, then pressed the wad of linen squares against the wound.

When Michaela's father walked over with the needle and boiled threads, O'Malley said, "Well now, that's generous of ye." He wrapped an arm around his wife. "Mayhap we'll be naming our son Patrick Robert O'Malley."

"Do I not have a say?" Michaela asked.

"Oh, aye," O'Malley replied. "As long as we name him Patrick in memory of me da, and Robert in honor of yers." When she frowned at him, he laughed. "After all, 'twas yer da's teaching ye that saved me…even if I've never heard of such before."

"I have had very few instances where I've had to use the technique I read about when I was studying medicine," Colborne said. "I enjoy reading about different methods. The one I taught Michaela was first documented in the mid-1700s by a Dr. Tossach, who reportedly revived a suffocated coal miner using mouth-to-mouth resuscitation a dozen or so years earlier in Scotland. Thirty or so years ago, our Royal Humane Society proclaimed the use of bellows was preferable to mouth-to-mouth for artificial respiration."

"I recall Lieutenant Sampson mentioning the use of bellows," Tremayne said. "He grumbled that he wasn't about to carry a bellows along with his other medical equipment on the battlefield."

"I did not have time to sterilize the kitchen bellows," Michaela murmured.

"Ye did a fine job of it, lass," O'Malley said. "Even though I don't remember it, I prefer knowing yer lips were on mine when ye gave me the gift of yer life-giving breath, lass. Though I think I could have done without the pounding me ribs took."

"*Hmph*. Next time I won't bother."

He pressed a kiss to her forehead as Tremayne moved to stand behind him and place his hands on his right shoulder. Garahan moved to do the same on his left side. Knowing what was to come, O'Malley pressed his lips to Michaela's temple. "Ye know ye would. Ye cannot live without me."

"Mayhap I can," she grumbled.

"Ah, it must have been another angel with soft brown hair and moss-green eyes that wept, saying if I died she'd have no reason to live."

Michaela sighed and leaned her head against his shoulder. "Forgive me for being cross with you when I nearly lost you. The very least I can do is speak the truth and tell you that you are right—I would give my life for you."

"As I've already given mine for ye, could we try to avoid doing that again? At least until our son reaches the age of maturity, when we no longer have to worry about him."

Her father began the arduous task of cleansing O'Malley's wound. It felt as if a hot poker was laid against his back. "Nearly finished with the easy part."

"Easy?" O'Malley grumbled.

"Aye. From the scars I can see, you are accustomed to the pain required to close the wound," Colborne said.

"Ye have the right of it," O'Malley agreed, and braced himself for what was to come.

While he threaded the needle, Michaela's father told him, "A parent never stops worrying about their child. No matter how old they are. King and I had an agreement, Michaela, one that I never intended for you to know. You wanted your independence, and I wanted you to have it for as long as possible. I hired a few of King's best men to follow you and keep an eye on you."

Michaela, firebrand that she was, asked her father, "Why did you not tell me that?"

"You must admit that you have a tendency toward stubbornness," he said before nodding to Garahan and Tremayne, who braced their hands on O'Malley's shoulders, holding him still.

"I do not—"

"Please be silent while I sew your husband back together." To O'Malley's surprise, his wife obeyed her father. "I shall tend to you next. You were fortunate the blade missed several organs, O'Malley. The blood loss must have hit the critical level that had you falling unconscious."

Garahan grunted, though Tremayne remained silent, ensuring O'Malley did not move until the physician finished sewing him back together.

"I wasn't expecting Haversham to have a knife," O'Malley admitted. "I felt the blade go deep, and I started to feel numb… Then everything went black."

"Despite what you think, Papa," Michaela said, "I know what I know. O'Malley wasn't breathing and had no heartbeat."

O'Malley observed the way the doctor listened intently before asking, "Would you tell me more of what you experienced visiting with your father, O'Malley? I've always believed in the hereafter, but have never been able to verify my ideas."

O'Malley told his father-in-law of his family, and the family farm, while the doctor deftly sewed him back together, applied the healing salve, and placed a thick bandage against the wound. "You cannot afford to lose any more blood. Rest and an invalid's diet for at least a fortnight."

Garahan and Tremayne finally let go of their hold on O'Malley and stepped aside.

"I'm living proof that a man can recover from dying," O'Malley boasted. "I'll only need to rest a day or two."

Michaela did not disagree with him. He turned to ask why and saw the anguish on her face and the tears that accompanied her pain.

"Forgive me for being glib, lass. 'Tisn't something I'll ever jest about again." He pulled her close and nodded to his father-in-law. "I'll hold her still while ye take care of the stitches she ripped open."

"My daughter has always been stubborn," Colborne admitted, "but she has a forgiving heart."

O'Malley wiped her eyes with the handkerchief Tremayne handed him. He pressed a kiss to Michaela's forehead while her father washed his hands and walked back over to inspect her wound. "Me ma prefers to say 'pigheaded.'"

Colborne chuckled and set out more of the sterilized threads and another needle. "You'll have to take extra care with this wound, Michaela. It is inflamed and could easily become infected. Lead poisoning is a possibility, as it was a lead ball that did the damage."

She glanced at her arm and sucked in a breath. "That does look a mess."

"*Mo ghra*, ye shouldn't have ignored yer wound to tend to me," O'Malley said.

"I would do it all over again if I had to." When she leaned against him, he felt her flinch and knew she was trying to ignore the sting of the needle, and the pulling of the threads, as her father replaced the stitches. "You are my life, Emmett."

"Ah, lass, I'd have no life without ye." She lifted her chin, and O'Malley saw the love he felt for Michaela reflected back at him. He lowered his head and kissed her gently. Reverently. "I'm thinking ye need to work on yer temper, lass." Before she could reply, he soothed her with another kiss. It must have worked, because she sighed and tucked her head in the hollow of his shoulder.

Colborne washed Michaela's blood from his hands and said, "O'Malley, tell me again who was on the farm when you arrived."

"Me da, grandda, and grandma… Da told me they are me guardian angels."

"Is Siobhan one too?" Michaela asked.

O'Malley's laugh filled the room as he pressed his lips to Michaela's. "Aye, ye minx. Did ye not know cows earn their wings, too?"

Garahan shook his head. "I am still recovering from the thought that I'd lost the only sainted O'Malley cousin I can tolerate, and ye're laughing, telling me cows are guardian angels, too?"

O'Malley shrugged. "I know what I know, Darby." He looked at Tremayne and asked, "Have King's men arrived?"

"Aye, been and gone," Tremayne answered. "They've taken the prisoners to Bow Street for questioning."

"Aren't ye going to ask about Haversham?" Garahan asked.

"He wasn't there when I opened me eyes," O'Malley said. "I thought Tremayne or Findley collected him and brought him to the stables where the others were tied up."

Garahan shook his head. "Do ye want to tell him, Michaela?"

She shook her head.

"Lord Haversham," her father rasped, the depth of his emotion evident on his face. "Can you ever forgive me, daughter? I have never so misjudged a man before."

"Yes, Papa. I can."

Colborne turned to Garahan. "What happened to the man?"

"Michaela wasn't strong enough," Garahan said. "So I pulled the knife out of Emmett's back while Michaela pressed the stack of linens to the wound."

"Wise decision," the doctor replied. "What about Haversham?"

"When I turned around with the knife he'd plunged into me cousin's back still in me hand, Haversham lunged for me with his hands outstretched, reaching for me throat. I didn't have a chance to warn him or move the knife out of the way."

"I arrived in the kitchen in time to witness what happened," Tremayne said. "The look of anger and determination on Haversham's face changed to one of horror when he realized that he'd impaled himself on the knife in Garahan's hand."

"Papa, you should tend to Haversham next."

Garahan shook his head. "No need—he bled out."

O'Malley felt relief, though his wife seemed visibly upset. "Will there be an investigation?" she asked.

"There's no need for concern, Michaela," Tremayne said. "I've spoken to King's men. It was agreed, given the location of Haversham's wound, and what Garahan told them, that it was an accidental death."

"I'm happy to hear that," O'Malley said. "I would have hated to have to explain to His Grace that me cousin went against His Grace's dictate that we may use force to subdue a prisoner, but never kill anyone."

Garahan shuddered. "Aye, His Grace has a wicked punch. Ask this one's brother Patrick when ye meet him, lass."

Tremayne nodded. "I have heard that particular tale before. His Grace would do anything to protect his wife and family. Before you worry unnecessarily, Michaela, Haversham would likely have been sentenced to hang for attempted murder." He turned, nodded to O'Malley, and added, "He nearly succeeded."

"Ah, but I'm still here," O'Malley reminded him.

Tremayne grinned. "Coventry will be here in a moment—"

"Where in the bloody hell are O'Malley, Garahan, and Tremayne?" a deep voice bellowed.

"Ah, there's the captain now." Tremayne chuckled. "In here, captain!"

Coventry stepped into the room, and his head swiveled from left to right as he took in the pile of bloody bandages by the pitcher and bowl, the fresh bandage on Michaela's arm, and the thick one wrapped around O'Malley's back.

"I take it your injuries have something to do with Haversham's death?"

"Aye," O'Malley, Garahan, and Tremayne answered simultaneously.

Coventry stared at the ceiling. "God help me, if the three of you are in agreement, that means you're covering for one another." He shook his head and asked Michaela, "Would you please tell me what happened?"

"Of course, captain." She laid a hand on her husband's arm and said, "It all began when O'Malley carried two little moppets, who were clinging to him like a vine, into my rooms proclaiming to have rescued them from a brothel…"

Coventry shook his head, turned to Tremayne, and asked, "Is there any rum left in your flask? I have a strong feeling it will take O'Malley's wife a while to get around to telling what happened here today."

Tremayne grinned. "A few sips will make for a better tale." He reached into his waistcoat pocket, pulled out his flask, and handed it to Coventry.

"Now then, as I was saying," Michaela continued, "the two little ones had their arms wrapped around his neck and were holding on for dear life. They knew what I sensed in that moment… Emmett O'Malley was a man I could trust to protect me with his life."

O'Malley grinned. "Ah, lass, I *would* give me life for ye."

Garahan groaned. "You nearly did, so don't start that again!"

⸻ ❖ ⸻

EPILOGUE

A fortnight later...

"ARE YE TRYING to keep me from me duties, wife?"

"If you have to ask, then I am doing something wrong," Michaela grumbled. She whirled around and stalked over to the dressing screen in the corner.

"Oh no ye don't." O'Malley grabbed hold of her hand and gave it a tug until she tumbled into his embrace. "Ye aren't stomping off in a temper again, lass. Ye saw for yerself that me wound has healed. It doesn't pain me nearly as much as I know yer ribs still pain ye. Especially when ye lift something ye shouldn't."

Hands on her hips, she demanded, "How would you know that unless you have spies?"

"Ye'd be amazed what a man would do for a steady supply of Mrs. O'Toole's scones."

"Garahan is spying on me?" Michaela asked.

"Nay. He and I already have an arrangement with Mrs. O'Toole. She keeps a separate plate of scones on the sideboard for us."

"Who is it?"

"Why would I be telling ye all me secrets, lass?"

Her shoulders slumped. "Because you know all of mine."

"If I didn't have me spies, how would I know that ye're doing too much work, lifting things ye'd best remember not to? Patrick Robert needs to have the chance to grow strong and be ready to battle his way into the world when ye give birth."

He drew her into his arms and held her to his heart. "I love ye, lass, more than life itself, but I'm hoping ye'll listen to reason and not tempt fate by ignoring what ye know is sense. Ye're carrying, lass. Ye need rest and to put yer feet up. Isn't that the advice ye gave to Aimee?"

"Well, yes, but—"

"Aren't ye a woman, the same as Aimee?"

"Of course, but—"

"And do ye not love me more than life itself, Michaela-mine?"

She relaxed in his arms and sighed. "I do love you more than life, Emmett."

"Well then, that's grand." He swept her into his arms, walked over to the door, and turned the key in the lock. Staring down at her, he asked, "What was it ye had in mind to tempt me away from me duties?"

"I'm not the expert, you are." She slipped her hand behind his neck and pulled him closer. "I just want you to make love to me."

She pressed her lips to his in a kiss that rattled his brains and had his body rock hard in seconds. He leaned his forehead against hers. "The door's locked. I'm thinking we have a bit of time before I'm late. Why don't I teach you how satisfying it is to make love with yer back against the wall?"

Her eyes widened, and she slowly smiled. "Aren't you too tall? How will this work?"

"First we need to rid ye of yer clothes." O'Malley lifted her gown and chemise up and over her head. "Now then, lass, there isn't time for me to remove all me clothes. Unbutton the placket on me trousers." He moaned when her hands brushed against his erection, but gathered himself enough to shove them off and step out of them. Naked from the waist down, he growled, "I'm going to put me hands around yer waist and lift ye up. When I do, wrap yer legs around me waist, and yer arms around me neck."

Her sharp intake of breath when their loins met had him aching with need. He walked toward the wall that faced the gardens and braced her back against it. "Let's see if ye're ready to receive me, lass."

Her moan of ecstasy when he slid one, and then another finger inside of her ensured she was ready to take him. Bringing her to the brink took but moments. Her excitement mirrored his as she begged, "Make love to me, Emmett."

"With pleasure, lass." He surged home into her warmth and began the rhythm that would take them where they both wanted to go—a world of love all their own. She screamed his name as she trembled from the orgasm that ripped through her. He shouted hers as he plunged one last time, filling her to the hilt, releasing his seed. "God, I love ye, lass." He lowered his lips to meet hers.

"I depend upon it, Emmett."

The pounding on the door interrupted the tender moment and had them both smiling, ending the kiss. "I guess Garahan noticed I wasn't at me post."

"Open up, ye randy *eedjit!*" Garahan demanded. "Ye're late for yer shift."

"I'm busy," O'Malley grumbled, and slipped out of his wife. He held her to his heart before sighing and letting go to find his pants and pull them on. "Fasten me up, lass, and then we'll find yer chemise."

Michaela quickly fastened his trousers, and O'Malley slipped the chemise over her head. A loud thump had him chuckling and her asking, "Did Garahan just pound his head on the door…again?"

"Aye, lass, 'tis a daily occurrence, and ye should be used to it by now. Haven't I told ye that ye don't need to worry? Garahans are known for their hard heads."

"In that case, can we make love like that again?"

"Not right at the moment. Me poor cousin is on the verge of

apoplexy."

They were laughing as he helped her don her gown then drew her into his arms. She quietly moaned when he nibbled on her earlobe.

"Meet me here midday, lass."

She traced the line of his jaw with her fingertips. "For another lesson?"

His green eyes glittered. "Aye. 'Tis time I taught ye how to make love with lips and tongues only."

"I thought you were jesting about that," she whispered.

"I never jest about lovemaking."

Their lips were a breath apart when Garahan started pounding on the door again.

"I'm coming!" O'Malley shouted.

"*Feck* me," Garahan grumbled from the other side of the door. "'Tis what I'm afraid of."

O'Malley strode to the door, unlocked it, and yanked it open, and quickly closed it behind him. "Don't just stand here, cousin—we're late for our shift." Garahan stuck out his foot to trip O'Malley, who leapt over it and nudged his cousin into the wall with his shoulder. "We can go a few rounds after teatime," he promised.

"Why not midday?" Garahan asked.

O'Malley grinned. "I've a previous engagement."

"Bollocks!" Garahan swore.

O'Malley's laughter filled the hallway and drifted under the door to their bedchamber, where Michaela stood staring at the closed door. Laying a hand protectively over her belly, she whispered, "Now then, Patrick Robert, I want you to grow up to be as broad and strong as your da, though I'd prefer it if you weren't quite as fond of bare-knuckle fighting as he is."

Eight months later...

PATRICK O'MALLEY RAISED a glass of the finest *poitín*... After all, he *was* in Heaven. His father did the same, saying, "The Lord must agree that we've done a fine job watching over Emmett and Michaela."

"Though they're in for a surprise, Da."

They were laughing, while down on Earth, O'Malley gasped. "What do ye mean there's another babe?" He tried to soothe his wife, bracing her against his broad chest, holding her with the strength of his arms. Sweat slickened the both of them as Michaela fought to catch her breath after another brutally long contraction.

A short while later, O'Malley marveled at the miracle of their twin sons. He lifted his gaze and smiled at the love of his life, who sat beside him on the bed, holding Robert, their youngest, while he held Patrick, the older twin by four minutes.

Michaela brushed the tip of her finger along the curve of Robert's cheek. Lifting her gaze to meet O'Malley's, she smiled. "We've been blessed, Emmett."

"That we have, Michaela-mine." His heart full, he sent up a prayer of thanks to his da and grandparents for keeping watch over Michaela through the birthing. He leaned toward her and rasped, "Kiss me, lass."

Her eyes sparkled. "Where?"

O'Malley's joyous laughter filled the room and soared up to Heaven, where two of his guardian angels were still congratulating themselves on a job well done. Patrick refilled their glasses. "Here's to two more!"

"Twin daughters this time," his da predicted.

Patrick met his father's gaze and said, "Where there's love…"

His da smiled. "There's life."

About the Author

If we have not met yet, I'm delighted to meet you. Here's a little bit about me…

I have been writing romance novels for almost half my life—well, at least for the last thirty years. I'm a die-hard romantic and have to confess the broad shoulders and wicked glint in the brilliant green eyes of a stranger had my breath snagging in my breast, my heart beating madly, and my future flashing before my eyes. At the age of seventeen, I'd met the man I knew I was going to spend the rest of my life with.

I write Historical & Contemporary Romance featuring characters that I know so well: hardheaded heroes and feisty heroines! They rarely listen to me, and, in fact, I think they enjoy messing with my plans for them. Over the years I have learned to listen to them! I have always used family names in my books and love adding bits and pieces of my ancestors and ancestry in them, too! Visit my website to learn more about my books.